"Holder, Oklahoma Senior Police Officer Aaron Clement is out for justice above all, even if he irritates the local hierarchy. Hayden in *Dry Bones* gives us nothing-barred investigation and plenty of nitty gritty police procedure—which makes for a real page turner." —Marianna Ramondetta, author of *The Barber from Palermo*

"*Dry Bones*: flawlessly presented and deeply moving, a smart and compassionate cop deals with cases in his own way. Hayden, in her inimitable style, has provided us with another character that we will not forget!" —Pam Brown, author of *Statue of Death* and *Mission of Death* in the California Lighthouse Mystery Series

"In *Dry Bones*, G. Miki Hayden brings us Senior Police Officer Aaron Clement of Holder, Oklahoma. He's both in step and out of step with the town—and the P.D. Clement has been given the bones of two unnamed boys buried in a local park years before, then is called to the scene of a vicious knife murder—just in Chapter One. What follows is a riveting story full of twists and turns, secrets suppressed and uncovered, all animated by a surprising cast of characters. Miki Hayden is a great storyteller, and this is one of her best.: —-Walter Sutton, author of *Finders Keepers* and *Losers Weepers*, with *Knick Knack Paddy Whack* coming soon

DRY BONES

BOOKS BY G. MIKI HAYDEN

Pacific Empire
By Reason of Insanity
New Pacific
Question Woman & Howling Sky
Strings
The Heroine's Journey
*Writing the Mystery: A Start-to-Finish Guide for
Both Novice and Professional*
The Naked Writer: A Comprehensive Style Guide
Rescued and Re-live, books one and two of the Rebirth series
Dry Bones

G. MIKI HAYDEN

DRY BONES

Down & Out Books
3959 Van Dyke Road, Suite 265
Lutz, FL 33558
DownAndOutBooks.com

Cover design by Margo Nauert

ISBN: 1-64396-371-6
ISBN-13: 978-1-64396-371-6

CHAPTER 1

The jumble of bones brought to Aaron Clement six weeks before had taken on a shape inside of him, and though they hadn't been identified, a sort of individuality. He'd insisted on having them back in his office after Dr. Neal, the forensic anthropologist, reported that these were the bones of two young boys between 10 and 12 (a determination made after DNA analysis).

Holder (Oklahoma) Senior Police Officer Clement should have known that *two* victims had been recovered, but he'd been inobservant and fooled by the fact that a single skull had been found. So after finding out that he had two boys to attend to, Clement had requested a team of searchers in the park for the second skull. Since animals like to gnaw on bone to file down their teeth, they might sometimes carry away the bones of the dead. Of course a skull was heavy, but Clement felt that looking around was worth a shot.

The skull remained missing, but the bones were now laid out on the air conditioning unit that formed a shelf below the window in Clement's office. He'd asked for a table of sufficient length to lay out the boys, yet that, reportedly, wasn't to be found—even though Clement was aware that the cafeteria in the police academy building across the street had a few, and he'd pointed that out.

1

Then he'd requested to have the one skull they were in possession of sent for the face to be reproduced by an artist. But when Chief Munson had discovered the cost, he'd told Clement such a proposition wasn't in the budget, either.

Although DNA had been extracted from the bones to determine sex, that had done no good right here and now in identifying the children. So these days, the stark, dry bones lay gathering dust within Clement's sight and very much on his mind.

Children. Two young boys. Buried or half-buried in Holder Park. Could Clement drive around town and not think about the children murdered? Could he go home at night and not think about the children murdered? Oh, yes, the two boys had been murdered, one with knife marks scoring some ribs and the other with the hyoid bone more or less crushed, indicating strangulation.

Today, Clement sat and looked at the boys, trying to decide what he must do. Maybe he could find someone who wanted to practice up, or who was charitable, to produce a model of the one boy, for free.

To find the killer, Clement had to identify the boys, discover when they'd disappeared and who might have been seen with them. People often came forward long after the fact—that was part of the cold case approach. But without the boys' identity, how could Clement proceed? He had searched through years and years worth of microfilm of the local paper, *The Holder Press*, as well as the department's reports of missing persons for the last 30 years. But he hadn't gotten a hint of two boys who'd disappeared simultaneously.

Well, a reporter had written a couple of articles in the *Post* about the case, one when two kids had found a femur in the park and another when department investigators had dug up the rest. Might someone know something and eventually contact the police? Maybe one of the parents of the boys?

The bones Clement was looking at right then had lain in the ground for many years, however. A heartbroken family or families might have moved on, while a murderous parent would likely never speak. Or the parent or parents were themselves dead.

And because Chief Munson had been under the odd impression that the murder was recent, Clement—the totality of the Holder cold case initiative—hadn't been at the crime scene on the initial dig. He'd been there subsequently, several times, of course, wondering where the boys might have come from. Had they been met at the scene and murdered there? Brought there dead? Or, brought there, and then killed?

Boys. Clement had one boy of his own, all grown up: Rod, a cook at one of the almost-decent local restaurants. Clement was extremely proud of his son. And that reminded him. Tomorrow night was a potluck supper at their church, where Clement and his ex-wife, Judy, were due to meet Rod's new girlfriend.

Clement struggled with the thought of bringing something— roasted chicken from the grocery off Osage, maybe. He could practically smell the bird right now and was reminded that lunchtime today had come and gone, and suppertime was almost here.

He made himself look at the tidily set forth bones on his way out...Children murdered.

Clement wasn't a good sleeper at best and though he fell asleep at one o'clock that night and slept an hour, once he woke up, he was wide awake. He dressed, went outside, and sat in one of the swings on the set he'd erected for a seven-year-old Rod. Always in an interior holster in Clement's pants, he wore a gun. At 47-years of age, though a police officer and a one-time MP in Afghanistan, he had to admit that sometimes too great a sense of caution overtook him. He lived in isolation in the country, and when he went outside into his own back yard at night, he was armed.

His mind returned now to the two dead children (brothers?

cousins?), and as his thoughts whirled around the case so unproductively, he hoped for a distraction. He knew what unstoppable rumination was, as well as lack of sleep.

Children in danger—what could be more upsetting to any policeman? But these children were beyond his help, and that was particularly troubling. He wanted to...at the very least he wanted a measure of justice for the boys. And he wanted the killer to have no more opportunities to destroy lives.

A car came up the road, and Clement tensed. This was a public roadway, of course, and sometimes a driver would be very late getting home to the housing development further along—or a worker would be very early traveling in the same or the opposite direction. But then the car pulled into Clement's front drive, and he saw that it was an RMP—a radio motor patrol vehicle, marked with his department's logo.

He recognized her from the brief academy class he sometimes taught on investigations. Not a pretty girl exactly—still a girl, rather than a woman yet—and not awkward, but gliding across the drought-nubbed grass.

"Sir?" she inquired when she was near enough.

He waited until she was even closer. "I'm not on call to-night," he said.

She stood in front of him, undoubtedly slender, but bulky in her uniform and gear. "Chief Munson told me that I was to come for you. I tried your phone numbers."

"I'm not on call," he repeated. "But wait in the car. I'll be out in five." He went in to dress.

Driving to the scene, watching the periodic swaths of fire-burnt land roll on ahead of them, he decided this was the distraction that he'd wanted. When he arrived home a few hours from now, he'd be able to sleep.

Or maybe he was wrong. Officer Bradley didn't know much. The homicide they were going to could be ugly, distressing, puzzling—sickening. The odds in favor of all those things weren't exactly bad.

Bradley slowed the car and started looking at the numbers, but Clement pointed to where the other RMP was parked half a block ahead. This was North Lake, and the lake was an artificial one, yet another pull on the area's slender water resources, but no doubt bringing absolutely seconds a year of joy to any busy, affluent homeowner who inadvertently happened to glance across the landscape. North Lake was still within Holder city limits but sooner or later would become part of its own incorporated suburb, probably dragging Clement and his acreage with it.

He supposed that Munson knew Clement wasn't on call, but figured the SPO was closer than anyone else he would likely send.

The officer standing guard outside the door raised his hand to Clement and Bradley in recognition. Or was he greeting Bradley, maybe a schoolmate? Some of the kids more recently out of the academy got the midnight to eight tour. They cycled from there to days, to the late tour, and back.

"What's up?" the senior cop asked the boy supposedly keeping the public at bay. Clement glanced around at the houses on the street. People were awake and looking out their windows. Only a few at the end of the block had ventured outside.

"Homicide," the kid assured him. "Husband's dead."

Clement nodded and walked in, Bradley at his heels like a baby chick imprinted on a substitute mother. No investigation, but evidence gathering would be the order of the day.

He couldn't smell gunpowder, and the living room showed no evidence of upset, aside from that caused by the cops milling around.

SPO Woodruf was already there, though on the phone, but he acknowledged Clement, who told Bradley to stay out here and do whatever Woodruf asked her to. She looked rebuffed.

Clement stalked further on. Nice home, immaculate more or less. In the hallway, however, he both saw and smelled a quantity of blood. He tapped quietly at one of the doors and opened it. Inside, a female officer looked up when Clement peeked in. She sat in a chair beside the bed of a sleeping child. The SPO gently closed the door. All of a sudden, he *did* feel tired, as if he himself could lie down and go to sleep, too, right this moment.

In the master bedroom next door, another woman officer sat with the wife. Clement wouldn't have guessed they had all these females on duty these days in the Holder P.D., but he recognized those he had seen tonight.

He came deep into the room, close enough to the wife sitting on the edge of the bed to witness a trembling underneath the liberally blood-splattered skin, where the muscles jumped of their own accord. Then, when she turned her face to him, he saw a frozen, wild expression in her blue eyes, as if she were from another realm. But Clement had seen such eyes before. Victims' eyes. Terrorized eyes. Eyes from which all humanity had fled, leaving the physical shell to survive—or not.

Clement gestured at the female officer to leave the chair at the bedside, which he then appropriated while the woman in the blue serge pants took up a post alongside the bureau. What must be in those drawers? Just the most usual of personal items—underwear, socks, handkerchiefs—set in organized rows or in disorder all around, and waiting to serve. The socks, pilled or new, didn't know that anything was wrong. They were stoical in the face of what undoubtedly was a human disaster.

Clement didn't say a thing but debated touching the wife's hand or trying to catch her eye once more. He shifted slightly in the seat and waited to see if she would come to him before he had to go to her.

She looked up at Clement sharply, then glanced around. "Shhh," she said. "He wants to kill us."

Clement nodded sympathetically. He tried to think what

might have happened here and decided on a home invasion and that the husband had been killed. But still, he was reluctant to reach out his hand and comfort her. Sometimes they grabbed onto you. That was better.

"Can you tell me what happened, ma'am?" he asked quietly. He wasn't sure he expected an answer. He wasn't sure if she knew she was in the same room with him or if she was in a state allowing her to interact.

"He's dangerous," she answered, however. "He's going to kill us."

"I won't let him," Clement told her.

But the wife looked around wildly. She tried to stand, which was when Clement finally reached out with a reassuring hand that coaxed her down.

"He wants to kill us," she repeated. "We need a knife."

"I have a gun," Clement offered, and she sighed and settled, lax, on the edge of the bed.

"He'll be back in a minute. I tried..." she said. "But nothing helps." All at once, tears streamed down the sides of her face and Clement took that as a good sign that she might come to her senses.

"Your husband," he suggested, wanting to hear if she knew that he was dead.

"Yes," she agreed, wiping at her eyes and streaking blood across her face. "I tried to stop him," she said. "But he'll be back."

"No," Clement insisted. "I won't let him."

"I stabbed him, stabbed him, stabbed him," she said. "But nothing kills him. Now I've lost my knife." She stood and Clement stood, too, trying to persuade her to take her seat, while the officer at the dresser made to come forward, and Clement had to signal her to stay where she was.

"Who? Who did you stab?" Clement asked, gently grasping the woman's wrist. "Who was he?"

"My husband. I told you," said the wife. "I stabbed and stabbed him, but he just wouldn't die."

7

* * *

Out in the back yard, Clement saw that she was mistaken. Gregory Holmes had died with as much ease as any other man who'd been stabbed so many times the medical examiner would have to count two or three times to be sure of the number. Clement had seen a lot of corpses is his career, but this one was so brutally hacked that it looked more like flesh pulp than a former human.

Clement, his feet planted carefully on the flagstone of the patio, watched two techs in white Tyvek coveralls extricate the corpse from a mound of dirt under which it was half-buried, an interesting touch. Woodruf emerged from the house and stood beside Clement. "Did she talk to you?" Woodruf asked. "An assistant district attorney will be out shortly."

"I wasn't on call," Clement said. He wasn't sure what he wanted to say.

"She talk to you?"

The two SPOs looked down at the body being disinterred. "Who called it in?" Clement countered. The two techs, removing the oozing corpse as best they could from the soil, had all the appearance of archeologists unearthing some rare find.

"A neighbor wasn't sure exactly what he saw," said Woodruf.

"I wasn't on call," Clement complained.

"You're good with the ladies," Woodruf said.

Clement turned and stared at the other SPO. He had known Louis Woodruf a long, long time although not well. "I'm good with the ladies because I like them," Clement answered. He had asked Christine Holmes who he might call for her and she had given him her sister's number. On his phone, he'd walked out of the female officer's earshot. Then he'd told the sister to get a good attorney out here immediately.

"Mrs. Holmes is afraid her husband is going to get up out of his grave and come after her," Clement now said. "Something wrong with this picture."

Woodruf frowned.

The medical examiner's assistant had the body on a trolley, which she rolled past a row of well-manicured azalea bushes and toward the garden gate.

Clement had suggested a couple of sharp defense attorneys to the sister before hanging up. And that was more or less why some disliked him in the department, or why the D.A. hated him, anyway.

He was supposed to want to see that frail, frightened woman put in prison. And she would be anyway, because the prosecutor was going to be unrelenting and the jury unforgiving. But Clement didn't have to be.

This wasn't going to be his case, and he wasn't an investigator for the defense, but he could undoubtedly prove that wretched mass of flesh they'd just hauled out of here deserved exactly what his wife had done. Clement simply knew it in his gut, and though the defense would show it to Clement's satisfaction, the jury would still put the woman where she only through bad luck and cruelty belonged.

"You know why she killed him," said Clement calmly, "just as well as I do."

"No," answered Woodruf in a neutral voice. "I don't." And, done with one another for the moment, the two SPOs turned almost simultaneously to reenter the house.

CHAPTER 2

When Clement arrived at their little three-room church home, erected about 20 years before by the small congregation, he remembered he had forgotten to stop for a potluck contribution. He had no time now, but hurried in past a few of the regulars chatting outside the door so he could take some time to quiet his mind.

Their church was a little bit unique, founded a quarter century before by Emmet Harding, a minister who believed that no man could exhort another in the right direction, but only the Christ could bring true guidance. Therefore, the minister, when they had one, didn't preach, but merely conducted the services, while others read from the Bible and such. The church wasn't evangelical then, but was democratic in its organization, and glad to have members from any denomination.

Clement sat with his eyes closed, but opened them with each arrival in the sanctum. He was eager to see his son's new girlfriend, Shelly. Shelly and Rod. Rod and Shelly. Would Clement like the combination? And did the father's opinion of the girl really matter at all?

The surge of love he felt when he thought of his son was unbelievable, strangely close to what he felt when he thought of God. That must be why God had given men fatherhood, so that even those who had no inkling of the Creator might experience such a devastating emotion.

When Clement finally saw the girl, he knew immediately that he didn't like her. She was young and pretty, but something about her struck Clement as all wrong. She would lead Rod away from his roots and suck him dry, bring him from exploring the depths of his existence to the surface of experience, turn his life into a husk of what it might have become.

How did Clement know that? Was this just his prejudice, or an insight? He closed his eyes again and tried to pray.

"Mr. Clement, I'm so happy to meet you," Shelly said when they were introduced in the basement, their tornado bunker/potluck hall. Dressed in a pristine red business suit with a short jacket, the girl wore large gold earrings that commanded attention. Shelly looked exactly like the corporate pharmaceutical saleswoman that she was. Clement was repelled by corporate; why wasn't his son?

The cop tried to expand his civility to embrace the girl, but only managed to sketch out a smile.

"I made a cherry pie, Dad," said Rod. He grinned. Clement loved cherry pie.

Judy came over and put her arm around their tall young son. Yes, Clement had lived with Judy for 15 years, and they'd had a son together. He tried to recall the circumstances of their marriage but what came to mind were some major cases he had worked on during that time.

"I brought a whole tub load of chicken salad," Judy said. She and Shelly evidently had met before. Clement eyed them as he would a pair of suspects, and Judy smiled as if she knew exactly that.

About 30 people had showed up for the worship, and a couple of dozen stayed for the meal. The four got in line to fill their plates.

Standing there, Clement folded his arms across his chest and tried to recapture the feeling of tranquility that had descended on him during their time in the sanctuary. Still, an uneasiness threatened to break through. Small talk grated on his nerves, and he left before the others did.

First thing Monday morning, the bones met Clement's eyes like a sock to the stomach. He was glad they were there. He *must* start on a few begging calls to find an artist who might put some flesh on the skull. He intended to make at least a little progress today.

Could he ever do enough, however? His will felt weak, and his determination started to sink. He sat and drank the coffee he had brought into the room.

The phone rang, and grateful for the distraction, he answered it. "Clement..."

After the desk sergeant let him know a visitor was here for him, Clement put the top back on his cup and went out to see. The sergeant's eyes traveled to a thin male figure in a not-too-crisp checkered shirt seated in one of the plastic chairs against the wall.

The man, 55 or so, Clement guessed, had the leathery face of an outdoor worker, maybe a farmer. What was left of his hair wasn't much, but had been slicked down, though Clement doubted that he'd done that in the course of an actual shower. On his lap, the man held a wrinkled paper bag with something in it. Sometimes families brought some sad gift of gratitude or other after a case had been solved. Clement hoped this wasn't one of those.

"Sir?" Clement addressed him as he approached; at which greeting, the visitor stood. "I'm Senior Police Officer Clement. What can I do for you?" Clement failed to extend his hand. Many years ago he had done so and the man turned out to be a murderer who had come to confess. Clement was sure he had shaken hands with other killers, of course, but that one irked him.

The man mumbled his name and Clement made him repeat it.

"Jessup Jenks."

Clement took Jenks back to his office where the man's eyes alighted on the bones lying across the extended windowsill, and he failed to notice Clement offering him a seat until Clement spoke up a second time, a bit more loudly.

Mr. Jenks sat, but his eyes swiveled again in the direction of the bones. Then he cleared a rasp of phlegm from his throat. "I have the other one," he said.

"The other one?" Clement repeated, not following at all.

Mr. Jenks opened the bag and out popped a skull onto Jenks's lap.

"Oh," exclaimed Clement, in astonishment. He could hardly have been much more startled by a head that still bore flesh and hair. "The other skull."

"Yes, sir," said the visitor. "I'm sorry I kept it."

Clement was glad he hadn't shaken the man's hand. "Tell me," he invited stoically, open to any type of statement or confession and a little excited that the case of the two boys had perhaps just solved itself.

The visitor shrugged. "I found it in the park some years ago and brought it to home. I liked it for a decoration out in the shed. I never thought I ought to turn it in. It never struck me." He shuffled his feet aimlessly.

"Of course," Clement agreed, once the man stopped his speech. Oh, sure, and where did Jenks think the skull simply lying around was from? Why would he not imagine that a skull found in the park ought to be brought in to the police? Had the man ever thought of *who, how, why*? If he had brought in the skull, they would have combed the park years before and could have started on their search for the killer or killers way back then. Clement waited for the rest of the story from Mr. Jenks.

"A guy visiting me last week told me you all were searching for another skull." The man put the skull back in the bag, then reached forward and placed the bag on Clement's desk. "So I brought it in."

Clement nodded as if people brought skulls to him all the time. He was energized though because somehow he imagined this would make the job easier. Of course it might not, really...

He asked Jessup Jenks a few more questions and then let him go. Jenks, whether he'd killed the two boys or not, could be a piece of a start. The possibility was that Jenks *had* killed them, had kept the skull as a souvenir or had retrieved it and had only turned it in because someone had seen the skull and might follow through with the police.

Stranger things happened every day of the week. Leads came walking in on their own two feet and this might be one.

Clement had been called over to the prosecutor's office and here he stood on the dun-colored carpet that made him think of the layer of dried weeds spread across the fields alongside his land. He was worried, very worried, about the coming summer fires. If the county, which owned the adjoining property, didn't get onto the land soon, he'd have to ask Rod to go in there with him so they could create a wide firebreak.

"The Holmes' murder," said assistant prosecutor Janet Enkan, turning toward Clement with a cold look from where she sat at the desk of power. A plump, middle-aged woman with a streak of orange across her lips, Enkan was known for her ruthless pursuit of...well...criminals to be sure, but also the prosecutor's top position.

"Yeah," said Clement. "A nasty business." He braced himself. The very appropriate phrase, *called on the carpet*, made its way through his head. He had put in enough years with the department and could retire, but he liked the job and what would he do then? He hadn't a single hobby that he could think of.

"Sit down," she said, as if startled that he hadn't already

taken a seat. He obeyed. "We're preparing for the grand jury," she explained.

"Ah," agreed Clement, noncommittally. He wanted nothing so much as to be back in his own office doing paperwork, which he hated.

"You spoke to Mrs. Holmes at the scene," prodded Enkan.

"I did," he acknowledged.

She glared at him. He supposed he was expected to be more forthcoming, and he was going to have to be.

"What was the tenor of that conversation? Did she admit to killing her husband?"

"She was disoriented. Her belief seemed to be, if I can summarize, that her husband was still alive and a danger to her safety." He spoke mildly, in a professional tenor.

He had accustomed himself over the years to saying the most disturbing things in neutral tones. The last report he'd made in front of cameras had been several years previously, when he'd explained that the killer of a ten-year-old had been prepared to cannibalize her, and that meat tenderizer and skewers had been found ready for use in the kitchen. Once Clement had been able to give that information in an impersonal manner, he knew he could say anything.

At this moment, though, Enkan looked annoyed. "She knew she'd stabbed him?"

"Yes, she knew."

"Well, just say that," concluded Enkan.

"I think I'm supposed to answer whatever I'm asked," Clement responded, his voice remaining entirely unemotional, though he had begun to feel a wee bit angry. Angry because? Angry because she was trying to coach his testimony. However, he could see the entire case unraveling for him should the question of what he'd said to the sister on the phone come up in court.

He hadn't been altogether professional at that point. At least not as the department defined it. He'd told the sister to arrange not only for the best defense attorney in the area, but for an immediate psychiatric examination and he'd suggested that she get over there immediately. He'd done the *right* thing, but not the most cop-like thing. He'd been sympathetic.

While Enkan was undoubtedly debating how to rake Clement over the coals, he put in another sentence that would, though not designed to, certainly provoke. "The victim may be shown to have been an abuser."

"That's possibly so," Enkan shot back, "but a strong sedative was found in his system—drugs prescribed for Mrs. Holmes. And residue was discovered in a water glass on the nightstand. That's quite a case for premeditation."

That was a point Clement hadn't heard back at the station, and one that gave him a certain amount of pause. Not about the woman's motivation necessarily, but in regard to any chance in hell Christine Holmes had of getting off.

Using the same tired brown paper bag in which Jenks had brought the skull to him, Clement transported the cranium to Dr. Neal, a forensic anthropologist at the Oklahoma Science Tech campus about 15 miles northwest of Holder proper. Since Neal had initially examined the bones for Clement, Clement knew when Neal had his office hours and hadn't called first.

Neal's office was smaller than Clement's because Clement had lucked into a closed-off hall end to call his own, while Neal was housed in a cube-shaped space in a row of similar-seeming offices.

Neal was there, talking to a student, when Clement tapped on the door and more or less barged in. He was eager to see what Neal might make of the find. "The second skull," he said and took it out of the bag without hesitation like a magician pulling a rabbit out of a hat.

Neal didn't react by more than a raised eyebrow, though the young male student in jeans and a blue polo shirt who sat across from the professor looked highly intrigued.

Neal's desk overflowed with all kinds of books and papers, and Clement saw no room to set down the skull, even if he could have sucked in his breath and sneaked past the student to reach the desktop.

"How do you know it's the second skull?" asked Neal.

"What do you mean?" asked Clement who realized at once exactly what the professor meant. How did Clement know for sure that this was the skull of the second victim? Well, it was small, a boy's skull, he figured, and it had been found by Jenks, the man had said, in Holder Park. But of course the assumption was a thoughtless one, a stupid and unscientific leap to judgment.

"I need the whole set," Neal went on. "I need the whole set of bones in order to make that determination. Bring me back the whole set and be careful with them."

Clement's mind cycled quickly through a file cabinet of ideas, trying to come up with some way to get around having to bring the bones back to the older, black-eyed man with the slovenly gray beard who sat not four feet from him at the other end of the narrow room. Clement liked having the boys' bones with him during the day. He felt comforted by them and he felt he, in turn, comforted the two.

And maybe that was how Jenks had felt about this skull. Maybe that was why he had kept it with him. Not that Jenks hadn't understood the enormity of a skull discovered in the middle of an urban park, but that he hadn't wanted to relinquish such an object to which one might sense some heartfelt link.

But that was also what lay behind a killer's taking of a souvenir that cemented forever his connection with the victim.

"Stupid of me," said Clement. "I wasn't thinking. I'll pack up the bones and bring them all back. Shall I leave the skull?"

By way of an answer, Neal stood up and reached out to take the head. At the same time, the student leapt up and pushed his chair closer to the desk to facilitate the transfer. The one man now passed the skull to the other, and the transaction was complete.

"I'll let you know then," said Neal, and Clement gestured agreement and left.

CHAPTER 3

The closer they got to the summer—and early April really should be nowhere near—the more nervous everyone in Holder became. In fact, everyone in the whole Southwest and up through Colorado was waiting now for the other shoe to drop, for more fires, for a ruination to rival the Dust Bowl of the 1930s.

Driving into town, Clement kept thinking about the dry land next to his house and decided to arrange to have someone out to plow the land and get rid of the thick, desiccated brush. Going onto county property on his own initiative probably wasn't absolutely legal, but he'd be darned if he was going to wait until fire season and let the house he'd lived in for nearly 25 years catch a spark from next door. Not that he relished the idea of the soil that would be released by a plow and blowing into his yard.

Good solutions to prevent Oklahoma and those states contiguous from going up in smoke were in short supply. Clement considered rigging up a water tank on his roof, but he was afraid that the house, a nice-sized country home from the 1890s, might collapse.

Clement stopped his car at a light and glanced at the newspaper on the seat beside him. Eighty-eight degrees was hot for this time of the year, but isolated thundershowers were predicted for the day after tomorrow. He hoped the area would get a corking good storm, and that the promise of precipitation wouldn't fade.

Five minutes later, he arrived at the courthouse. He wore the sole court-worthy suit that he owned, and this and funerals were the only places where he wore it. He supposed the purchase of a new suit wouldn't really be amiss, but he hadn't gained any weight in the last few years, and he hated to sink two or three hundred into something he didn't wear all that often.

An avid throng of reporters had gathered in front. Some cases were like that, and the case of a wife killing a husband was going to be hotter than a Billy goat in a red pepper patch. As sleepy as Holder might once have been, the town had grown by leaps and bounds in the last decade or so, and no towns were that sleepy anymore these days.

Of course if the drought got any worse this year, so would the economy droop, and people might move along out to California or up to the northern plains as they had in the '30s. Not Clement though. He was comfortable here—and he had a pension coming even if they kicked him out of the department.

Inside the old building, the air was hot as sin, but it was too early by the calendar for government offices to have on air-conditioning below a 90-degree exterior temperature. Clement paused to unbutton his jacket. The shirt would have to go to the laundry, without a doubt, but if he could get by a couple of hours in here, he would save the suit a cleaning.

Chief Munson and SPO Woodruf were in the hallway inside the grand jury waiting area in the basement, but Clement didn't go over to speak to them. He sat on a blue plastic chair and closed his eyes, trying to stay cool.

He was bothered by the idea that Gregory Holmes had been drugged. Of course Mrs. Holmes—Christine—had done the drugging. Clement had no illusion that anyone else had come into the house and drugged the man, and Clement knew that

Christine had been afraid of her husband.

But still, as a cop, he wasn't all that comfortable with the progression of events and the woman's obvious premeditation. Because she hadn't drugged Gregory simply for the night, but in order to kill him. And either Christine had been crazy before she'd planned to drug and stab her husband to death (in which case, what kind of crazy, really?) or she'd gone a bit mad before or during the stabbing.

Or, of course, Christine hadn't been that crazy at all, but had been shamming. And Clement couldn't believe he'd been that wrong. He tried to accept that he might have been fooled, but he knew he hadn't been. She'd been out of her mind. But could that insanity have been intentional, in some way, too? Could she have been medicated for schizophrenia, maybe, and stopped taking her medication because she wanted to get away with killing her husband?

He had a moral dilemma here and the consequences were serious for all concerned. He'd given the sister advice because he'd come to a snap decision about the case—just as he'd come to a snap decision about the skull. He was probably right in both instances, but neither conclusion had been well thought out. Clement already knew he could get kicked out of the department for what he'd done in counseling the sister, and he was concerned. But maybe even more worrisome was that he didn't want his sentimentality to taint a case against a killer.

Finally, he conceded to the heat and took off his jacket, but sweat was seeping into his pants. He stood up to let his pants dry and went over by the fan, then poured himself a glass of water from the pitcher on the table.

Clement had testified before grand juries in the basement grand jury room many times before, and so when he was called in a minute later, he wasn't nervous but simply shocked and relieved by the cold in the relatively small space he stepped into. Here, the air conditioning was an absolute necessity. So, let his sweat freeze!

Enkan asked Clement his name and such routine questions as how he happened to have been at the Holmes residence that night.

"When you spoke to her, did Mrs. Holmes acknowledge that she had stabbed her husband?"

Clement hesitated. Well, the woman might as well be indicted—and she would be if Enkan wanted her to be. "Yes," he said.

"She said she stabbed him?"

Clement tried to recall exactly the words that Mrs. Holmes had spoken. "Yes," he repeated. He felt uneasy, though, because how a person might most sensibly regard what had happened depended not just on Mrs. Holmes' words and not just on Clement's "yes." The matter wasn't so very simple.

"Thank you," said Enkan. She paused and looked at the members of the grand jury, her fingers moving in mid-air in an impatient wiggling, though not directed at Clement. None of the jurors—entitled to ask whatever questions they wished—raised a voice. "Thank you," repeated Enkan.

Clement stood up. They were all just going through the motions here, but that was all right, he reassured himself. The trial would be the real deal. This was nothing.

He ought to have said more, maybe, taken the initiative. But really, his not having spoken wasn't so bad. Especially if the murder had been premeditated. Clement pushed the door to the outer chamber and was once more enveloped by the circulating fetid air, intended to cool them. He nodded at Munson, now sitting by himself, and hurried off.

That Jessup Jenks had met two boys in Holder Park not far from his house and had killed them was as likely as his simply having found the skull there and taken it home. Clement drove from the park to the address Jenks had given him, a short drive, but about a 20 minute walk. Interesting, because Jenks hadn't seemed in very good shape physically, not the kind of shape you'd expect an habitual walker to be in. Twenty minutes each way, after all, was 40 minutes—a good long walk, especially if he'd then walked in the park a while as well.

The man's residence was a little more isolated than Clement had expected, being on the edge of the neighborhood and up an oddly slanted incline. That also meant that if Jenks had walked to the park and back, he'd climbed up a steep slope at the end.

The house was a rather old one-story and beat up. No pretensions here. Clement rang the bell and waited a bit. Eventually, Jenks opened the door and peeked out. He appeared startled. Clement reminded the man that they'd spoken very recently. "Did I forget something?" Jenks asked. Clement didn't really quite know what he meant.

"Nice location," said Clement. "You're near the park."

"Yes, convenient," agreed Jenks, who didn't seem disposed to invite Clement in.

"Can we talk?" Clement asked.

Jenks looked clueless as to what the two of them had to discuss. "Can you meet me out back...in the shed?" he suggested.

An odd request, but one that Clement acceded to. Walking around to the back of the house, the SPO felt spooked.

Inside the shed, a startling vision met Clement's eyes: bones, bones, bones—an incredible mess otherwise, with all the usual paraphernalia of a working man's shed, but with bones on shelves everywhere, most of them small, like the bones of babies. The flesh had been removed from them and the bones were dry, heaped up for some unobvious reason.

"Oh," said Jenks weakly. "Yes, the bones. I...I..." Whatever the man was trying to say didn't come straight out of his mouth. "I forgot..."

He'd forgotten that he had piles of bones in the shed when he'd asked a homicide investigator to meet him there? Clement went over to the shelves and looked without touching them. The rib cages and limbs of babies? What type of hellacious charnel house had he wandered into?

"I like bones," said Jenks, apparently by way of rational explanation. "They're very mysterious. We all have bones, but most of the time our bones are covered."

Clement turned and looked at Jenks. The man was insane and had killed the boys. How easy was this turning out to be?

"That's why I kept the skull. What a great find. I wasn't thinking..."

The man had kept the skull for a dozen years and now he said he "wasn't thinking"? For 12 years, he "wasn't thinking"?

"And where did all these bones come from?" Clement asked mildly, pointing around. Perhaps in a not-thinking state Jenks had committed a few other atrocities.

"Oh," said Jenks, again confounded. "These are mine." Clement didn't respond, and Jenks seemed to realize that the policeman had taken his words somehow differently than he'd meant them. "Here, I'll show you."

Bigger and better revelations?

Jenks led Clement out onto the property and around a bend. As they neared a structure further along, Clement caught wind of a somewhat rank smell and heard an uproar of odd squawking. "Oh, because I'm here, they think it's feeding time," said Jenks.

They'd arrived at a wired-in pen with an attached coop, inside which were chickens. Clement didn't know his chickens, but he felt sure that these weren't ordinary ones. "What are they? Show chickens or something?" Clement asked.

Jenks seemed pleased by the question. "They're pretty, aren't they? Shaver Reds and a couple of D'anvers."

"The bones are theirs?"

"I've had a lot of hens over the years. Sometimes they die," Jenks said sadly.

"Then you eat them?"

"Good heavens, no. We only eat the eggs." Obviously Jenks was shocked by the callous sentiment of Clement's ignorant question.

After a short walk back to the house, Jenks finally invited Clement in, and they entered by the yard door. The display inside was the culmination of all that the SPO had already seen. "What do you call it?" Clement asked, goggle-eyed.

"Chicken art," Jenks replied promptly.

Jenks had rebuilt a number of his dead chickens. Dead hens stood everywhere like statuettes—some only skeletons wired together (and Clement now could see that the bones in the shed were indeed chicken bones) and some with feathers, beaks, and even eyes. Not all were the types Clement had seen outside in the chicken run, either, but all were really quite beautiful, he thought—for chickens, anyway.

"Remarkable," Clement observed.

A woman of about Jenks's age emerged from another room. "Oh, you're getting the grand tour," she said. She looked around as if seeing the chicken art for the first time. Then she made a gesture of resignation. "It's his passion," she remarked. "We used to go around the Southwest to the state fairs and the 4H shows. We sold a lot of them. Now we stay home and just sell the eggs."

"Making these is a lot of work," added Jenks, "but I love doing it." He turned to the woman. "He's here about the skull, Goldie."

"I told him time and time again, he shouldn't keep it," the woman said. "But would he listen to me? No, of course not. He'll only listen to someone else. He'll only take advice from a man, don't you know?…I hope he isn't going to get into trouble."

"No," said Clement. "I don't think so." Jessup Jenks was a man obsessed with chickens, apparently, and probably not boys. He was, to come right down to it, typically Oklahoman, in his very oddity. Once Clement got the idea of where the man was coming from, Jenks didn't seem all that strange, actually— just a guy who…well, did whatever he did, because he liked it. The skull? The matter of the skull, of course, remained to be seen.

* * *

Rod's apartment door opened before Clement even rang the upstairs bell. Of course Clement had buzzed first in the lobby. Now he smiled stiffly at his son and handed him a bottle of wine. Clement had been told that Shelly appreciated a glass or two with dinner, and he was trying to make this evening work.

Clement thought his son's smile was both knowing and intend to reassure.

"Hello, Mr. Clement," Shelly called from the depths of Rod's black leather lounger. Clement tried to smile in response, but didn't seem to do too well at it. That she was relaxing while Rod worked nagged at Clement. But the reality was that the nuances of the relationship were none of his business.

"Sit down on the sofa, Dad. Shelly, look what Dad brought us. Very thoughtful—chilled, too. Sauvignon blanc. Wow, Dad, you're really learning." Of course the sophisticated vintner hadn't been Clement, but the clerk in the store who had alerted on the pricey Napa Valley wine like a K-9 sniffing out a bag of cocaine.

Rod looked back at his father. "I'm going to finish off a couple of things in the kitchen now, guys. Shelly, why don't you pour the two of us some? I don't think Dad wants any of that."

Rod stepped into the narrow, contemporary apartment kitchen that he'd outfitted as a chef's paradise. When had Clement's son gotten as deft at social maneuvering as he seemed to be? Had he gotten that from Judy? Or on his own? Surely not from Clement.

Shelly had hopped up and was uncorking the wine with expertise at the dark wood sideboard. "Of course you'll have a glass," she said to Clement.

"Really not," he disagreed. Why hadn't she accepted Rod's word concerning his father's preference? Oh man, he felt irritable tonight. That really wouldn't do. He struggled to right himself. "What is it you sell, Shelly? I know it's pharmaceuticals, but what, exactly?"

"Oncology drugs." Having filled two long stemmed glasses with the white wine, Shelly popped her head into Rod's realm and handed him one. The apartment was small and the living room and dining room more or less merged, but everything was perfect here. Rod's life was as well-trimmed and neat as his sandy-brown hair. Maybe that was it—Shelly was the type of groomed and professional girl who fit well with Rod. But she wasn't exactly "Oklahoma." Possibly that was what Clement objected to.

Shelly returned with a plate of crackers and cheese. Even the food, Clement thought, wasn't quite what he was used to.

She sat again. In Rod's chair, a chair Rod had been rather excited about buying. "Rod tells me you work on unsolved cases, 'cold cases,'" she said.

Clement nodded. He picked a fancy cracker off the decorative plate. "No statute of limitation for murder," he told her, merely to say something. The cracker was the type to break an aging man's teeth. He crunched on it for a while.

"Yes," she said, seeming to think over this comment. "You really wouldn't want anyone to get away with murder."

"No, you wouldn't," he flashed. "Nor anything else criminal in nature. Or at least I wouldn't. Why they have a statute of limitation for any class A or B felony, I don't know." He did feel strongly on that topic.

"But surely someone might...turn his life around...and not really need to be prosecuted over something he did, well many years before..." The girl's own smile was tight and glasslike. She could be nervous, herself, or angry at Clement. She saw him as coming between her and Rod, or...well, he couldn't really know what the girl thought.

"People have to pay for what they've done," Clement said.

"Is that in the Bible?" She sipped at her wine and stared at him.

"No," Clement acknowledged, as if she'd caught him in an

unchristian attitude. "'Vengeance *is* mine; I will repay, saith the Lord.' That's what's in the Bible. But an organized society of more than 300-million people in this country can't let it go at that." Then he grew silent. He believed. He believed both what was in the Bible—and what he experienced every day he was on the job.

CHAPTER 4

Clement sat in the cramped station house "lunch room" eating slices of leftover brisket on thick seven-grain bread. The beef was tough, so Clement hoped he could chew and swallow, but his boy had insisted Clement take all the dinner fixings when he left—pecan pie included.

Just about to call Rod and leave a message as to how great the dinner had been and how tasty the sandwich, Clement was joined by two uniformed officers with their Chinese takeout. This was why Clement didn't like to eat in the lunch room, which had only two small tables. But while a cup of coffee in front of "his" bones was inevitable, Clement didn't want to eat in front of the remaining slain boy in his office. It seemed disrespectful.

"How's it going, gentlemen?" he asked the two. Stan Running horse, the perennially worried-looking one whose uniform had begun to bulge at the hips, had come onto the force a couple of years after Clement, and Clement recalled him well from years of roll calls. The other, older one, Martin Burks, was so grey in every respect he just about blended into the government-issue grey-green walls.

"A rash of house robberies out past North Comanche around Horn Ridge," Burks answered.

Clement didn't know how they could eat the nasty concoctions that came from Luck Sun takeout around the corner.

Burks' meal emerged from the cardboard container pre-congealed.

"Is that a development out there?" Clement asked.

"Some older ranch style houses. Afternoon robberies. Break-ins around the back, either the door or the windows," Burks told him through a mouthful of his dinner.

"We have a missing schoolteacher from Holder High," put in Stan. He opened up a can of soda and poured the super-charged liquid into a plastic cup. "A local beauty queen a few years back. She left one of those, like, giftware parties that the women have and wasn't seen after."

"Probably won't be seen again," offered Burks. "Know how that goes."

The three men chewed stolidly and considered the proposition for a long moment. Not a single one of them could say that of course the woman would be found.

Clement shook his head in general annoyance at "civilization."

"Turn up anything on those bones of yours?" asked Burks.

Clement fought to swallow a lump of beef. "Someone brought in what's probably the other skull," he said hopefully. "I just don't understand why a parent hasn't come forward, or why I can't find a report of two missing boys in the files. I've been through the past 30 years and the guy at the university said the bones can't have been out there more than that long." He heard himself sounding as frustrated as he felt. "Two young kids and no one reports them? Unless the parents are the ones who killed them."

Some other cop would have been cursing by now, but Clement hadn't been in the habit since he'd come back from the Army and found, well, yeah, "religion." A warm glow gripped his heart and he relaxed.

Stan Runninghorse spooned some rice onto a noxious-looking main dish. "I know one possibility," he said quietly.

Clement zeroed in on him and waited for more.

Stan shrugged. "Tolliver," he told Clement. "I rode with him for a while back in the 1980s. He didn't like to take reports on missing kids. Well, not on what he called 'the riff raff.' He always said the kids must have run off. I'm not claiming we had a lot of these, but we did have a few."

Clement's stomach began to churn along with his mind. He stood up and pushed in his chair, then brought the plastic bag with a couple of crusts of bread and the last slice of beef and shoved it in the trash. When he turned back, the two uniforms were looking at one another as if they feared Clement might flee in pursuit of what he'd heard from Runninghorse.

"How the hell did he get away with that kind of crap?" Clement asked. His voice was choked with the blatant wrongness of Tolliver's misdeeds.

"That's the way things were in those days under the old chief. You know it. You were here," answered Stan.

"I don't know it," Clement disagreed.

Neither man answered him. They looked away. And maybe— well, undoubtedly—Clement did know.

When he walked off, he felt as if he were slinking away, avoiding what they were all aware of. He knew. And they knew why and how he knew.

He didn't want to go back and face the remaining boy's bones with so much on his mind, and his lunch sat like a lead weight waiting to be digested, so he got in his car in the station lot and drove off without a thought of where he was going. Out of downtown and the congestion of humanity, that was all he knew.

He ought to like people better, and he wished he did. He didn't blame God exactly for how he'd turned out, but at this moment he felt terribly mediocre at everything. He couldn't rise above his own conventional nature spiritually, and he wasn't much of a success as a cop these days, either. He was middle-aged all of a sudden and indecisive about right and wrong.

Though maybe not knowing which way was up was better than feeling he knew something for sure. Still, sinking in quicksand wasn't an especially comfortable position.

Out near the Cherokee Natural Gas pipelines, he turned around and drove back to the WalMart. He could at least get something for the headache that had begun to creep up his neck.

He would've imagined that at this time of day everyone over the age of 20 would be at work, but no. Men and women, and not just the retired set, seemed bent on spending all the income that they weren't busy acquiring. None of his business, either, was it?

Inside the store, he picked out a few cans of dog food for the stray that, without taking actual responsibility for, he'd been feeding lately. If Clement was going to feed the animal, he ought to take it in, let it get dog hairs on his sofa and chew up his shoes, and take it to the vet. Then Clement would have to come home early enough at night to keep the dog company. He had to laugh at himself.

He knew the painkillers weren't good for him, any more than the over-the-counter stomach medications would be. He walked along the rows of shelves in the pharmacy section evaluating what remedy he might buy. He examined the boxes but couldn't decide and so went to the pharmacy counter to find a package of mints, instead.

Bradley, the girl cop whose first name he could never re-member, stood there, waiting, wearing a regular office skirt and blouse, as if she'd been to a job interview, her eyes blank even when she looked straight at Clement. He figured maybe she was picking up a prescription she didn't want anyone to know about, and when the pharmacist came over, he stepped back by the teething rings and plastic bottles in order to be tactful and not eavesdrop. But then she showed her identification. "Holder Police," she said. "You're the pharmacist?"

The boy on duty acknowledged that he was.

Holy cow, someone up there in the ranks had taken a liking to Officer Bradley and was giving her a tryout in investigations. That was interesting as no promotions would come through until the fall.

The gist of what she wanted, and he wasn't reluctant to listen in at this point, was the prescription orders for Mrs. Holmes. Legwork—and she was probably quite pleased to be able to do it in her civvies and not in blue serge at this time of year. He peeked at her legs to see if she was so foolish as to wear nylons or whatever the women called those things these days. He didn't think so.

"Can't tell you anything," objected the boy. "The federal regulations are strict on privacy. HIIPA." As if that meant anything to the general public, though Clement knew the government had regulations.

"She's gonna get a subpoena later on anyway, Bobby, so you might as well tell her something now for her to carry back to the D.A.," Clement butted in. He supposed Bradley's glance at him was a hostile one, but he actually was trying to do her a good turn. Bobby and Rod had gone to Holder High together a ways back. Then Rod had gone on to work in a restaurant and learn to cook, and Bobby had finished at Oklahoma State.

Did Clement wish his own son had become a quasi-professional like Bobby Winters? Well, maybe. Or maybe not. Then all the girls Rod met would be like Shelly, cold and snobbish; whereas with Rod's current job, once he got past this particular woman, he had a chance of doing better for himself. Or, in the eyes of some people other than Clement, less well. Rod could meet a more natural, down-to-earth, less materialistic girl.

Clement sidled back toward the counter, a conciliatory smile on his face. Confrontation wasn't his style, especially in a circumstance like this. His best approach was to let Bobby feel that not giving in made him a bad sport.

"You know," Clement said, "a murder investigation." He

reached for a nail clipper and turned it around in his fingers, his gaze on the object rather than the pharmacist.

"Oh well," said Bobby, "but don't tell." His eyes were on Clement and not on the girl. "I could lose my job." He tapped some computer keys and slowly told Bradley what she wanted to know, letting her take notes and spelling out the drug names she hesitated over.

Clement dropped the clippers and decided he'd get a soda on the way out. "Thanks, Bobby," said Clement at the end.

He waited for Bradley and walked her toward the door, and when he said he had to get something to drink, she stopped with him, and he asked her whether she, herself, would like a soda.

Outside the store, he expected her mask to slip and her annoyance at his interference to show, and he prepared to be defensive. "My kid went to school with Bobby," he began. He put his hand out to stop her from crossing into traffic.

"I don't get a training class until August in Boise City," she said. She hesitated and sipped her cola through the straw he'd given her. "Did I sound stupid?"

They two crossed into the parking lot and stopped again. "No," he said. "I didn't think that. I just know him. I didn't really mean to interfere."

"Oh no," she said. She looked around as if to orient herself to the location of her car. "That was great. I can look good now when I go back. Thanks."

He had anticipated a stern reaming out for being such a chauvinist and was suddenly relieved. He swigged at his club soda, glad for his final choice of remedies. "See you back at the station later," he told her and grinned.

She didn't walk off but held him with what felt like a reluctance to leave. "The sleeping stuff in his system was hers then," said Bradley.

34

"Uh huh," Clement acknowledged. "But I've been thinking about that." The sun had peeked out from behind a transient cloud, and he started to bake. "He could have taken her medication himself—trouble sleeping or whatever."

"No," said Bradley. "It was dissolved in the water."

"Oh yeah," he recalled. "But I'd love to see all her medical records. The D.A. will get the files from the defense though, during disclosure...Whoa, it's hot out here. What do you want to bet on how many broken bones from 'falls' off the patio and walking into doors? Ever break a bone walking into a door?"

Bradley appeared reluctant to agree. She wiped a fingerful of sweat from atop her upper lip and shook her head. "Even so," she said, "it's not a license to commit a premeditated murder."

"I didn't say that," he responded. But he could well imagine that such abuse might be exactly the permission needed for someone who had few inner or external resources to lean on.

Backing away toward the promise of air-conditioning, he made a gesture of finality with his palm, then turned and hurried along the melting tarmac until he found his car. *She's wayyyy too young for you*, he reminded himself. She looked a whole lot better today in her regular clothes than she had the other night.

She'd built his ego up, he guessed, and something in him had opened to her. But not only was he too old for the girl, who was no more than 30, he felt entirely wary of such entanglements. All he really needed at his age was his God, his boy, his work, and his house. If he could make it through the next 30 or 40 years on any combination of these things, he would be able to die in relative peace, he figured.

But who knew what might come next on the grand agenda. He sure didn't.

CHAPTER 5

Clement realized he had come out in this direction for a reason and not just randomly. He hadn't seen his dad in a good long while, and despite everything between the two of them, he couldn't just let the relationship slide. But then again, he had to be honest, that wasn't really why he wanted to see his dad.

The homes in the Cherokee Wash area were old and small. Clement hadn't grown up out here, but when Clement's mother had died, the senior Clement had sold the house nearer town and bought this place on the cheap. The problem, of course, was that this was a river basin from a prior era and subject to a real danger from flash floods. When the ground was dry as it had been the last few years, heavy downpours were a definite threat to life and property. That was something people maybe didn't consider could occur with a drought.

The area was seedy and gave off a heavy sense of economic and emotional downturn, with homes needing maintenance, and flaunting browning, uncut lawns that would invite the spread of flames when wild fires started for the summer—and they would. Even if Clement got out here and did something about his father's lawn, the house next door was less than a dozen feet away, and any fire there would easily leap to his father's little cottage.

Clement knocked, then rang the bell. In a moment, he felt his father staring out at him. "Police," Clement announced in a voice as official as he could make it.

The door opened. "I called you guys two hours ago," his father said, and Clement smiled. Despite the joke, he couldn't detect any sign of pleasure at the visit on his father's face. He came into the house and followed his dad into the living room where the TV was on. The old man's arthritic limp seemed bad today.

"Where's Maria?" Clement asked.

"You come to see her?" His dad sank into his recliner and heaved his legs up onto the foot rest. He didn't turn the television down and they were soon engrossed in a commercial featuring a talking gecko with an Australian accent. Although the little guy was terminally adorable, Clement figured the lizard should, by rights, have a Southwest twang.

But he didn't say anything and neither did his dad until the commercial was over and the news started in with its summation of everything that everyone already knew.

"So?" his dad asked him.

"Just checking up."

"In the middle of a work day? You do still work, don't you?" His father glanced from the set to Clement.

Clement didn't answer but thought about what he was going to ask now that he had his dad's attention. "Henry Tolliver," he said.

"Oh, so it isn't a personal visit," his father answered and turned his head back to the TV.

The two men watched a report on the missing schoolteacher while several pictures of her were flashed on the screen, including one of her in a bathing suit taken when she'd won a local beauty contest a few years back.

"Christ!" said his father in irritation. "It never ends."

Clement blinked.

"I hope I don't offend you with my blasphemy," his father added, looking at Clement with something of a sadistic smirk.

"I've heard worse," Clement answered woodenly. "Was Tolliver as bad a cop as they say?"

Clement's father had joined the department when only 20 officers patrolled in three shifts. In those days, the three homicides per year, tops, came out of the occasional Saturday night drunken sense of a world gone wrong.

"Well, that depends on what you think a good cop or a bad cop is," his father said.

Clement reached from the sofa to the arm of the recliner and picked up the remote. He punched the mute button. He didn't want to argue policing philosophy, however. "If someone reported their kids gone missing would he have filed on it?"

His dad, whose eyes had followed the movement of the remote, now nodded in a regretful acknowledgement of the truth. "Depends on whose kids."

Clement, angered, shook his head. He tried to clear from his mouth the words that arose, though they stuck insistent on the edge of his tongue. "And Chief Kenny tolerated that?"

The old man picked up the remote, though he didn't turn the sound back on. "Kenny let a few things slide," the older man muttered.

That told his son a whole lot more than he wanted to hear. Clement worked on just breathing and saying nothing.

"How's Rod?" asked his father, abruptly veering from things neither one of them wanted to discuss.

"Has a new girlfriend." Clement also didn't want to talk about *that*. "He's a real good cook." The lump had just about disappeared from Clement's gut. Wasn't the boy's fault that the beef had been tough.

"You should have sent the kid to college," Clement's father said.

Clement got up from the sofa. "I'd come out and mow your lawn, but you don't really have one." Rod hadn't wanted to go to college. Clement would have paid anything for the boy to go.

And then another constant theme from his father. "If you'd given Judy the house and the kid had grown up decently..."

Funny how instead of talking about his father's dismissal from the department for having been dirty, they'd shifted to Clement's imaginary misdeeds. His father knew that Judy had wanted to move back to town.

On his way to his office tucked behind the stairs to the second floor, Clement happened to run into the chief. Munson had brought a breath of life into the department, had gotten rid of the lazy cops and those collecting money that, one way or the other, wasn't rightfully theirs. On that basis alone, Clement appreciated Munson, though the new chief had anticipated an entirely different attitude from Clement when he'd edged out the SPO's father.

Still, as pure as Munson had seemed at the time, he wasn't pure enough for the son of the grifter. Munson was entirely too political to always gain high marks for law enforcement from his subordinate.

Now, he asked Clement to step into his recently recarpeted sanctum sanctorum. Munson wasn't on the take, but he pretty much did well for himself, as Clement could see. The chief stepped behind his desk and settled his bulk in a black leather executive chair. The recliner in Clement's dad's house had been well-worn. This piece of furniture radiated a new leather smell.

But at least Munson hadn't taken away the old man's pension, Clement reflected.

Clement took the padded, green visitor's chair without being invited to.

"I've been looking for you all afternoon," Munson complained.

"You want me to account for all my time?" Clement asked. "I'm not cheating the taxpayers." He tended to become hot under the collar with Munson, and today he felt as if he could easily step away from the job, go home, and happily become a hermit.

"No, no," said Munson. "That isn't it. It's about Enkan and the Holmes' case."

Clement shrugged. "She got her indictment." Enkan couldn't have found out he'd helped Bradley investigate not two hours before, and if she had, why would she care?

"Yes, and Enkan's going to trial with this soon. She wants to know she can rely on you." Clement respected Munson for his lack of apology, but the SPO didn't feel the chief should try to help a prosecutor mold a detective's testimony.

"I didn't say anything she didn't want me to at the grand jury." Clement knew he was being stubborn, of course, and that his response was indirect.

"She's going to trial ASAP, and she doesn't feel comfortable with you." Munson's stare would make a younger man squirm but Clement had no such sense of fear.

"Few do," answered Clement. Surely he had friends, however—at least at his church. Didn't he?

"Get out of here," Munson told him. "But promise you'll cooperate."

"Yeah," said Clement. He pushed himself up from the guest chair. "That is, I'll try to tell the partial truth and not the whole one."

Munson half-closed his eyes in annoyance, but he was through and picked up the phone to get on with his business.

Instead of inviting Clement to take back the second skeleton and skull, Dr. Neal at the university asked the officer to visit and bring the first skull along. Considering how much Clement owed the scientist for the forensic assessments he performed without any payment, late Friday afternoon, no questions asked, the SPO turned up as requested.

The heat had eased, with a hint of rain in the air. As much as everyone in the panhandle had been praying for exactly that, the clouds had to arouse a certain amount of anxiety as well. A gentle rain today and another tomorrow and the day after would be a welcome relief, but one disaster they didn't want to accompany that would be a twister.

When Dorothy realized she wasn't in Kansas anymore, Clement liked to say, she probably had been blow off into nearby Holder. Yeah, all of Oklahoma lay in Tornado Alley, which wasn't exactly something for a homeowner to be pleased about.

This time he'd conscientiously packed the skull in a layer of bubble wrap in a cardboard box. He wondered if he was becoming overly obsessive as well as possessive in regard to "his" skulls.

Clement met Dr. Neal in his lab, and this time Neal was smiling. He beckoned Clement over, extricated the skull from its priority-mail packing, and examined it as if greeting an old, familiar friend. Of course Neal knew the skull from his previous time spent with the skeleton and Clement wondered if the scientist also had a relationship with the boy the skull had once been. By "also," Clement meant as Clement himself did. He certainly wasn't about to ask, however.

Neal gave over the head to a female assistant, who put it on a stand next to what Clement believe to be the other skull that he'd brought in a couple of weeks before. He looked around at the individual bones tagged and scattered about, as well as at the complete skeletons that hung from stands, hooks, and pegs. Where had they come from, he wondered and had the obtaining of all these human remains been strictly legal?

"This is Margery," said Neal and Clement wasn't sure if Neal meant the other skull, and he himself had been mistaken as to its gender, or "Margery" was the name of the female assistant.

Ah. The assistant, no doubt, as she looked up from the computer where she'd settled herself and smiled.

Both Neal and Margery seemed almost breathless and Neal gave her a signal to get started at whatever she was now to do.

"The idea is so simple, I'm surprised no one in the field thought of it before." The forensic anthropologist's words actually tripped over one another on the way out. He leaned over Margery's shoulder. "Show the sequence," he told her.

The image of a skull imposed on a grid popped onto the screen and turned slowly to present a complete 360 degree view. "That's the skull kept in the shed that you brought last week," Neal explained. He turned and pointed at the skull on the stand, so Clement knew he had been right in identifying the second skull that had been missing all this time.

"What Margery did was to scan exactly—and I mean exactly—for each parameter, so that the program could give us the three-dimensional view of the skull as it is." Neal tapped his assistant on her shoulder and the screen changed. The skull began to grow flesh over it.

"This program...we didn't write it here, by the way—I learned about it at a recent conference—does what an artist will do when building a lifelike model from the skull of the person." Neal went on and detailed the steps as the skull continued to flesh out as a boy, trying on one face and then another.

"Everyone knows about how artists such as Frank Bender and Oklahoma's Clyde Snow and Betty Gatlif originated creating full dimensional reconstructions of homicide victims from the skull—well, this program we have hold of does something of the kind from the scan." Finally, the screen offered three versions of the face, each quite similar to the other.

The eyes of each boy showed the warmth of breath and the sparkling enthusiasm that comes with youth. The wide lips of all three clones of the skull offered pleasant, upturned smiles. The nose of each similar child was broad and distinctly African-American. The flesh the program finally filled in was dark, defining the child's lineage without denial.

"I thought you said you couldn't guess race from just the skeleton," said Clement. "Are you sure?"

"The structure doesn't lie," responded Neal with evident delight. "I also had probable race from the DNA, but apparently the structure itself simply is what it is." He turned to Clement who could hardly tear his eyes from the boy. "It's wonderful, isn't it? What a tool."

To think that someone might well have reported two children missing, and the Holder P.D. had simply turned its official back. "Yes, wonderful," said Clement slowly. "Now if people could only transform into real, decent human beings..."

CHAPTER 6

The days had become so scorching that Clement felt he ought to keep the stray inside, in the air conditioning. Of course he was afraid the shaggy black dog would have wild and destructive habits that would turn a relatively orderly home into a stable. So he gave the dog a bath and when he went to work put the nameless animal in a spare room with food and water.

The dog behaved in a civilized fashion on his own—knew enough not to empty his bladder or bowels inside the house— and lifted his head calmly from a day of rest when Clement returned.

That weekend, Clement gave "Buddy" free rein of the place, and the dog's manners were impeccable. A visit to a nearby vet and flea medication were the final, domesticating moves.

The next Saturday, Rod called, wanting to drop by the house with Shelly, and Clement said he'd be glad to see them. He looked in the refrigerator for something he could serve. Though he did have most of a pint of ice cream, he had carelessly put his spoon into it the night before. He quickly made a pitcher of iced tea.

Buddy barked when the doorbell rang, and Clement, a clean shirt on, let the two young people into the house.

"You have a dog, Dad." Rod seemed taken aback. He reached out to touch the animal, who moved away.

"I guess so," said Clement, leading them into the living room to sit. He wasn't so sure. He preferred to view the dog as a guest in the house, perhaps one who would extend his stay if he liked the place. This wasn't a matter of Clement's "having" a dog. The two weren't exactly on such terms as of yet, though the dog took "his place" on a pillow near Clement's feet.

"I didn't think you liked dogs," Rod added as he sat on the couch and pulled Shelly over to sit there with him.

"I don't know," said Clement. He was still deciding if he, in fact, did like dogs.

"You never wanted to have a dog when I was a kid." Rod seemed a bit put out by the idea that, all of a sudden, a decade later, Clement would take the first opportunity and acquire a dog to frolic with on his own.

"That was a long time ago," Clement observed somewhat dryly.

Clement looked around at his furniture, which was neat and clean, and really not frayed because Clement mostly only sat in his one bulky chair, aimed directly at the television set. He'd bought the couch, a sort of velveteen green, after Judy had taken a nicely padded beige one. He supposed the green couch wasn't very attractive, really, and undoubtedly Shelly saw it as something a country hick cop would have in his old farmhouse. He glanced at the girl. She was looking around as he just had.

"What a nice house you have here," she remarked. He felt that he did, but he didn't believe she meant what she said.

"Thank you," he answered. She wouldn't want the house, would she, for when she and Rod got married, if that was what she had in her mind? No. A girl like her wouldn't want to live all the way out here. Judy hadn't liked it out in the sticks and Shelly certainly wouldn't. But the land could be worth quite a lot for development, eventually. Clement surely dreaded the day the developers came knocking.

He went out to the kitchen to get their iced tea and glasses and returned to find Rod and Shelly kissing. They broke it off at the sound of his feet and the tapping of Buddy's nails on the wooden floors.

The plastic serving tray went on the coffee table. Clement hoped Shelly would be careful with the glass, and he put a coaster in front of each of them. "I don't have any cookies..." Clement apologized.

"Oh, we had some dessert at grandpa's," Rod told him. He wiped the sweat from the glass with a napkin, then drank the tea, which probably was still a little bit warm.

"Grandpa's?" Clement and Buddy returned to their spots. Judy's father had been dead a couple of decades already, which only left Clement's own father. Why in the world would Rod take Shelly there?

"Shelly and I are engaged to be married, Dad. We would have come out here first, but it just worked out this way." Rod seemed to flush.

"Well, congratulations, you two," responded Clement, trying to sound happily surprised, rather than sour. He replayed it in his head a couple of times after, instead of listening to what the two of them were talking about. He tried to smile. He'd sounded insincere and pathetic, and he could feel the smile as a sort of grimace. He wanted to focus on what they were saying.

He wished he could be a little happier for his son.

The thing that got Clement about Shelly today as he stared at her on the not-quite-cheap-looking sofa was that she wore a dress. Today was a Saturday, not a Sunday. Any normal young woman would be wearing jeans, or at least some kind of chino pants. This was a dress, as if she were on her way out to dinner—and she wore big pearl earrings.

That was why he didn't like her? Because of how she was dressed?

But really, something about her just didn't seem right and he didn't like her at all, and he was sorry his son was going to marry her.

Oh, hell, all right, he had to concede. These days the father didn't get to choose the wife for the son. He'd help them buy a place to live in, in town. That was it. He kept on trying to smile and to show how pleased he was for the two of them. He absolutely wanted to feel pleased.

The only way for a police official to answer the phone was to bark his last name into it. Clement very well knew the industry standard. On, the other hand, when something was so set in stone as that, he preferred to find a technique that suited him better. Thus, when the phone rang that next Monday afternoon, he enunciated his name politely into the receiver.

"SPO Clement?" asked the female voice.

"How may I assist you?" Clement responded. Hadn't he spoken clearly enough?

"Officer Bradley," she explained. "Can you meet me somewhere later today?"

"Why don't you just come to my office?" he suggested.

"Better if I don't."

She was undoubtedly making something of nothing, since subterfuge had never struck Clement as an approach required at the Holder, Oklahoma Police Department. Sure the force had its fair share of malicious gossip and venal backstabbing, but nothing that couldn't be pursued around the office water cooler, or by a pair of good old boys leaning back at their desks.

He agreed to meet her at a roadhouse out along North Cimarron.

Then he got up and went to the personnel department. Oh, yes, they now called it "human resources," although the sign on the door still said "personnel." And no matter what the office was called in departmental memos, staff continued refer to it in the same old way.

Then, too, the identical efficient secretary sat just inside, while the man in the inner fortress, who changed his name and face from year to year, earned all the dollars. Clement, though, knew where the real power lay and had courted Madge's friendship for the last 20 or so years with a mild flirtation, not his usual style.

In fact he now winked at Madge when he walked into the room. "How's my favorite 'police department ancillary'?" No, he wasn't capable of going too far.

"Aaron," she acknowledged with a quizzical smile.

"Remember Henry Tolliver?" he asked. She gave a quick nod. "I heard he moved out of state and I need to contact him regarding an investigation."

Madge punched a few buttons on her computer without missing a beat. "You didn't get anything from me," she stipulated.

"Naturally not."

The printer clattered and in a minute he picked up the top page and blanched. She was giving him Tolliver's entire personnel record...All Clement had asked for was the current address. But he didn't say anything. Madge had gone back to doing whatever she'd been doing.

He waited until the last page came through, then picked up the rest of the bundle.

Madge looked up. "I hope the investigation is of him," she said.

Madge was no fool, and Clement made a wry face. "There's no going back to whatever happened in the old days, for the most part," he remarked. "But we never know, do we?" He would have liked to have gotten a better idea from her as to what she thought Tolliver guilty of, but after a further sharp-eyed smile, she returned to her paperwork.

He did have allies.

By the time he pulled up at Bar None off the highway, Clement was starving. Places like this usually had hamburgers at least. He went inside where a few after-work rig workers of some kind were shooting the breeze and looked around for Bradley, but didn't see her until the occupant of the last booth turned around and stared. This *was* conspiratorial. He walked back and sat down across from Bradley, who was drinking a soda and eating French fries.

When the waitress came over, Clement ordered a lemonade and asked for a menu. "You mean a cooler?" the woman asked.

Clement couldn't exactly decipher the word. "You know what a lemonade is?"

"No alcohol," intervened Bradley, interpreting his request for the other woman.

"We don't have anything like that." The waitress still seemed mystified and Clement wondered if he'd crossed the border into New Mexico, where maybe they didn't know what lemonade was.

"An iced tea then and let me have a hamburger. Well done."

He waited for her to go away, then looked at Bradley. "You come here often?" Bradley just laughed and Clement smiled in return. "It's your kind of secret meeting place?"

She pushed the fries forward, offering him some. He shook his head. "Thanks for coming out this way," she said.

"It's my pleasure. But what do you want?" He scrutinized her face for an indication of what in the world she was up to. Sure, half of him wondered if she was interested in him in "that" way, while the other half refused to entertain the topic whatsoever. His solution was to avoid bridging the gap between his two warring halves.

She leaned forward and whispered. "I have a copy of the hospital file on Mrs. Holmes."

He pursed his mouth. People were throwing files that they thought he should have, his way. For sure he was curious, and for sure being able to look through such material made him uncomfortable. "Why tell me?" he asked.

"I thought you cared."

Her eyes locked onto his and he broke the gaze." I do care," he answered. "Though why I should, I don't exactly know." That was a lie. He knew why he cared. He hated to see an injustice done. Society ground the weak down every day and Clement turned his head, but he hated to see the action up close. "And I thought *you* didn't care."

"He kept on breaking her bones," she said.

Clement struggled with thoughts of the natural law of self-defense, the laws of society, and the ideal of higher law—the laws of God. "That gives her license to kill?" he put to her as she had to him.

"I don't know—it might."

She hadn't stopped looking at him, and now he met her stare. "What about the boy?" he asked.

He saw no recognition in her. "Christine Holmes' son. The child. Was he beaten by the father?"

She recoiled. "I don't know." The words were a confession of forgetfulness. She obviously hadn't thought of the child at all.

The two of them spoke softly as if to avoid being overheard, but they were alone in the back, and the only sound until the waitress approached with Clement's order was an occasional round of laughter from the oil or gas workers up front. Clement gulped down some iced tea and dug into his food. "The attorney is Frank Rich?" he went on.

"No," Bradley objected. "Why would it be him? It's a public defender."

Clement swallowed and frowned. He'd told the sister to call Frank Rich first. Rich was both clever and aggressive. "What do you mean?" he asked.

"That Rich isn't her attorney. She doesn't have any money, I guess."

"Oh for heaven's sake..." He was disgusted with the sister. He'd told her to ask Rich to take the case on pro bono.

"You never swear, do you?" Bradley asked. She popped a fry into her mouth as if for something to do.

"You got me," he admitted. "A cop who doesn't swear."

The smile she gave him lit up her youthful face, softened her, made her look prettier than he'd noticed before. He returned to the topic at hand. "But the information about her abuse will come to the public defender through discovery, since you found the reports for the D.A."

He began again to eat his hamburger, paused, and put some catsup on as she replied. "No, they won't get the hospital report from discovery, and that's why I thought I should bring what I have to you—that you'd know what to do. The D.A. asked me to get it from the medical center. Then, when I brought it back, they didn't like it. When I was leaving, I heard them say they could ditch the document. Is that really legal?"

"If the record is exculpating," Clement responded, "or at least goes to a possible motive of self-defense, it might be prosecutorial misconduct if they throw it out without handing it over to her attorney."

He tried to dissect the situation as clearly as he could from his secondhand knowledge of criminal law. The prosecutor had to hand over anything she'd come across that could show the charges against the defendant were false. But Clement wasn't certain about the fine points. The fact that Mrs. Holmes had stabbed her husband to death wasn't really contested. Nor could the hospital record show that she hadn't done any such thing. On the other hand, the woman's having been brutalized multiple times would surely go to state of mind...

The waitress came with the check and Clement took it out of her hand without allowing her to put it on the table. Bradley reached out to take it from him. "Never mind," Clement told her.

"Let me pay for mine," said Bradley. "Don't be sexist."

"It's more like an age thing," Clement asserted. "The old guy gets to pay for the kid."

When she opened her purse a minute later, Clement thought she was going to insist on paying for her food. Instead, she brought out some folded sheets of paper, and after turning around to check if anyone was looking, then facing him again, she handed over Christine Holmes' hospital records.

"Both of us can be fired for this," Clement said. But he took the pages from her, anyway, feeling as if he were walking through a field of landmines.

CHAPTER 7

Once home, Clement took the papers from the trunk of his car and went into the house, nearly tripping over Buddy just inside the door. The dog must be pretty happy to have company after a full day at home alone. Clement would walk the stray after dark, when it cooled off a bit, but for now he opened the back door and let the dog out into the yard and then, a few minutes later, invited him back into the cool interior.

Buddy settled at his new master's feet by the all-important chair. Clement, however, still wasn't sure he wanted the dog as a permanent responsibility. He'd have to look online tomorrow for a no-kill shelter, just in case.

First, Clement straightened the pages that Bradley had handed him and then he scanned them for the highlights. Christine Holmes was a very clumsy, accident-prone woman. She'd broken the suborbit of her right eye when she'd pitched herself down the basement stairs—a real feat of gymnastic targeting.

On another occasion, she'd pulled her right arm straight out of its socket so that the tendons were ruptured. The patient wasn't sure what had caused the injury, but it looked to the doctor like an athletic one. Similar injuries were seen in baseball players or small children whose parent had jerked violently on the child's arm. A doctor said Christine might require surgery, but she didn't return for further examination.

A broken tibia, a severely sprained ankle—no break detected—and two fractured fingers spoke volumes in small, unremarkable black type on the printout.

Clement sighed and mulled over what to do with this unexpected documentation. He had a moral responsibility, now that he'd taken part in the unethical action of receiving materials he shouldn't be privy to.

Buddy also sighed and put down his head. Apparently his sigh was one of relaxation. His world seemed to be in good shape now, Clement judged. All the dog's wants and needs were accommodated and he enjoyed enough entertainment just having a friend by his side.

If only Clement operated under an equally simple set of requirements. Instead, today, he felt increasingly edgy at being on the wrong side of the law—or at least departmental regulations.

He picked up the unfolded mass of papers he'd gotten from Madge and began to skim those. Tolliver wasn't an exemplary, commendation-winning cop. He'd been brought up on various disciplinary actions early on in his career: kipping on the job—parking at an out-of-the-way spot and sleeping—too many sick days, too many late arrivals, and such. In short, he was lazy. No doubt not taking the report of a missing child was all in a day's work, or minimization of work, for a cop like that.

Clement's head began to throb. But how could a cop ignore a report of a missing child? The entire situation struck him as sinister in a way. If this one case of murder had finally come to light—and he couldn't yet be sure that the two boys he was now the guardian of was a case reported to Tolliver—then other murders (reported first as a child missing) might have occurred. This was something he could look into, and he would. Relentlessly. Because he had nothing else to go on right this minute.

He felt dispirited, however. Because while catching the killer after the fact and seeking retribution was good, that wasn't the same as preventing terrible events of this kind in the first place.

"Although if we punish this one now, we have the slender chance of warning off another one," Clement told Buddy.

Buddy appeared to be not just surprised to hear such a comment coming from Clement, but rather skeptical as well. "I'm not sure I believe it, either," agreed the dog's human friend.

He must have fallen dead asleep because when the phone rang and he looked at the clock across the room, the time was 8:30. Oh, he *had* eaten—at the roadhouse.

"Clement," he said into the phone.

"It's me," said Judy.

"Oh, yeah, okay." She sounded just a little annoyed and he tried to think why. Tonight hadn't been a church night, had it?

"Aren't you happy for the kids?" she asked.

Kids? He'd been thinking about the two murdered boys and couldn't quite put two and two together for a moment. "Yes, of course."

"We might have to decide a few things about the wedding. Can we both throw in some money for something nice?"

"Sure," he said, though an actual ceremony seemed so final.

"Her parents will be here Saturday and Sunday. What's a better day for lunch for you?"

"Parents? She has parents?" That might have occurred to him, but it hadn't.

"You didn't spend any time talking to her about herself?" Judy questioned.

"I guess not," he admitted. Clement sought out an excuse, but anything he might say felt too lame.

Judy made a condemnatory sound. "She's a very nice girl."

"Oh, yes," he agreed. "Either Saturday, or Sunday after church, would be fine. They can all come to church." Maybe Judy didn't realize exactly how freed up his schedule was, or maybe she just inquired to be polite.

"I certainly don't want to make them come to our church,"

she objected—an indication that his manners were, as usual, lacking. "I'll get back to you when we settle on a time and place. Or *you* can call *me* for a change."

"I will," he promised. "Either that, or I'll check with Rod."

He hung up. Buddy was looking at him with some circumspection. Perhaps the dog wondered at the oddity of the relationship between the two humans. Clement certainly did. "Did I just insult her?" he asked Buddy. "By saying I'd call Rod instead of her? Well, probably."

Hadn't the two already divorced a long time ago? Why wasn't that enough to end the quibbling?

Because he was antsy waiting for the university to develop a picture of the second boy, Clement decided to do a canvas in the black neighborhoods with the several computer-developed pictures of the initial child.

He had, when he'd first come on the job, been in a sector car that patrolled Whirlwind Avenue and its side streets. He'd known the neighborhood well at the time, so he started there.

As a child, Clement hadn't learned about the difference between black and white much because primarily in this part of Oklahoma the low color on the totem pole was the red. Out here, the real question for the older whites had been the Indian population—after which a growing concern had arisen over the numbers of Hispanics—legal and illegal, and all called "Mexicans"—streaming up from Texas.

He parked just off Whirlwind and put a police sign on the dash.

On the street, he stopped by three men, maybe in their 30s, who tried to avoid catching his eye. He took out the pictures and showed them around. The men shook their heads.

"Look," said one abruptly. "If these kids have been missing for something like 25 years, why didn't you start your search all those years ago? What's the point of asking us today? Where was your law enforcement then?"

One of the other men made a gesture to calm his friend down.

"This isn't a question of that," said Clement. "I'm trying to do today what can be done now. It's the only thing I know to do. It's what you ought to want me to do."

He'd expected some of that hostility to the white police, but as he went along, going into the grocery store, a barber shop, and a liquor store, he received rather a lot of friendliness as well, from both older residents who had worked their way through the questions of racism and had come out standing tall in their own self-assessment, and from the younger ones who hadn't really taken on the burden of the racial division that their elders had.

In a small variety store of the old-fashioned type, Clement got into conversation with the elderly owner who only rarely had to pause to deal with a customer. Business, he explained, was slow. The bigger chain stores in the mall had co-opted all but the sudden impulse purchase.

"Do you think the police used to ignore reports of missing children?" Clement finally asked. The question pained him.

"Everyone knew that," answered Mr. Biggs. Even a dyed-in-the-wool Oklahoman like Clement had some trouble with the thickness of the older man's drawl.

"They knew that the police didn't take seriously reports from the black community?" Clement probed.

"That, too," agreed Biggs. "But lots of children went missing back in those days. You heard stories."

"You're saying the police routinely didn't take any of the reports? Or was it one or two of them who wouldn't take them?" Clement got a soda out of the old-style soda chest then took a dollar from his pocket and put it on the counter.

Mr. Biggs shoved the single back at him, but Clement shook his head in refusal. As the son of a dirty cop, he never would take those little freebies.

"I don't know," said Mr. Biggs. "I always thought of all those police officers as the same. I never thought of any of them as any better than the others."

"Lots of children?' Clement repeated and Mr. Biggs nodded sadly. Clement lowered his head and gazed at the floor. Something here was glaringly wrong. Then he considered whether his father had ever patrolled around Whirlwind Avenue and whether Sam Clement had declined to turn in any reports of missing children.

On Clement's way back to his office, he stopped at 125 South Comanche, a high-rise building near the courthouse where many of the lawyers had their offices.

In the elevator, he pondered the idea that "lots" of black children had gone missing in those days, that a predator had run loose in the community and that no one had cared to stop it from happening. All across America—hell, all across the world—communities had cops for a reason. To not live up to that purpose was to let the devil win.

Clement felt sick at heart and was glad when the attorney couldn't see him right away. He picked up a *People Magazine* and tried to distract himself. He doubted that the things the magazine said were true about these celebrities though. Even Hollywood types, even the extremely beautiful and rich, must be more real than they were depicted.

In a little while Rich's client—a middle-aged man Clement didn't recognize—left, and a minute later Rich came back out and called to Clement to come in.

"Not a criminal case, huh?" Clement pointed back toward the door.

"Do you have to know *every*thing?" Rich asked.

The two had been somewhat friendly ever since high school, and Rich also had been in Afghanistan. Moreover, Clement admired Frank Rich for his basic decency and his effectiveness as an attorney.

"I like to know as much as I can." Clement smiled and took a chair.

Rich sat, too. The office wasn't fancy, but Clement thought Rich did okay. Or as okay as he wanted to, anyway. Rich liked to fly down to the Texas coast or up to Michigan to fish.

"You're aware of the Holmes case," Clement began. He had no doubt that Rich was aware. You'd have to be dead or deaf and not looking to be unaware. And everyone in town had an opinion.

"Yeah?"

"Would you do the case pro bono?"

"Who are you, all of a sudden? A member of the family?" Rich stood up and took off his jacket. "Hot," he said.

"I know something about the situation," answered Clement cautiously. He crossed one leg over the other. He didn't like to sit that way as it could throw out his back, but the chair was a killer. "I interviewed her right after the murder. I'm also privy to information I shouldn't actually have."

"I really can't hear this," Rich cut in.

"I wasn't going to tell you anything specific," said Clement, "but the woman ought to have a good attorney. And whoever she has as her attorney could likely get some notice in the press. For some people that would be payment enough. But not for you. No, you'd take the case just to do a good deed for a woman who doesn't deserve to go to prison forever."

"I like a quiet life," Rich objected.

"You do not."

"She has an attorney, a new kid on the block, a public defender. I saw it in *The Holder Press*."

"Sometimes an attorney will offer to take on a client he feels he can help," suggested Clement.

"Not me. I don't bust in on another man's territory."

Clement stood up. "If the sister asks?"

"Well, why should I?" Rich wanted to know. He followed

Clement's lead and got out of his chair.

"Could be she did what she had to, and with a little due diligence you'd find that out. Due diligence the new kid doesn't understand. And information the D.A's office might have seen and decided to suppress." Clement knew Rich must have some feelings about the D.A.'s office after all these years of opposing the prosecutor's team.

"That's quite a statement," responded Rich after a momentary pause. "I'd be open to hear from the family," he added as he came out from around his desk.

CHAPTER 8

An email arrived for Clement from the university late Friday afternoon, at which time he downloaded the attachments slowly over the telephone wires still used by the Holder P.D. Miraculously, the files weren't corrupted by their journey, and he was able to make the multiple images of both boys appear, and play the video of their 360 degree perspectives. He tried to imagine the two as grown men now, with sons of their own.

Then he went down to the basement, the city's combination tornado shelter and one-time Y2K command center (sadly unprepared for possible flooding) to apply for help from Jan Whitetree, the department's communications director. That was to say, he needed her okay to release the files to the media.

This was tricky. Jan was a dud, but an entrenched dud, who in the eyes of the police commissioner, a tribal relation, could do no wrong. Jan, though incompetent in many aspects of her job, liked the work she did and enjoyed controlling all police outreach to television, radio, newspapers, and now the internet outlets. Normally, for the big news of the day, her handiwork hardly made a dent in preventing or promoting the flow of information.

But in this case, although the boys had both lain in the park dead and only shallowly buried for many years, Clement was eager to send their pictures out immediately and obtain an identification.

Jan Whitetree, however, was not a fast worker. So Clement approached her with an excess of humility and a pretense of technological naiveté.

"This whole internet craze." Clement stood in front of Whitetree's cluttered desk and wrung his hands. "Yes, yes, it's convenient. But you've got machines, you've got problems."

Mrs. Whitetree gazed at him benignly. That was the thing—at least she had no malintent in her narcissistic idiocy.

"Maybe I can just have the university send the pictures to the...well, maybe *The Star*?" *The Star* was a Holder weekly, mostly a shopping rag with lots of ads. Clement frowned in pretended concentration. Was he being too disingenuous? If he'd said *The Post*, that would probably have sounded more reasonable.

"Have the university email the photos to me," said Whitetree. "I'll have one of the staff produce a written release to go along with it."

"Oh, good. I'll just ask them to email the photos on," Clement agreed. "Thanks a lot." He retreated. Unfortunately, he was going to have to look as if he was contravening her orders. But, well, he had gone to her first, as periodic memos insisted on. In this case, however, he'd become confused.

He'd have to abase himself afterward, when she confronted him on it. He'd misunderstood her. He always seemed to be thrown when talking to her—distracted by her powerful presence, perhaps—and turned out to be unable to listen to exactly what she said.

At least the last couple of times that he could remember, he'd followed her instructions and had her do the work. Those cases had already been solved, after all, and Clement's priority hadn't been the public relations.

He went back upstairs and emailed the photos to the police journalist at *The Post* and the video to channels 2 and 4. Then, for good measure, he emailed pictures of both the boys to a couple of police reporters he knew at the Oklahoma City and Tulsa papers, and finally to *The Star*.

Then he went downstairs to the department library, hoping he wouldn't run into Whitetree again, lest she repeat her decision on the photos. *Oh, I didn't realize the other files were videotapes…Oh, I just hit my media mailing list. I didn't realize who all I was sending these too. You said I should send the photos to* The Star? Oh, hell, he was doomed. Never disrespect the police commissioner's tribal relative.

In the library, Clement went through the last few issues of *The Post* and found the name of Christine Holmes' sister. Then he snuck back upstairs to his office where he used the online Holder telephone directory, updated weekly by the telephone company, and to which only the telephone operators and the police department had access. The directory was a great database that could be used as a reverse directory to find the name associated with a number. But Clement didn't need that now—only the sister's street address.

He also saw that he had gotten some telephone messages. The reporters must check their email every two minutes. He was pleased and spent the next hour and a half on the phone. He decided not to worry about explaining all this excess of enthusiasm to Mrs. Whitetree. Any good will he'd generated with her over the last year or so was fried in batter. He could eat crow until the cows rode to the stockyards in Chicago…his butt was grass with her. In fact, he was burning through his career here quickly and was likely to follow his father out of the department in short order.

To top it all off, he was late to church.

Saturday morning after a brisk walk during the coolest part of the morning with Buddy, who did surprisingly well on leash (which Clement concluded meant the dog had been born into captivity—well, had been someone's pet), Clement showered and shaved. He actually had two addresses to check out for the sister since he didn't have the husband's first name, but he didn't want to be too early at either home. Nor too late, either, since he didn't want to miss them. On Saturdays, people shopped and ran their errands.

What would he do if he weren't a policeman? He supposed he could be a freelance investigator for some attorneys downtown. But he wouldn't have access to the department databases, and why would anyone hire an old guy as opposed to a young one with energy?

He hoped Munson would let him collect his pension and supposed the chief might, but couldn't be sure of it. He could sell the house and the land—but he wouldn't. Oh, surely someday Rod would, after Clement was dead, and the developers would swoop down like a pack of turkey vultures. Clement hoped Rod would get a good deal at least. Clement was relieved to find he still loved the boy more than his property.

"I'm leaving you here in the AC," the man told the dog. "I'd take you with me, but I don't want to keep the AC running in the car. It's really nothing personal."

He put out food and water, locked the door and left.

Clement parked along the curb at the first Cline household and watched for signs of activity inside. He had a 50/50 chance of this being the sister's house. The odds were in his favor today. How many times had he tracked a person with a name similar to dozens of others? Redhawk, say.

The door opened and a woman came out dressed in jeans accompanied by a little dog on a leash. Hey, a dog "owner." Did people actually *own* dogs? Did he own Buddy? No. That made no sense. The relationship in the case of Buddy and Clement was a voluntary one.

"Excuse me, Miss." The woman stopped and Clement looked down at the little dog, who, until the woman jerked at the leash, seemed inclined to sniff and jump at him. The jerking at the leash, for some reason, bothered Clement. "Is your sister named Christine?" If she was the other Cline, he didn't want to alert her to his snooping around, so he didn't use the Holmes last name.

Mrs. Cline tensed. "Yes," she said. "I already talked to you people."

"No. You didn't talk to me. Well, yes, you did. The night your sister was arrested. I'm the one who called." Clement looked at her and tried to see if she remembered, and she nodded. "I suggested an attorney at the time," he added.

"I don't have any money," Cline lowered her voice and glanced back at the house.

Ah, men everywhere had their women too cowed to speak in a normal tone of voice, or maybe the sisters had grown up in a household with an abusive father. And if that was so, Rich would bring that fact out in court. Would the public defender?

"I think Frank Rich would do it pro bono." Clement handed Cline the business card he'd taken from Rich's secretary's desk. He was conscious that he'd left a drop of sweat on it with his DNA, along with a fingerprint. Of course he wouldn't deny that he'd given it to her. He wouldn't lie about what he'd done if Munson got wind of it.

"She has a lawyer now," Cline said.

Clement shook his head. "She's your sister. You have to give her the best chance possible. And all you need to do is call Frank Rich and hire him."

She appeared reluctant, and he didn't want to be in the position of "selling" Frank. He turned away and then turned back. "A lot can be done," he said as a parting shot. He didn't bother to add something stupid about not saying he'd been out here. He had been here, after all. Why ask her to lie?

After driving around a while, he went into the WalMart where he'd run into Bradley. He somehow kept looking around for her, although he realized she probably didn't live anywhere in the neighborhood, had just been here as part of the investigation. He bought the more expensive dog food, as he guessed it would be better for the dog. Or so the label would have him believe.

At home, Clement was changing into a pair of shorts when he realized today was the lunch with Shelly's parents and that he was already late. Maybe this explained why Judy had left him. Or had she left him? Maybe he'd left her emotionally before the marriage finally had ended. He washed his face and hurried into a suitable pair of pants and a clean shirt.

He arrived at Pertita's an hour late and apologized at once to the five who were finishing eating. Rod smiled, but Shelly's brow wrinkled a bit.

Clement's face was flushed again with the heat of the day, but the restaurant was like an ice box and he sat there in relief. The Marshalls forgave him graciously and he took their measure while peeking up from the menu. More or less, as he might have suspected, they were too well-groomed, overdressed for a Saturday in his view—the man had a suit on, for goodness sake—and too...what was the word...upper-class looking? He was satisfied that he didn't like them.

"What do you do?" he asked Mr. Marshall. Why did he ask? And why did he ask the man and not her? He must think that Marshall was the primary provider and did quite well. Yes, he did think that.

"I'm a lawyer." Marshall seemed pleased with himself.

But he had managed to pique Clement's interest. "What kind of law?"

"Corporate."

Ah, that made sense, but Clement was disappointed to hear the answer. That was the boring side of the law. He could chat with a defense attorney, like Rich.

"Aaron's obsessed with crime," Judy explained. Clement didn't deny it. But was it crime that preoccupied him, or was it justice on this earth? And how justice could emerge in the here and now—and whether humans could determine the parameters of righteousness. Corporate law surely didn't involve any such questions or such a search.

Appropriately though, the conversation shifted to the happy couple and the upcoming wedding. Clement wasn't one for such domestic and girly conversation, but he tried to put an oar into the water here. Marshall turned out to be a good talker at least, and Clement gladly shut up and let his mind drift.

After lunch, they drove out to see the countryside and Clement's house. He had put in sodas for the occasion. Buddy ran and hid under the bed. If only Clement could do the same.

CHAPTER 9

On Monday morning, Clement was eager to get to work. The pictures of "his" boys had run in the paper both Saturday and Sunday, while the video had shown locally as well as nationally—on CNN—since technological forensic approaches were so trendy these days. Now Clement wanted to see if anyone had recognized the children.

Too bad he had to wait around for calls, as this left him a sitting target for probable internal (Whitetree) complaints.

By noon, he had received 17 calls and had both recorded them and jotted down notes. Of course he was going to look into each lead, but none sounded all that promising. Still, he couldn't ever discount that the killer himself had been at the other end of the line on one of the calls, and every tip was worth looking into.

After church the evening before, he'd bought a roasted chicken for his dinner. He'd strangely *not* been invited over to his dad's supper for the kids, rather a nice relief, although, at the same time, somewhat hurtful. He was a big boy now, but still didn't like the idea of being left out of a family gathering. Not to mention by his own father. His dad's house was small, however, and after all, Clement and Judy were divorced.

Now he forwarded his calls to his cell and took his next-day chicken sandwich down to the lunch room. Some new academy graduates said hello; they knew him because he'd taught a couple of classes across the street, and though he recognized their faces, he didn't know their names. Munson had done a good thing in starting the academy, despite the small class size. Clement himself had gone to a regional academy in Boise City, although he'd really trained in Afghanistan—poor benighted country now gone back to the devils. Still, civilian policing had constitutional constraints that didn't apply in the military, and he'd had to learn them.

He sat at the second table by himself and hoped no one would dare to join him. He was pretty sure that Whitetree never stopped by here with her homemade lunch or a takeout container. He held back a snort. No doubt her lunch was with the commissioner at the Holder Inn. No, he wasn't thinking *that*, though obviously it occurred to him as he considered the imaginary scene.

His phone played its signature ringtone—a simple one that had come with the phone—and Clement swallowed the last bite of his sandwich so he could answer. Between the noise of the new recruits talking and the softness of the woman's voice, he had trouble hearing and walked out of the lunch room into the corridor. He leaned a notebook against the wall and wrote, while balancing the phone in the crook of his neck.

She sounded old and tremulous, which seemed right to him considering when the murders might have occurred. "I'll come to you there," he promised her. In consideration of her age. Moreover, an interview in her own home would allow her some sense of relaxation, and she might be able to remember more than in an official atmosphere. "In an hour?"

He felt a presence behind him, hung up, finished scribbling, looked at his watch, and turned.

Jan Whitetree stood there smiling at him. Too bad he'd eaten because he suddenly felt as if he might throw up.

He elevated his forehead in an attempt to force his own face to smile back.

"Now don't forget to send that to me," she told Clement. "We'll get right on it."

"Oh good. Thanks." He smiled with a little bit more conviction this time. "I won't forget." A communications director who didn't read the newspapers or watch TV. Kind of scary. But nice to know.

The woman lived downtown in the old Chisholm area, which had gone from the site of the finest homes in town built for the wealthy in the 1870s, to a middle-class area of boarding houses—a district of transient cowboys, salesmen, and oil field workers—transitioning with the new oil boom in the first decade of the 1900s. Then, during the 1930s, this whole area of the state had been hit hard by a series of dust blizzards, with Holder in the central part of the Depression-era Dust Bowl.

As the oil expansion died along with the economy of an entire world, the Chisholm neighborhood reinvented itself as apartment houses for black sharecroppers who had gone bust elsewhere and never made it as far as California. These unfortunates soon settled into a collective, impoverished lifestyle in the previously elegant mansions, and there they and their descendants remained.

Clement loved the old buildings, though he hated their collapse. He reveled in the reminder of his home state's interesting history: the period of the stage coach traveling through what was then Indian Territory—and then the rise of the railroad—the Oklahoma land grab in 1889, and the oil boom that pretty much made the state wealthy until the Depression.

Inevitably, within the next decade from now, developers were going to come into the Chisholm section to buy the buildings and renovate for the younger, trendier, moneyed class. If the national economy and the latest oil boom held.

Then where would Mrs. May and her neighbors go? Clement found the building and buzzed from downstairs. "Buzzer don't work," said a little girl who sat on the steps. "The door is open."

Clement pushed in. The tilework inside was intricate and would need an acid bath to remove the dirt. Once-exquisite marble steps looked well beyond restoration.

He walked up to the second floor and knocked on the door marked *1A*. The apartment numbers were one lower than the actual floor number—probably to minimize the idea of the walk up. Someone inside called out, and Clement waited. Finally, the door opened, and he was face to face with a very elderly and frail black woman whose complexion had been lightened by the passage of the years.

"I'm Officer Clement, ma'am. You called me earlier."

"I know." She let him in and they walked down a slanted corridor to a small room that featured a sofa bed and card table, on which stood a hot plate. The building had obviously been chopped up in pragmatic but irregular ways to house the impecunious many, in place of the privileged few.

"I love these old buildings," Clement said.

"That's cause you don't have to live in one. Sit down there." She indicated a dining room chair with arms that looked as if it would hold his girth and muscle. He sat carefully.

"I live in an old farmhouse," he told Mrs. May. But he didn't mention the hours he'd put in stripping the paint off built-in cabinetry so he could revarnish it to a pristine condition. He didn't mention replacing all the windows and the window frames, the lighting fixtures, and the door knobs. Or pulling off the porch because the floor boards were rotten and putting in a new and wider one. Or...but that was all irrelevant.

She picked up a copy of *The Holder Post*. "Someone gave this to me," she said. "Did you put the pictures in here?" She pointed.

"Yes, ma'am," he answered.

"When the officer came to take the report the first time, 21 years ago, he didn't call me 'ma'am' then. Or Miz May. He

71

didn't call my daughter Miz Parker." She looked at him sternly.

"No, ma'am. I understand," Clement answered, chagrined. And what she said was what everyone would say when all this came out. He just now realized it. What had happened all those years ago wasn't simply a private disgrace for the Holder P.D., but a very public one, of the type that movies or television magazines were made. This was going to be a scandal up for discussion in the papers and on the talk shows. He had opened a local, maybe a national, can of worms.

"Please tell me," he asked humbly. "Tell me as much as you can."

"I can tell you everything," she said. "You don't forget a time like that, when you lose both your grandchildren at once." Her eyes rimmed red and he was afraid he must now wade through the deluge of her tears.

But she didn't cry. She simply went on and told him the story in her old lady voice and he took notes and at the same time recorded through his cell phone of a type sold exclusively to law enforcement.

She hadn't been living in this house at the time, but a few blocks over, where she'd had an apartment with her daughter and the two boys—Moses and Ezekiel.

She said she remembered, but maybe she didn't recall everything exactly—just thought she did.

The day the two boys, Moses, 13, and Ezekiel, 14, had simply vanished, they'd gone to the park on their secondhand bicycles bought for them a couple of months before, for their Christmas. They loved those bikes, and their father—who didn't live with them—had fixed the bikes up just like brand new and had painted one red and one blue.

Mrs. May had watched them go, from the window.

Had anything struck her? Had they been followed? Had anyone unusual been in the area?

No.

The boys weren't home yet when their mother had returned

from work as it was nighttime. Loretta Parker became frantic when she heard the boys hadn't come back. She got a neighbor with a car to go out with her. They drove the streets. Mrs. May stayed back in case the boys showed up there.

The next day, two local white policeman came. They said the children couldn't be reported missing this soon, that they had probably simply run away. Mrs. May and her daughter explained how young the boys were, how respectful of their elders, how well they did in school, how they would never stay out late at night and certainly never until the following day.

The two white policemen said to come into the station once the boys were missing for 48 hours.

The next day, the two women had gone to the station and had filed a report. In the days following, they had called again and again, each time being told that the officers "were working on it." After the first month or so, conceding defeat, the mother and grandmother had called no more. "We wanted to, but they seemed bothered by it, and we got to feeling they weren't doing nothing about the boys, anyway."

The boys—Moses, 13, and Ezekiel, 14—were not seen again, though the women waited. Ten years later, their mother died of a fast-spreading breast cancer, brought on by grief.

Mrs. May still had the phone number and the policeman's name on his card and she brought it to Clement, who asked if he might keep what he considered might be evidence. Mrs. May said he could.

The card said *Henry Tolliver*. The phone number was the old one used at department headquarters before they'd moved and gotten a whole new telephone system.

Clement nodded and put the card in his notebook. "And he never called you?"

"No, never even called." She bowed her head.

"And they never found the bikes?

"Don't suppose they were ever even looking for them. Do you?"

73

She gazed up at him, and he said something like what Tolliver should have told her all those years ago. "Well, ma'am, I'm so very sorry for your loss. I know it's too late to make any difference, but I'm going to try to do everything I can."

She nodded as if she believed Clement, despite all that had gone on before with the police. "Thank you," she answered. "I know that we'll never get no real good explanation now, and that I won't know much until I get in front of the Lord, myself, but those boys deserve to be cared about. We always cared about them, but no one else did."

"I care about them," Clement said, pausing a moment so his voice wouldn't choke. "And I'm going to arrange for their bones to be buried in a real nice funeral. I hope that will mean something to you even after all this time."

She seemed surprised, but following a moment of thought, she smiled. "Yes, yes, it would. Thank you very kindly then. I know the boys will rest the better for it."

Clement felt as if he had just climbed a mountain and had made it to the top. He looked down with triumph, but then looked up. He hadn't arrived at the summit at all. This was only the first leg of a daunting journey. He braced himself for the ascent to come.

CHAPTER 10

Clement told Munson that he'd made progress, and he requested a second detective to help him out with a canvas of the Chisholm area. He neglected to mention that the investigation was likely to tarnish the reputation of the whole Holder P.D, as well as focus on at least one specific officer.

Munson thought over Clement's request. "Don't have anyone," he answered after looking at some sheets on his desk top.

"How about Officer Bradley? Don't know her first name. The girl." Clement was relieved Munson wasn't going to offer him any of the old guard. They might have known Tolliver and might want to protect him.

Munson gave his subordinate a curious look. "And you know her from...?"

"You had her drive me over to the Holmes' house that night. I heard she was making investigator." Yeah, right, he was so plugged in.

Munson didn't seem overjoyed. "Okay," he said. He marked something down.

Clement backed away. He'd learned not to turn his rear on potential danger, and his instincts were right this time, too.

"Did you go through Whitetree before you went to the papers?" Munson asked.

"Yeah," said Clement. "I went to her first." He didn't like to lie and he wasn't entirely lying now. Or maybe he was. Certainly he wasn't conforming to the spirit of the law.

Munson nodded and Clement walked face first out the door.

Clement called Bradley and told her she'd been assigned to help him canvas in the Chisholm neighborhood. "What do you mean?" she asked cautiously over the phone.

"I mean you can come down here and step into my office like a normal person. Then the two of us will go to Chisholm and do a canvas."

In a few minutes, she arrived, but in her uniform. Ah, that's what had made the girl look homely.

She explained that she'd been returned to radio patrol until she trained in Boise City in the fall, and then she'd be on standby for the detective squad. Clement sent her to the locker room to change into street clothes.

Outside, in the parking lot, he sat in the car with both doors open, waiting for her. Funny that when they'd erected the building, no one had thought of a covered lot for summer, but they hadn't. Therefore, the cars simmered and broiled in the sun.

She got in the car and closed the door. Her hair down, she looked more female. "What's this about?" she asked.

"My boys," he said. He indicated a set of pictures on the seat next to her. "I'll tell you the questions we want answers to on the way." He started the engine, eager to be off and to turn on the air.

"You didn't do anything about Holmes," she accused as they pulled away.

"What was I supposed to do?" Funny how traffic had increased in town in the last few years. Why would anyone in his right mind move to Holder in Tornado Alley, a place with periodic droughts and in the wildfire zone? He liked it here, but he'd never been much of anyplace else, outside of Afghanistan and Germany.

"What were you supposed to do? Nothing I guess." She

sounded disappointed.

"Lose my job?" he asked.

"No."

"Well, I went to the sister," he told Bradley. "I can't make her ask for a better lawyer. I can't fire the one Christine has right now. I can't go into the jail and tell the woman what lawyer to ask for."

"No. I'm sorry," she said. "I didn't know you'd tried."

"I hope no one else ever knows," he said. He glanced at her. "I shouldn't involve you in this thing with the boys, either, because it's going to blow up in my face. Almost guaranteed. Munson was a reformer when he came into the department and he'll probably look golden whatever happens, but I don't know how he's going to take my casting a black mark on the whole P.D."

A surprised, alarmed, expression crossed Bradley's face. "What in hell are you talking about?"

"Moses and Ezekiel Parker, for two dead boys, and probably others."

Her jaw dropped.

"At best, police racism and negligence. At worst, a murder by a policeman. Maybe that's an illogical conclusion, and I don't conclude that yet, but I'm kind of a suspicious guy."

His eye was on the road right now and he couldn't see her reaction to his last statements, but something in him felt relieved to have said all that out loud. He wondered if Tolliver was just a lazy, no good cop, or if the man had killed "lots" of black children. But that was a stupid idea, no doubt. Probably Tolliver had "only" taken a bribe or two to cover up the real killer's work.

Clement would be a very bad cop, indeed, if he only provided a picture of the suspect, as opposed to an array. He'd made an arrangement of pictures on the computer in Madge's office while her eyes were averted—and her boss was out. Clement had strewn in almost too many photos, including several cops who had patrolled both the Whirlwind and Chisholm areas and a couple who had just about exclusively worked the suburbs or other white areas. The array would only be shown to anyone who seemed to have some information that might lead him to be able to identify a suspect.

Clement had also included a photo of his father. Not that he thought his dad had been involved in killing children. No, in fact, that was why he'd included his father. Whatever his father was guilty of, it wasn't child murders. No, really not.

Additionally, Clement had scanned and printed out photos of the two boys that Mrs. May had given him—including one of the boys on their bikes.

He divided the territory between himself and Bradley and was prepared to spend the rest of the week here. He was ready for the second leg of the long climb up.

Stores and the street were the places with easy access—lunch counters and bars. *Do you remember these boys from the 1990s? Maybe you went to school with them? Moses and Ezekiel Parker? Did you ever see anyone else riding a bike like either one of these? Did you hear of any other children missing around that time? If you think of anything or if you know anyone who might know, here's my card…Yeah, this is the case that was in the newspapers. I know we're 20 years too late, and believe me, I'm very sorry about that. If I could change that, I would.*

In and out of air conditioned establishments, by the time he'd set for meeting Bradley at the car, he felt like raw meat handled by a careless cook. Bradley looked about the same—wilted, her face red and black eyes serious.

Before she got in the car, Clement suggested they eat up the street at Manna, a diner type place. "We'll attract a little attention and can show our pictures around," he said.

They walked across the hot sidewalk under the midday sun

to the restaurant. "Get anything?" he asked.

"Sort of hit on," she said. "Plus some hostility. You."

"Not hit on, for sure." He grinned at her. "But no. Don't worry, though. I didn't expect this to be easy for us. That's part of the fun."

"Fun? Ha ha. You have an oddball sense of fun." Her eyes seemed to follow every eye on the street that tracked her passage.

"It's a guy thing," he said, opening the diner door for her to enter.

With no tables available, Clement and Bradley had to sit at the counter, but the counter had old-time swivel seats with chair backs, and Clement didn't mind. "Like the old Woolworth's on Black Mesa." She looked at him blankly, and he remembered that she was very young.

Clement put the pictures of Moses and Ezekiel on the counter, face up, and the counterman, when he came to wait on the white officers, regarded the photos and not his customers. "Oh Christ," he said, giving Clement a double jolt from the curse using the Son of God's name and from the vehemence of the exclamation.

"You knew them both?" Clement asked.

The counterman continued to stare at the pictures. "Moses was my best friend." His voice cracked.

Ah. "Had anyone been bothering Moses and Ezekiel around that time? Do you know anything about the night they disappeared?" The cafe seemed to have gotten a whole lot quieter. Clement looked around. Yes, people were listening. The fact that all men everywhere in this country had been declared equal, didn't mean that real, full integration had taken effect. Holder, Oklahoma still had a black section and when two white people ate in the diner there, they must be cops. And this time, they were, and something worth eavesdropping on was happening.

The counterman wiped his eyes and face. The sight of his childhood friend had forced tears from him. He shook his head.

79

Clement wasn't satisfied. A best friend should be a source of information. The cop pulled out the composite sheet of officers and laid it on top of the photos of the boys. In an instant the counterman put his finger on the old photo of Henry Tolliver. "He used to bother us," the man said.

"He didn't seem to have pursued them sexually though," commented Bradley on the drive back to the station.

"No," agreed Clement, "although Moses or Ezekiel could have been the target, and not Walter. Or Walter feels too embarrassed to mention the fact. Or he's suppressed the memory."

"Tolliver sounds mean. I don't understand why he would have stopped them all the time and yelled at them that way. They were just kids, just playing. I wonder if he treated all the kids that way. But I still don't think he sounds like a molester." She reached over and tried to turn up the air conditioning, but Clement had already put it on maximum. "Is this a department car?" she asked. "Can you use it in the evening and on weekends?"

"*My* car," he told her. "I get mileage."

Clement wanted very much to talk to Tolliver, but he couldn't forget Mr. Biggs' mention of "lots" of children going missing and Clement had to verify or discard that possibility before he traveled to San Diego to confront the ex-cop. In fact, the minute he'd heard the story in the P.D. lunchroom of Tolliver's refusal to take reports, he'd known that he had to speak to the ex-cop in person.

"Do you want to do this again tomorrow?" he asked Bradley. "Start in Whirlwind?" He needed as much background on Tolliver as he could get.

"Yes," said Bradley.

"Are you sure? It's not as much fun as I might have promised, and it's hot."

"Hot as hell," Bradley agreed.

"Actually not. Hell is a whole lot hotter," Clement said as if he'd been there. "We're in luck here in Holder."

He reached to turn the air conditioning higher, then realized, as she had only a moment before, that it was on max.

CHAPTER 11

Clement woke up with the sun at about 6:30. He'd slept, more or less, from one in the morning or so, on—pretty good for him. But Buddy wasn't on the pillow that Clement always set on the floor for him at night, so the little guy must be waiting for his breakfast in the kitchen.

Clement walked into the living room and for just a second he became utterly disoriented, and his heart stopped, then skidded into overdrive. Someone was lying on the sofa, while Buddy lay on the floor, alongside. Clement wondered if he himself was lying there, if he'd fallen asleep last night on the couch, and if he was dead or somehow outside his body standing here.

In considering the situation carefully and pausing to actually look, he realized that the man stretched out prone on the couch was Rod, his son. Buddy raised his head, gazed at Clement, and let out a soft "woof"; then Rod rolled over and saw his father, too.

"Are you okay?" asked Clement. "You still have a key?"

"Yeah, I'm okay. Sorry if I startled you." Rod sat up straight.

"I could have come out and shot you as a burglar," Clement said, irked.

"You wouldn't shoot a sleeping man, would you?" asked Rod. He smiled faintly.

"In my own home, I'm allowed to," Clement said. "And what if I'd woken up when you were coming in and I thought you were a burglar then?"

"Sheesh, Dad."

Clement sat on the couch beside his kid. "Okay, what is it? Something wrong with your car? You weren't out drinking?"

"We had one of our arguments and Shelly left me."

The boy seemed lower than a snake's armpit, but Clement felt a sudden surge of happiness. "She'll be back," he said. "Couples always argue."

"Yeah," Rod agreed. "She'll be back today. I thought she'd be back last night. Then I went out and looked for her. Then I came here. But maybe she's home now." He brightened and pulled out his cell phone and dialed. And listened and left a message while Clement petted Buddy for taking care of Rod.

But the relationship between Clement and Buddy was basically a commercial one, and Clement wasn't going to kid himself that the dog loved him. The dog was working for meals and flea collars, so Clement got up and went to the kitchen.

Buddy followed, as did Rod.

"I know you don't like her, Dad," Rod said. He opened the refrigerator and stood there considering the limited offerings inside.

"I like her fine," said Clement. "I'll make us some oatmeal."

"I know you don't like her, but I don't know why. Mom likes her. Grandpa likes her." Rod reached into the stove and pulled out a pan. "I'll make the oatmeal. Butter and cinnamon?"

For a minute Clement had forgotten that Rod was the cook, and the idea of the butter and cinnamon made his stomach roil. "Great," he answered. Then he let Rod talk about Shelly and how sweet she was and how funny, and how he hoped she wasn't really angry.

Clement was pleased that Rod had come to him in his upset and disappointment, and he prayed that the relationship with the girl was finally over, that his kid would recover soon and that he would find someone who was firmly in their church or who could be.

Clement and Bradley started with the on-the-way-to-work breakfast crowd on Whirlwind, each taking a different side of the street and going along to all the food places, talking to people who would have been either the age of Moses and Ezekiel or older. Then Clement decided that the killer could have committed atrocities later as well—even to the present day, for all Clement knew—and he began to question everyone.

He spoke rapidly because people were in a hurry to go to their jobs, and because he wanted to interview as many potential witnesses as possible. His tongue grew weary and his throat became increasingly dry.

"Oh yes, when all those black kids were being killed," said one young woman, a few years younger than the Parker boys would have been today. A chill of excitement ran through Clement at hearing her acknowledgement.

The girl had a white paper bag clutched in her hand and her eyes rotated toward the bus stop. She refocused on Clement since the bus to the commercial district hadn't arrived. "My mama walked me to school and picked me up every day afterward, and if I wanted to go out and play with my friends— unuh. I couldn't do it." She laughed. "I was mad at my mama, but she was scared to death."

"Was it in the newspapers then?" asked Clement.

She looked puzzled. "I don't think so."

"How did you find out about it? Are you sure kids were killed?"

"Well, that's what everyone said." Her eyes were on the street once more, and he could see the bus lumbering toward its pick-up spot.

"Can I talk to you again? Can I talk to your mama?"

"Mama's dead," said the woman. "I have to catch the bus..."

She walked toward the stop and got in the line and Clement walked with her, then stood alongside. "I need to talk to you about it," he said.

"Is this guy bothering you, sister?" asked a black man ahead of them in line who had turned to check them out.

"Mind your own business," said the girl sharply. The man gave Clement an angry stare, and Clement returned a blank look for the hostility. He wasn't at an age for pissing contests.

The SPO handed the girl his card and let her go ahead. Maybe she knew something and maybe all she knew were the rumors of the time. And while her mama's worries could have been entirely groundless, two sets of bones proved something dreadful had happened here once.

When Clement arrived in Mr. Biggs' store, Bradley was already in there talking to the merchant. Clement tapped his temple with his index finger in a salute to the man and stood to listen to the conversation.

Everyone in Oklahoma had a twang—Clement, too, though he didn't really think he did and generally didn't notice or acknowledge it—but some of the blacks in Holder added the Oklahoma accent on top of a rural Southern one.

Even though the facts of black migration to Oklahoma from the land grab to the 1920s or so wasn't actually taught in the high schools here, Clement, who took an interest in his state's historical roots, had read all about it. The eastern part of Oklahoma had been a popular destination for blacks moving out of the South in order to have a less constricted life. Part of that new sense of living freely had propelled the blacks who came (first, to the Oklahoma Territory, and then to the newly named state) to form all-black towns.

The all-black townships had made the whites nervous and had been discouraged through economic discrimination against the blacks. Eventually, too, the hardships of the Depression had broken up the black townships in the east, and the blacks had moved on further west and north, where they'd lived in segregated sections of mixed race communities, such as Holder.

Even if they themselves had never lived anyplace but here, the Southern part of the accent was simply the way their parents spoke—along with everyone else they knew. So Mr. Biggs, though an Oklahoman all his days, spoke in a drawl that Clement had to edge closer to try to decipher.

"Sir, you told my partner here that a lot of children from around this area had gone missing during the time these two children disappeared?" Bradley said.

Partner? Clement hadn't looked on it in quite that way. He'd cast her in the role of...well, sort of like a human Buddy...Instead of food, though, he doled out the opportunity to do the job—and some instruction.

"I know the name of one boy who disappeared," Biggs told them after careful consideration. "His name Lawrence Harding. His father worked for the Department of Transportation as a road worker or something." He looked at Clement who was making notes. "I recalled that after you were here and was gonna call you, but I didn't think...You seem like a very sincere person, but...This is many years later and I didn't think you'd want to bother with any of this." He opened his hands wide to indicate everything around the three of them.

"Bother with it?" Clement reacted. "Someone killed at least two children in this town and has never been punished for it. I don't think doing what we need to do to finally catch him is a bother."

All in all, the day so far had been wonderful. Rod and Shelly had broken up, and Clement had a solid clue to work with: the name of another child.

Rather than suffer in the heat any longer, the senior officer took Bradley to a Denny's closer downtown. He felt like gloating. "Persistence pays." He couldn't help but grin. "Even if the father isn't still alive, someone will know."

"I hate to burst your bubble, Aaron, but what if it isn't true? What if Lawrence Harding is still alive and he just moved out of town, and with the rumors running all over, people just added his name to the gossip." Bradley had begin to work on a double cheeseburger, shedding pieces of the bun as she went.

"You don't have to worry about your weight," Clement observed.

"The bread isn't healthy." She pulled some more or it off her meat and cheese.

Clement issued a skeptical look. Hadn't the experts just been saying that what wasn't healthful was red meat and high fat? Not that *he* paid any attention. He was happy to eat his own burger and not worry about the aftermath. "Sure, Lawrence Harding could still be alive. I hope he is. I hope his parents are. I hope they have grandchildren from him. I don't conclude anything until I've investigated, but now I have a possibility to look into. If this one doesn't pan out, well, maybe something else will. Just identifying the boys is a start, a gift, and now I'm rolling."

"Can't you say 'we'?" she asked, though a little timidly.

"Oh, the partner thing." He laughed practically in her face. "Didn't they tell you I don't work well with others?"

"Yeah," she said. "But I'm different than anyone you worked with before. You're going to be glad you're working with me."

Clement laughed again. "Okay," he said. "We'll see. I'll show you what I do from here. You might as well learn some stuff while you're waiting for classes. But we're not partners yet, Officer Bradley. I'm just barely tolerating you right now because I need some manpower."

Bradley smiled. Her plate was a disgusting mess and he pulled it from in front of her and put it on the next, empty table.

* * *

Some of the Board of Education's old records had been computerized, but not back that far, Clement didn't think. He supposed that Lawrence Harding had gone to Chisholm Trail Junior High, which at the time had been all-black and segregated—and now was "resegregated" and predominantly black.

Chisholm Trail, unlike Holder Middle School where Rod had gone, had no parking lot for the teachers, so Clement left his car in front of a hydrant and put his police notification on the dash. He gestured at Bradley to get out. He recalled hearing an old-time female officer recount her early days on the force, how her partner had kept trying to open the squad car door for her. Clement smiled.

"What?" Bradley asked.

"Can't I think my own thoughts anymore?"

She looked at him suspiciously.

In the school office, Clement didn't wait diffidently to make himself known, but rapped on the counter as if he were in a bar or hotel. Not that he didn't understand that being a cop had ruined his manners in many situations, but he believed a cop should act efficiently—and aggressively. They didn't call the police a paramilitary organization for no reason at all.

He showed his badge at once and explained to the young black secretary what he wanted. "Those would be really old records," she told him, her voice shot through with doubt and negativity. The records were from a long, long-ago era, before she herself had been in school. Ancient times.

"I know exactly what year this is and what years I'm asking for, but I need to see those records, Miss. Where are they?" He hoped the "Miss" would make him sound a tad more polite, but he was impatient.

She left him without a word and went to the door of an inner office while Clement tapped the tips of his fingernails against the wooden room divider.

Another young black clerk looked up from her work. "What year?" she asked.

"Nineteen ninety-six or so," he said. "Lawrence Harding."

"They're in the tornado cellar, I believe." She got up from her desk. "Do you need a subpoena or something?" she wondered.

"Not when we have a nice, smart girl like you to help us out." He'd ask her if she wanted to come work for the Holder P.D., but she probably didn't. Who would? And anyway, he didn't know if he'd be there in another month or two himself.

He and Bradley followed the young woman through the hall and then down some steps into an environment that smelled horribly of must or mildew—probably killer black mold. The girl turned on the light.

"You can wait upstairs," he suggested to Bradley. But he definitely wasn't going to open the car door for her.

"No," she said.

"No windows?" he asked the office clerk.

"That's the point," she responded. "It's a storm cellar."

The files weren't as impossible to find as he might have imagined. And the papers themselves might smell a bit, but nothing seemed to be growing on them.

Harding, Lawrence went from being enrolled to school to "not attending." *Not attending* could mean anything. Hadn't someone from the school checked up on the child?

"I need a photocopy of the file," Clement said.

The three of them walked back upstairs. "I'll have to ask," the girl answered. "I don't want to be fired over this." Sensible girl. Much more sensible than some.

CHAPTER 12

Mrs. Williams, the principal of Chisholm Trail (as their helper, Adella, had explained), smiled at the girl when the three walked back in. The first clerk, however, shot daggers at her colleague. "These are the police, Mrs. Williams," said Adella. "I remembered that the files were downstairs." She laid the folder on the counter where the principal stood.

"A clever girl," Clement observed. He hoped the two young women wouldn't come to violence in their mutual dislike.

Mrs. Williams smiled again, and Clement made his request for a copy of the file. In response, she sighed. "I can't," she said. "I'm not allowed to." She gave him a regretful look. "You have to request the records, and the okay has to come from the Board of Ed. But you'd probably be better off having the district attorney's office send a subpoena. They can't do anything about a subpoena signed by a judge."

Clement nodded. He'd studied the file in the last couple of minutes in the hallway as they'd walked. "Were you here in 1996?" he asked.

"Yes," she answered. She beckoned them in through the opening in the barrier. "Come into the office where we can talk."

Without thinking, Clement gestured for Bradley to go first. What the hell was he doing?

They sat in the principal's office—about as stark as Clement's own, although she had no sets of bones hanging around—though neither did he right this minute, come to think of it.

Once they were all settled, Mrs. Williams sighed again. "Mr. Robinese was the principal then." She opened the Lawrence Harding file and skimmed through. "Why this boy? What's your interest in him? Has he done something dreadful?"

"Not that I know of," answered Clement. "In fact I'm trying to find out what happened to Lawrence. What does 'not attending' mean?"

Mrs. Williams shook her head. She studied the last page of the file. "Nothing. It doesn't mean anything. Nothing official, that is. Nothing that makes any sense." She stared at the two officers for an overly long beat of time. "Mr. Robinese was not the most careful administrator who ever lived," she said finally.

Clement made a small sound that combined interest, agreement, and an element of amazement. What surprised him though wasn't that Mr. Robinese was a lazy, indifferent leader of the school, but that his negligence might have been coupled with a similar lack of professionalism on the part of law enforcement. What the devil had been going on here?

Mrs. Williams watched Clement's face for a further reaction but his own eyes were intent on her and that was all the response he was about to give. He followed the old law enforcement adage that less is more. The less the officer speaks, the more he's likely to elicit from a witness—or a suspect.

Her head dropped as if in concession. "That was a terrible period around these parts," she said. "I was teaching here at Chisholm Trail at the time and a lot of talk went on about missing children. I don't really think as many were missing as they said, but Lawrence Harding might have been one. He wasn't a student of mine and he may well have simply moved out of state." She gazed directly at Clement once again. "Ezra Jackson was my student who stopped showing up to class with no explanation. I went to his house and talked to his mother.

She was as frantic as any mother could be. She hadn't seen her son in days."

"And the police?" Clement asked with a sinking feeling.

"Said the boy had probably just run away. She knew it wasn't true."

At her words, Clement's emotions grasped him by every possible portal to his body and he felt the breath go out of his chest, while a darkness fell across his eyes.

Boys. All the missing children so far were boys. That seemed to tell him something about the motive. Like every other cop in the world, Clement was familiar with all the famous serial killers, and the category of men who killed boys now ran across the film screen of his mind. This was an obscene vision he didn't welcome, and he tried to dispel all these horrid pictures along with the thought that this could be the case that made Holder, Oklahoma famous and the Holder P.D. universally despised.

The three of them sat there and looked askance at one another. And that, Clement knew, was the consolation here: the ability of them as human beings to connect in their sadness.

In the interest of some kind of speedy justice, Enkan had pushed forward the Holmes' court case. She wanted the trial to be held immediately, which Clement guessed would prevent adequate preparation by the defense. But the judge apparently had room on his calendar, and Christine Holmes' attorney didn't object. Maybe he, too, was eager to have the accused squared away—forever—under state care.

This speed was unusual for a first degree, premeditated murder case, but then again, the prosecutor hadn't called for Christine's death. Nice of her, considering that Oklahoma was one of the top five states sending convicted killers off to execution. On the other hand, the death penalty for women wasn't a popular cause, and Enkan was unlikely to win such a sentence for the defendant.

Mrs. Holmes would be convicted, sentenced to life in prison, Clement was sure, and transferred to the Mabel Bassett Correctional Center outside of Oklahoma City—too far for her sister to visit more than once a year, following a protracted fight with the sister's husband.

The facility had been built just over a decade back, and Clement had visited a year after the center was opened. Already the odor of all prisons everywhere permeated the building—a smell of sweat, dirty water used by the inmates to clean, and desperation. The worst thing about prisons, both old and new, was the noise. The materials they were built of, whether brick or concrete, seemed to beam the sound of shouted chatter and the clanging of metal doors against their frames right back into the visitors' and inmates' ears.

Clement, who had been something of a mama's boy as a child, knew that he was a complete pushover where women were concerned—but was that so bad? In this world where so many men seemed hardened and predacious toward the weaker sex, was being inclined to protect their gender really a weakness?

Enkan hadn't tried to prep him again. Clement presumed she relied on Munson's having talked to him to bring him into line—or she'd been satisfied with how he'd done at the grand jury. But the grand jury, of course, was presented with only one side of the case, whereas in theory, a regular trial put on some opposition to the prosecution. Clement hoped that this might be the situation here, but he wasn't confident any great defense would be presented.

He shouldn't let himself be bothered about Christine Holmes. With the case of the missing boys, a situation burgeoning into something both grippingly disheartening and eminently media worthy, he had enough on his mind. His investigation wouldn't stay under wraps for too much longer either, he supposed. Someone in the black community would go to the press.

Meanwhile, he woke up early, dressed in his usual court-going suit, and shut Buddy into the cool of the house for a day-long siesta complete with kitchen sidetrips—and, okay, Clement had started to leave on the TV for the dog's entertainment.

Once outside in the morning air, Clement felt the sweat pouring down.

Even having the air on in the car didn't do much good. But he didn't expect it to. The outside heat was hopelessly oppressive. *Practicing for hell*, he told himself, though he didn't really believe in hell, nor did his church focus on such a notion.

Clement stood at the railing on the second floor where the actual trial was to be held. He looked down at the busy main floor and wondered what everyone was doing here. Lawsuits probably, over property and cattle; corporate oil and natural gas; slip and fall cases; and one man demonizing the other over this or that outrage; criminal prosecutions—rape, theft, as well as murder.

When he entered Courtroom Three after being called, Clement had a strong sense of disorientation. He had been in this courtroom many, many times before, and he felt those past cases crowding in on him. The clerk made him swear to tell the truth, and he settled into a chair that far too many had sat in over the years. The cop sensed the worry, the tension, the lies, the truth, the hope, the fear, surging up through the carved wood of the seat, to rest on his shoulders.

A real trial, Clement knew, wasn't like the ones on TV. The lawyers didn't speak as well as actors, and the action often halted for each attorney to find his notes or for the judge to tell his bailiff something.

So Clement sat for a minute or two unattended until Enkan came forward and asked the usual string of questions about his name, his position with the Holder Police Department, years served and in what role, as well as what he had been doing at the crime scene that evening. The answers spilled from his mouth, automatically—without the intervention of his brain.

But his brain had awakened from its absolute absorption in the world of multiple dead and missing boys, and he realized he hadn't considered what his testimony would be at this trial, here and now. He wasn't sure what his attitude was because, even knowing that his sympathies lay with the defendant, he didn't know what, well, what God would have him think of such a thing. Christine Holmes had killed and quite probably after premeditation.

Now he looked over at the defendant—a little too well dressed in a blue suit and white blouse and a little too well composed to present in the courtroom as the abused wife. Clement wondered if she was medicated since she looked so calm, so different than the last time he had seen her, the night of the murder.

"Did the defendant say anything to you about stabbing her husband?

"Yes. She said she stabbed him and stabbed him." Clement hesitated, gathering his thoughts, the words he might say if he was willing to say them.

"Did you coerce her in any way?"

"No." He would prefer to protect his own position, of course, especially as knee deep as he was in the murder of a series of boys, and, at best, negligence by the Holder P.D.—or a coverup.

"How long did you speak to the defendant, Christine Homes?"

"No more than 20 minutes or half an hour."

"So you didn't interrogate her intensively?"

"No." And maybe her attorney would ask him something helpful, a key question such as: *What was the defendant's mental state?* Of course Enkan would point out that Clement wasn't qualified to answer that question and then a competent attorney would point out Clement's expertise, an expertise the prosecutor herself had relied on, and then the judge would say that Clement might answer...

Enkan had walked away, and the defense attorney, a kid with glasses and arrogance written all over his beardless baby face came up to Clement and gave him a condescending smile. "Have you ever seen a defendant convicted that you thought was innocent?" he asked.

The question didn't register with Clement as it had no meaning in the current context, and he looked at the boy without comprehension. Then Clement thought over what he'd been asked. "I don't believe so. No," he answered. That was the simple truth.

But the boy's aggressive spirit wasn't dented. Nor, apparently, his stupidity.

"Tell me this, Senior Police Officer Aaron Clement." He paused dramatically. "Did you actually see my client stab her husband?"

Clement refrained from rolling his eyes in response. "No, sir," he said impassively.

Then the witness was allowed to leave the stand.

CHAPTER 13

Clement had spent enough time as an investigator to figure out how to find a man. But in fact, only seven Hardings were listed in the Holder telephone directory, and Clement simply had Bradley call until she located the right one. Then she made an appointment, and the two of them drove out to speak to Lawrence Harding's father.

Asking a man to report his son missing and presumed dead after 20 years of ignoring the case cannot be one of the more pleasant tasks a law enforcement officer has to face. Such a necessity makes up probably at least one reason why the typical emotional display of the average cop appears little more than stoical.

Jarvis Harding met them at the door displaying a demeanor rather similar to Aaron Clement's. The two men evaluated one another with not much greater than a glance and Clement stepped inside after Harding opened the door a little wider. This time, Bradley followed in the SPO's wake. *Better*, Clement told himself.

Harding invited the officers to sit and informed them that he was a retired trucker. He'd driven an 18-wheeler for about three decades until his back was nearly crippled with the constant pounding of the road against his spinal column. He'd gone to fat, either before or since, and surely that didn't help what he described as "eroded disks." Maybe he meant "herniated disks"—Clement's colleagues were always taking weeks off at a time for those.

"I'll get to the point," Clement said. "I'm looking into the disappearance of some children around 1996. Someone mentioned the name Lawrence Harding." Clement preferred not to discuss the file he'd seen at Chisholm Trail.

"We called him Lonnie, as a nickname," Harding said and a mist came to his eyes.

"What happened?" asked Clement.

"Just what you said. He disappeared. He went out one night to get some milk at the store for his mama, and 20 minutes later, he hadn't come back. 'Oh that boy is just messing around outside with his friends,' I said. But a while after, I went to fetch him. I couldn't find him and came home and borrowed a neighbor's car. Lonnie wasn't nowhere. Then I got a bunch of men to help and go look." The speech was accomplished with several pauses and much sighing over the past as if it were present with them at that moment in the room.

Clement remained silent, his eyes mostly on Harding but sometimes on the floor, his heart contracting in pain, and wondering how men endured these unendurable moments. Thank God his own child had grown up safely. And he prayed to God that his own son would continue to thrive.

"We called up the police," added Harding a second later, that inevitable, dreaded moment of truth. Clement had, of course, expected this, and he stared at Harding. "They took the report, but they didn't find nothing. And Lonnie never showed up again."

"I don't suppose you recall the name of the policeman," Clement said.

"I recall everything about what happened real clear," Harding answered. "Sergeant Howard Munson. I spoke to him. He was very sympathetic, but he never found Lonnie."

Well used to showing no reaction at all, Clement nonetheless startled. Of course he had expected Tolliver's name, and indeed Munson hadn't been on his list of officers assigned to patrol the black district in those days under Chief Kenny.

Clement speculated on the story behind this. Because he hadn't found a report of a missing young Lawrence Harding. If Munson had taken such a report and had filed it, where was it now? And, of course, the operative word here was "if." "If" he had filed it. Was Munson, who had always seemed very much the straight arrow to Clement, actually badly twisted?

At home that night, Clement turned on the news. He was quite concerned about the weather. Even though they were under drought water restrictions, he was willing to pay a fine in order to water the ground around the house. They were getting deeper into summer, and sometimes he could smell fire in the air from not too far a distance. The scent ignited a slow-burning worry in his mind.

He sat musing about that when the news caught his attention—a report on the day's proceedings in the Holmes' trial.

"According to forensic psychiatrist Norman Parks, not only was the defendant, Christine Holmes, mentally competent at the time, she based the killing on something that had appeared in a *Trial for Murder* episode on the Criminal Justice cable network," said the cute, blonde WHOL news anchor, Mary Anne Evans.

"In that episode of the show, for which Dr. Parks is a consultant, a wife drugged her husband's late night beverage and then stabbed him multiple times in his sleep. Dr. Parks, in testifying for the prosecution in the Holmes case today, contended the television incident was so similar that Christine Holmes must have based the murder of her husband on that show...Next up, after the break, a look at today's baseball with Keith, brought to you by Holder Auto Body Shop."

Shutting off the television although he hadn't yet found out the weather, Clement reflected grimly on what he'd just heard. Possibly Christine had committed a very premeditated murder modeled on something she'd seen on a television show. Of course Clement had already resigned himself to accepting some degree of premeditation on her part, but if the WHOL report was accurate, then Clement had to go a great deal further in acceptance.

Christine had sat in her darkened living room thinking how to kill her husband and learning from what some other wife had done. Clement supposed in the *Trial for Murder* episode, the wife had somehow gotten off or had been given a lenient sentence for some reason. He'd have to look into that in the next week or so. Just how calculating had Christine been?

Still, in thinking of the hospital report, Clement tried to reassure himself that the killing might nonetheless be justified. Not that what he thought made any difference. What mattered here was her attorney, and what he led the jury into believing. This case, especially, depended on sentiment.

Clement packed up his car for the trip to Oklahoma City and the flight to San Diego, where Tolliver now lived. Clement had been to San Diego once, and though he supposed both the dust bowl town of Holder and the Pacific Coast municipality were Western cities, the cultural gulf between them loomed un-breachable. Despite his having traveled here and there in the Army and as a cop, Clement was at heart an Oklahoma boy and used to this particular set of hardships and disasters. The older he got, the more he hated to leave his home.

Bradley arrived at his house in her car and he gave her the keys and showed her where he kept Buddy's food. He wasn't sure if he'd first asked her to look after the dog or if she had offered. Not that he didn't recall sort of what had been said, but he wasn't certain...Funny, because most times he was pretty definite about what had gone on between himself and someone else, and the nuance of the interaction. In fact, maybe he'd become a cop because of his habit of analyzing such things to death.

"You sure must love this dog," Bradley said now. She examined the plain old nonelectrical can opener he'd used for at least 30 years and set it back down on the table. He'd engraved his name on the thing with a metal cutter.

"I don't think so," Clement said. "Why?"

"You're leaving him in an air conditioned house for two whole days. Going to cost a lot to run the air all the time." She looked at him with curiosity.

"Cost of doing business," Clement said. "Can't take him in and not do right by him, can I?" Saying that, Clement knew that he was lying, that he cared for the dog, about the dog's well-being; otherwise, what was the point? "Love" though was an awfully strong word for the feeling.

A little uneasy because he wouldn't be here to oversee her work, he told her to follow up on the Ezra Jackson lead Mrs. Williams at Chisholm had given them. "You've got to be discreet," he told her. "We're stirring up a nest of something with this case. Something nasty." He totally shouldn't expose Bradley to the politics involved. She was young and just starting out in policing. Going on with this investigation, he, himself, understood that because of the politics he could easily lose his job—but she shouldn't have to. He'd warn her again when he got back. Maybe get her reassigned.

He showed Bradley how to lock the door. "Thanks," he said. "You have my cell, if anything comes up." He got in his car and drove off before she did.

Holder to Oklahoma City and then the flight to San Diego would take the day. He wasn't trying to surprise Tolliver, and, anyway, Clement couldn't have counted on Tolliver's being home, so he'd made an appointment for the following morning.

Clement didn't drive directly to the airport, but went, instead, to the Oklahoma federal building, kitty-corner to the one blown up in 1985. He'd been in this place one time before. Because he had an appointment here and then was going to fly to California, today was one of the few days he hadn't carried the holster with his cocked and locked pistol inside his waistband, a habit from, well Afghanistan.

Set back from the street so that the (God forbid) next car bomb wouldn't bring down the building as easily as the last, the place had security features up the ying yang. Clement pulled everything out of his pockets and was wanded. He showed his ID. This was the type of extra-careful scrutiny he got when he visited a maximum security prison.

FBI Special Agent Carrie Roberts came down to fetch him. They talked the weather on the elevator—hot—and only when they'd settled into her office did Clement glance at his watch and then broach the subject of what had brought him here. She was a profiler he had worked with on a case previously; now he had a situation...

"So far I have three boys missing, two sets of bones, confirmed identities. I have at least one other name to check out, but the total number, who can say? The boys were all around 13 or so. And all the boys so far were black." Only as Clement actually said this did he realize that he hadn't looked into the possibility of white boys missing during that same time frame, but of course the possibility did exist.

He handed her the reports the forensic examiner at the university, Dr. Neal, had given him.

"You don't have much," Roberts observed.

"I have a lot more than I had six weeks ago," he told her. "The case is finally in motion—at last."

"Well, I'll start by presuming the killer is a male in his late 30s, early 40s, and that's not invariable, of course." She stopped and looked at him, as if checking that he understood. But Clement already knew the general parameters and the impossibility of being really exact. He just wanted to see if he was missing anything, any scrap of an idea, and already he'd realized his failure to check around in the white community, maybe especially among the poor white "trash." Hadn't Stan Runninghorse said something about Tolliver treating anyone who didn't seem to be someone with disrespect? Maybe that meant more than Clement had seen it as at the time.

"What do you think, white or black?" he asked, but he decided as soon as he said the words that without knowing if white children—boys—had been targeted, they couldn't really know.

"Wayne Williams," Roberts said, naming the man, black, convicted after 29 black boys and men were killed in Atlanta in the 1970s and early 80s. Williams was only convicted of two 1981 killings, though.

Roberts seemed about to explain her comment, but Clement jumped in. "Innocent or guilty..." he countered, referring to the question of whether the police had actually gotten the right man. Although the killings had stopped after Williams' arrest, the man had never confessed to any guilt, and many thought he wasn't the killer—or wasn't the killer of *all* of the children.

Anything was possible in these situations. Maybe killers took the opportunity to stop and remain undetected when someone else was caught.

They looked at one another for a moment, each thinking about the ramifications of such crimes. "You don't know if the murders were sexual?" she asked. "Although...all boys."

"Hard to say at this point," Clement acknowledged, "but it could look that way, of course."

"And only the two bodies...well, sets of bones," she mused. "No other physical evidence. We usually work with physical evidence and we work with suspects that you establish first." She frowned. "We're no psychics," she added. She appeared exasperated, but he didn't suppose it was with him.

Of course he'd neglected to give her a key set of information, the fact that the cases of the missing children hadn't been properly documented or investigated after they'd been reported by the families, and Clement's sense that in some way this itself was related to the killings.

As if right on cue, she asked him a rather obvious question. "What about other reports of missing children during that period?"

"We have a problem in that area," Clement answered warily. "The records...the documentation...Something happened there."

She looked at him as if she were saying "hick cops" to herself, and he felt like one.

"If I mail you a letter, would you promise not to open it?" he asked. "I'd like to put something in writing for you at this time, just in case. But only in case I don't work this thing out."

"What is it?" she asked sharply. Obviously she didn't like the sound of that.

"In case I find a civil rights aspect to all this," he said.

She appeared thoughtful.

"Just in case," he added, as if he hadn't said that already.

She shook her head no. "All right," she agreed then, despite the signal she'd already sent.

He'd drop the letter he'd prepared in the mail on his way to the airport. Just against the possibility someone in the Department of Justice had to file a suit accusing the Holder P.D. of systematic civil rights violations. And just in case Clement was fired and his charges were suppressed on the basis that the accusations were from an angry ex-employee trying to get even.

CHAPTER 14

Clement enjoyed the descent into San Diego, although he'd heard this was one of the most dangerous airliner landings in the nation. Still, the view of the sparkling ocean was incredible.

Eyes on the palm trees and marinas, he rode the courtesy shuttle to the least expensive Holiday Inn, where he had made a reservation. Whether he was out of pocket for the trip or would eventually collect from the department, he wasn't exactly sure.

After checking in, he found the hotel coffee shop and had a small steak and a beer, then went to his room. Five o'clock and he was in for the night. He called Rod's home phone and left a message, telling him to hang tough and to call later if he needed to. Clement knew that the boy was still hurting after being dumped by his girl.

But the one Clement really missed he couldn't leave a message for. That was Buddy. Yeah, Clement missed the companionship of the dog, and a dog without a lot of personality at that. Some dogs were really cute or terribly amusing, had character, persistence, or a sense of showmanship. Buddy, though, didn't display any outstanding traits. He was just a dog, an average dog, one that didn't make much of a fuss or do a lot other than the usual. Sort of like the owner himself, Clement reflected.

He turned on the television for a moment, but wasn't interested in San Diego or California news. However, every hotel room Clement had ever visited, except for two vermin-filled nights that time in Kabul, had one thing in common, and that was a Gideon Bible in a drawer. At this moment Clement took a practically unbreached copy out of the nightstand, and he resolved to read until he was ready to fall asleep—which was what he did.

In the morning, Clement reached down for Buddy on the dog's cozy pillow, realizing at the same second that the little guy wasn't here, in this town.

Clement just about didn't know how to move forward into the day and appreciated that in a minute-to-minute sense he operated on a mechanical level rather than a spiritual, or even human, one. His life proceeded for the most part by rote. What would happen if he *did* get fired and he had no idea of where to go in the morning? And each day he'd be a little older and less capable of starting anything new.

With that debilitating thought, he bounded up to shower, and after he dressed he went down, ate, and got a cab.

Tolliver's house wasn't much of anything, probably would sell for under $80,000 back in Holder. Yeah, that was Holder, for a house of that size. In San Diego, well, Clement had looked in the newspaper classifieds at breakfast earlier and had nearly spilled his coffee over real estate prices. But Tolliver had moved here almost a decade before and the house hadn't cost anything like what it must now be worth.

Trying to estimate the square footage here, Clement rang the bell.

A woman Clement vaguely recalled opened the door. She was made up to beat the band, and extra poundage bulged from a stylish pair of navy pants. "Howdy, Aaron." She smelled like a drugstore cosmetics counter.

"Yeah," he said as brightly as he could muster. "Good to see you." He wondered if he was supposed to lean forward and kiss her on the cheek, but he didn't want to, so he didn't.

She ushered him in. The home inside wasn't too different than he had figured it: the furniture as predictable as his own (aside from his restored, antique pieces), but the space more cramped. "How do you like our San Diego weather?" she asked.

"A nice change from Holder," he reported, knowing that was exactly what she wanted to hear.

"We think so! Here, sit down." He had to sit on the plastic covered sofa. As bad as his own sofa was, at least it wasn't plastic-covered. "I'll go fetch himself for you."

Clement nodded and smiled—all his behavior totally mechanical, without any substance.

Truth to tell, he was a little bit nervous and almost wondering why he was here. He didn't have anything on Tolliver at all and didn't actually expect the man to adopt any attitude except hostile.

Tolliver came in, wiping his hands on a dishtowel, which he then handed to the wife who stood right behind him. She took the cloth and gave Clement an "I'll leave you two men alone" look and went back in the direction from which she had come. She probably was relieved to get out of the room and not have to listen to the conversation.

Clement stood and extended his hand to shake Tolliver's slightly damp one. He sat again immediately and stretched his arms across the back of the couch. "Looks as if you're doing right nice out here," Clement began carefully, choosing the most "Oklahoma" way to express himself. He watched for Tolliver to take the "master's" seat—the large cushioned chair across from his guest—which he unsurprisingly did.

"The weather's a sure sight better than back home," said Tolliver. He crossed his arms against his girth and stared at Clement. A challenge? Or simply the man's way of interacting?

Clement remembered Tolliver, of course, but just didn't remember him looking quite this gray, this old, this fleshy—though underneath the pounds Clement could detect a girdle of muscle. Cops used to have muscle, Clement reflected. A lot of the new guys—men included—didn't really. They relied on their wits, he supposed. Or the gun. Both good tools, actually, though a hint of muscle didn't hurt.

"The old days," said Clement. Tolliver wanted to get down to business, and so did Clement.

Tolliver's expression didn't change.

"In 1996, you patrolled the Chisholm Trail and Whirlwind areas," Clement remarked.

"I did that for years and years," the man agreed. "I had an understanding with those people." Tolliver relaxed, apparently no longer feeling threatened. He even smiled. So, had he thought to perhaps have been accused of something he felt guilty of, but nothing related to his work in the black areas?

"Can you remember—well, maybe you have your patrol notebooks?—in 1996, a number of reports of missing children?" As he said that, Clement felt his chest and throat tighten with the heat of a growing fury. He had been angry all along, he saw, but had tried to put it from himself. Now he realized that he hadn't done that, only delayed the expression of the anger. He had to remain rational here with Tolliver. He was after information and that was the important thing, not punishing Tolliver.

"Can't say I really recall anything out of the ordinary," answered Tolliver whose face contorted into a puzzled frown. "Seriously? Sometimes the little colored kids ran off. We'd look for 'em if their parents made some kind of a fuss, but we hardly ever found them."

Instead of speaking, Clement handed Tolliver the pictures of the two boys—his two sets of bones—given him by their grandmother. Tolliver shook his head. Not even a spark of recognition came into his eyes. Clement handed over a picture of Lonnie Harding.

No, nothing. Just some little colored kids who'd run off, in the ex-policeman's view.

Clement's breathing had eased a bit. "You never filed reports on these children? On any of the...runaways?" He tried to retain a neutral tone.

"Well, sure I did."

Of course that wasn't what Stan Runninghorse had told Clement, so the statement was definitely an interesting one.

"Hey, can I get you a cup of coffee?"

"No, thanks," Clement said as evenly as he could. "I'm already drowning."

"Bathroom's down that hall," Tolliver let him know. "And I'm going to get a cup for myself."

Tolliver had lied and then had broken off the intensity of the interview to collect himself, was how Clement saw it. Clement followed Tolliver into the little kitchen. "Nice," he said.

The ex-cop opened the refrigerator and took out what looked to be a pitcherful of filtered water. "You know Doris," he answered cheerily.

No, Clement didn't know Doris in actuality, but he forced a smile onto his lips. "A good housekeeper," he praised.

"Your dad still with Maria?" asked Tolliver. Clement nodded. "How's your dad doing?"

"Pretty good," said Clement. He didn't know if referring to his father's dishonesty—which everyone knew about, anyway—would help here or not. Something to imply that most of the officers on the Holder force had been cowboys in those earlier days.

"So you filed reports on all the boys," Clement went on.

"Maybe not all," admitted Tolliver. "Just the ones who seemed to really be missing."

Clement had said "boys," and he hadn't meant to. "Really missing," Clement repeated. "Boys and girls?"

"I guess," said the ex-cop. He had measured the grounds into a paper filter and had started the machine. Now they waited for the beverage to brew.

Clement went and looked out the curtain that hung on the

back door. The yard was small, but outfitted with a couple of chaise lounges and an aluminum table with a big umbrella to give shade. "You have it good here," Clement said. His anger had subsided by now and he only felt disappointed. He wasn't done, but he wondered if Tolliver was anything but an ignorant Oakie redneck, who, like Clement's own father, wasn't above a bit of graft.

At just that point, Doris stepped into the kitchen and went to the refrigerator, herself.

"Sure you won't have a cup?" Tolliver offered a second time.

"No thanks," said Clement. "I'm staying at the Holiday Inn downtown. Leaving about noon tomorrow to go back. Why don't you come and join me for breakfast first? I'd like to talk about the old days a little bit."

"Oh, well, if you're buying," said Tolliver.

"You can get an egg white omelet," put in his wife.

Clement walked back to the living room and used his cell phone to call a cab.

He'd had no intention of staying until the next day, but then he'd decided to try to talk to Tolliver away from his own territory. Clement got the room for another night and changed his flight. Being active law enforcement, not only did he get a discounted fare, but he didn't have to pay an additional charge for taking a different plane on his return.

He went and sat by the pool in the summer khakis he had on. There, he read the paper and drank an iced tea. His best guess was that he looked like a cop. Everyone else seemed to be on vacation.

He went back into the air conditioning and used the free Internet in the lobby. No one else seemed to want to grab the computer, so he stayed there a while. He went to the Criminal Justice cable network and looked up the descriptions of episodes on their *Trial for Murder* show. While he didn't find anything that Christine Holmes would have copied in killing her husband, the show might have been on during a prior season.

Clement could track down the production company and someone there would undoubtedly send him a full list of shows. He simply wondered. The idea that Holmes had committed a cold-blooded murder all along certainly bothered him, though not as much as it might have if he hadn't seen the hospital reports.

How much premeditation could he tolerate? Undoubtedly more than the jury could. He hated to see her go to prison for life.

Upstairs, he called Bradley and let her know he was staying another day and asked if she would take care of Buddy an extra 24 hours.

"He's a nice dog," she said. "You should put in a doggy door, so he can come and go as he pleases."

"I don't want raccoons in the house," Clement told her. "And we get the occasional bobcat out there. Buddy would make a good meal for one."

"You're kidding me!"

"No, not really. And coyote." He smiled.

"No wonder you always carry a gun."

"Who told you that?" He was sure he hadn't.

He waited a long pause for her to answer him. "Everyone knows everything about you," she said finally.

He was taken aback. He couldn't imagine *anything* about him being of interest to the rest of the department, much less *everything*. People gossiped about *him*? They must gossip about all the SPOs. He pretended she hadn't said that and went on to ask about the investigation.

Clement was packed up and in the lobby well before 10. He believed from his meeting with Tolliver the day before that the man wasn't a suspect in the children's deaths, though one should always be ready for a surprise in anything having to do with homicide. People weren't always what they seemed. Good

111

citizens, husbands, and fathers sometimes emerged as serial killers—Herb Baumeister's killing spree in Indiana turned out to be quite a surprise to his own wife, even though the kids had found human bones in the basement.

Clement assumed, of course, that his killer had to be a man. Female serial killers were an anomaly and most killed people they knew and didn't search the streets for victims. Moreover, eighty percent of known female serial killers had used poison as a weapon of choice. Of course Aileen Wuornos, who'd killed on the Florida highways, had been a single, convoluted exception.

Tolliver entered the hotel lobby, and Clement stood up. The older man walked heavily. Aging was hell. Clement, not yet feeling the effects of time all that much, feared the process. He went forward to meet the former cop and take him into the coffee shop, where a friendly hostess greeted them.

"An all whites omelet?" Clement asked as they studied the menu.

"Hell no." Tolliver grinned. "I'm not going to live forever, no matter what I eat."

"True," agreed Clement. When the waitress came, he himself asked for bacon with three scrambled eggs and buttered toast. He didn't believe that cholesterol count affected citizens of Oklahoma.

Tolliver ordered a stack of pancakes. "I was thinking of calling and not coming," he said when the cheerful blonde waitress had left. "But I came out of respect for your father. Your dad was a good cop and a standup guy. I want you to know that."

"Of course," agreed Clement, though he felt perennially ashamed of his father. "That was the way things were in those days," he added. He'd thought long and hard about how to handle Tolliver today and had decided on some of the old 'you might have done a few things, my friend, but that's normal' tactic. In this case, Clement Senior lent a hint of credibility to Clement's own supposed attitude.

And Clement seemed to have struck just the right note because Tolliver nodded, as if pleased, then quickly drank the apple juice set beside him. "The old days," agreed Tolliver. "We had different attitudes. You remember Chief Kenny?"

"Sure," Clement said.

"Look, we didn't have the kind of staff you have today. Everything was a bit rough and ready then."

Their food arrived. Clement, whose hunger had vanished when he wasn't looking, decided he had to eat, anyway. He had a flight and a long drive ahead.

"Kenny allowed a lot of things to slip by," Tolliver went on. "And, listen, in terms of your dad. He had a family to support and on not a whole lot of pay."

Clement nodded, but blaming his dad's dishonesty on that "family to support" always made Clement feel particularly bitter. He would rather have gone around in rags than have a scoundrel for a father. And he wondered if defending Clement's dad was Tolliver's way of saying that whatever he'd done to earn a San Diego retirement in a nice little house had been okay, too.

"Where are those boys—the ones whose pictures you showed me yesterday?" The stack of well-buttered and syruped pancakes was fast disappearing.

Clement swallowed a forkful of egg. "Moses and Ezekiel Parker are in two decent caskets at Russell's waiting for a proper burial." He could hardly pretend otherwise and he felt choked with the knowledge of the events Tolliver had played such a key role in.

"Damn," said Tolliver. "But how could I have known?"

By doing the investigation, Clement thought. He shook his head and bent his head down over his fork in motion.

"Of course I did file some of those reports, the ones that seemed serious," Tolliver added somewhat anxiously.

Clement had found none for the entire period. None. A little odd in itself. And other records—robberies and drunks,

113

domestic disturbances and theft of livestock—all were there. Clement looked up and stared directly into Tolliver's eyes. "Did you, Henry?" he appealed. "Did you file one or two?"

"I always did," Henry Tolliver assured the SPO. "We made judgment calls in the field in those days, of course. Kenny always said we should. Whatever we didn't bring back didn't have to be followed up. We didn't actually have the staff."

Clement stopped eating because he knew the food would turn on an angry stomach. "Yeah," he said. "But you filed some? Even among the...colored...folk?"

"Of course," Tolliver told him again. "I didn't pay attention to colored or white. If the case seemed serious, I filed the report." In a couple of swallows, the pancakes were gone. "I don't like to think I did any harm," the retired cop added. "I'm sure your father and I both feel the same way."

Clement nodded. He'd continue to jolly the old man along, not to miss anything that might be forthcoming.

Then suddenly Tolliver blinked and turned away. "Ohh, you don't understand," he muttered. "You've never done a wrong thing in your life, have you?"

"I don't like to make a habit of it," Clement said dryly. Though he knew he was willing to reinterpret wrong and right according to his own lights.

CHAPTER 15

Although to anyone else, the trip might have seemed like a waste of time and motion, Clement had found it valuable. Driving over the rough back roads in the panhandle, getting closer to home, he made mental notes of what to do next. To him the case was going swimmingly and had kicked into an up-phase of investigation. Police work was foot work, metaphorical or the type that wore down the detectives' shoe leather in actual fact. Clement had sat around for weeks on end having no place to go with the two sets of bones. He had searched the files for any hint of missing children—and had found nothing.

Now, that nothing was a significant clue, which, if it didn't tell him everything, was at least another starting point. He felt, for the moment anyway, encouraged.

He knew the back roads closer to home pretty well and he enjoyed them. He liked being away from the crowds. He liked being the only one on the road, the only human in sight. What must it have been like back in the day when men rode horses through these canyons? At one time, bison herds might have roamed through here. Certainly black bears had lived in the hills.

Those who went to the farthest reaches of the panhandle, to the Black Mesa Preserve, would find black bear still, as well as antelope, and not only bobcats, but mountain lions.

Clement's mind was so fixed on wildlife, that he needed a minute to come to his senses and analyze what he saw walking along ahead by the single lane road. The gait was odd and painstaking, and the creature was hunched. But it was two-legged he understood at last, and wore some kind of filthy, ragged clothes.

Clement stopped and rolled down his window. "Hello there," he called, not too loudly to scare a body, "can I help you out?" Maybe the person had been in an accident. "I'm a police officer. Can I call the highway patrol? Do you need a lift?"

The person approached the car and Clement unlocked the doors. Could the dead walk? No. Then the person, a woman, he guessed, but in bad condition of a kind he couldn't yet figure out, was still alive. Clement half-hoisted himself into the back seat and opened the door. He righted himself in order to drive away as the person came in.

The smell was unholy—yes, like death itself—and Clement, who didn't think himself a superstitious man, shivered. He said a short prayer. The female pulled the door to.

Clement took out his wallet and held it up so his passenger could see his badge. He didn't want to scare her further, if she'd gone through some trauma, though he, for his own part, was unnerved by her foul-smelling presence.

"Where shall I take you, Miss?" he asked, still quietly. He started his engine.

"It's Shelly, Mr. Clement," the woman in the back seat said. The words seemed garbled and his mind needed a moment to decipher them.

He looked back, using the rearview mirror. Her face was almost black with bruising and dirt and was swollen beyond recognition. Her eyes weren't normal and he couldn't imagine the last time her hair had been brushed.

"Of course it is," answered Clement in the calmest voice he could muster. "I'll take you to the hospital." He reconstructed his shattered emotional state as best he could, in order to drive.

* * *

When he got her inside emergency at Holder General, he showed his badge and told the nurse to be sure to do a rape kit. He checked more than once and that nurse and one other assured him that they would. He didn't suppose they were forensic nurses, but maybe they knew how, all the same. With growth and progress in their town, had come mayhem, including despicable and not infrequent incidents of rapes.

He sat and waited to hear more from the staff, his heart pounding and insides in total turmoil. *It's Shelly, Mr. Clement.* How could he have imagined...*If the case seemed serious, I filed the report.* Why hadn't he imagined? Why hadn't he, a cop, who didn't like to make a habit of doing anything wrong, or so he said...why hadn't he wondered at her disappearance. *I don't like to think I did any harm...*

He hadn't perceived the beam in his own eye, while focused on the mote in someone else's. He'd let down Shelly. He'd let down Rod. He'd deceived himself into thinking he was the pure and moral cop, while others were rotten.

The time passed. Clement went out to the car and fetched his Polaroid evidence camera. He returned and sat down. The rape kit alone could take a couple of hours, if properly done.

After a while a nurse came out. "She wants to see you."

Clement followed the woman into the treatment area. Shelly lay on a cot with a drip in her arm.

"Are you a relative?" asked a female doctor in a short white jacket. Clement nodded. As well as being a cop, he was her father-in-law to be. "She's dehydrated. We should keep her at least overnight."

Shelly shook her head decidedly. She looked petrified. "No," she said.

Now Clement realized that her problem in speaking wasn't just because her face was swollen, but because a couple of her upper teeth were broken. "Do you want to go home?" he asked coming closer. "To Rod?" The smell on her of decay and filth mixed with a medical smell.

She shook her head again in a definite no. No, she wouldn't want Rod to see her this way...or she wouldn't want to be so close to a man. Shelly's eyes sent him an appeal. "Can I come stay...width you? I know you don'e like me, but I know too many doctorth here." That was right, she sold pharmaceuticals.

"Of course. Of course."

"She'd be better off in the hospital," said the physician irritably.

"She doesn't want to be here," Clement countered. "She'll sign herself out."

"Well at least give her an hour or so to get some more fluid into her," the doctor snapped.

"All right, Shelley?" he asked. She'd closed her eyes and didn't answer.

"I gave her some sedation," the doctor added.

"Did someone do the rape kit?" Clement wanted to know.

"Yes," said the nurse. She handed the evidence case to him and Clement made sure the nurse doing the kit initialed it. He marked Shelley's name, the time, and the date on the plastic. Then he took a few pictures of Shelly, though the doctor looked at him in horror. In this instance, as was the more usual case, he was on the D.A's side. He initialed the rape kit himself and turned over the photos and marked them with time and date and his initials.

"I'll be back for her," he said.

He got in his car and drove to police headquarters, where he turned the evidence over at the lab. Then he went and knocked on Munson's door, which was open, probably because of the hour, which...Clement looked at his watch...was seven at night.

"What the hell are you up to?" asked Munson, glancing across the room. "You're never around."

"I'm an investigator," Clement said. "I leave the building in order to investigate."

"And?" asked Munson.

As a senior police officer, Clement would ordinarily have had to report to one of the sergeants, but he was the cold case squad—he and he alone—so he reported to Munson. "My son's fiancé was assaulted," he answered.

Munson's eyes widened. "Your son...?" His tone implied that Rod might have been Shelly's assailant.

"Of course not," Clement said in disgust. He came into the room and sat down. He felt that he smelled of what she had smelled of—death. He felt unclean. He imagined what the poor girl might feel. "This is a major case. I believe she was kidnapped, held captive, beaten, and raped." Even that didn't seem to be a full expression of what had happened to the girl.

Munson reached toward the phone. "I'll get someone on it."

"I'm on it," Clement countered. "She's sleeping right now, anyway, under sedation. She's in rough shape."

"I can't let you handle it," objected Munson. "There could be a suggestion of coverup. Something like."

"Isn't any coverup." Clement's tone was scathing. "I'll get her story and I'll do whatever has to be done."

"Sometimes I wonder which one of us is the boss," Munson observed.

Munson had capitulated, and Clement knew he'd done so because not only did Munson trust Clement, but everyone did. And see how he had handled this so far—like Tolliver had handled the disappearance of the boys. Clement got up. "I'll let you know," he said.

Then, when he got to the door, he turned back to Munson. "I have something else to talk to you about tomorrow," he said. "What time can we meet?"

"It's only because we don't have the manpower right now," Munson told him, sounding even more tired than Clement himself felt. "Our biggest problem is a lack of funds. So you take the case. What do you want to talk to me about?"

"Seven-thirty in the morning. I'll come by," Clement instructed his boss. "I know you get in early."

"You should be the chief," Munson said.

"Good grief, no."

Once in Fine Fare shopping, Clement checked his watch again. He called Bradley. Soon, he'd have her number memorized.

"Bradley." She picked up at once.

"Are you with family?" he asked. "Boyfriend?"

"I don't know how to answer that," she said. "Since I don't know if that's a personal question."

He smiled. He put a couple of packages of chopped meat in his cart. With the girl's teeth broken, this might work. What else? Nothing like cereal—oh, maybe soft grits. He'd want some photos of what the perp had done to Shelly's mouth. If he had a gun, he'd shoot the bastard. If he knew who the bastard was.

"If you're not busy," Clement began again, "can you meet me at my house? As soon as possible? I'll make dinner if you haven't eaten. And bring an extra pair of jeans, if you have one and a couple of extra shirts."

"Jeans? Shirts? Dinner?"

For the moment he was able to feel amused. "And two pair of pajamas, if you wear those..."

"I'm spending the night?"

"I'd appreciate it," he said sincerely. "If you don't have anything else that's urgent." He had begun putting all kinds of things in the cart that maybe Shelly could use or would like. Yogurt—girls ate that stuff all the time. A nicer soap than he himself used. A bath powder. His head ached for what the woman had gone through.

"I'll be there," Bradley said. He guessed she'd heard the kidding go out of his voice and her own attitude had gone from lighthearted to deadly serious.

Once again, he heard the woman in the back seat say, "It's Shelly, Mr. Clement." And he'd said, "Of course it is," but he had needed more than just a second or two to understand that Shelly really was who she said she was. Thinking of it now, the horror of that moment, of what this young girl had suffered, resonated through to his deepest, usually inaccessible self.

Though she was still not completely awake, at the house he let Shelly get herself out of the car. He imagined she wouldn't want to be handled or moved around as if she were a thing.

At about 8:30 at night, the temperature was still in the 90s. Dehydrated—no kidding. The radio, which he'd played quietly during the drive, said that Holder's "cooling centers" were in operation.

Bradley's car was already here and she came out of the house and approached to help. Yes, that was better. Shelly might not mind a woman helping her so much. "Shelly, this is Bradley," he said. He wasn't sure if the girl was tracking that well.

"Anna," said Bradley. "Hi, Shelly." She seemed to know just what to do and Clement was pleased. *Anna*, he thought, though. That wasn't right.

They'd finally cleaned her up at the hospital and had put her in a pair of green cotton scrubs. He was glad about that, too. That was a step toward getting rid of the smell, though the smell lingered in his nostrils, and probably in hers.

Bradley assisted Shelly in walking into the house, and Buddy, who'd stepped out, seemed interested in doing the same. When the dog came over to sniff at Clement, the reunion was cool. Did that mean Buddy had expected Clement back inevitably? Or that the dog was too outraged at the desertion to make a fuss over Clement's return? Then again, maybe he thought he belonged to Bradley now. The dog tried once more to assist Bradley with the girl.

"I'll make up both the other bedrooms," Clement said. His voice sounded rusty in his ears. "Shelly, do you want Bradley in the same room with you? There's twin beds in there... Otherwise, you two can each have your own."

He brought in the groceries and then fixed the beds so Shelly could lie down and get some sleep. Trauma—that would knock you out without any drugs. He expected she'd be sleeping a lot in the next week or so.

He was going to call Rod later tonight, but Rod shouldn't see Shelly until she was willing. Clement couldn't imagine she'd be willing right away. Or would she be?

People thought cops were unavoidably hardened, he guessed. Well, he had seen an awful lot, and he supposed he could stand up to what he needed to. But that didn't mean the brutality didn't hammer at him—inside. And maybe because he couldn't really tolerate the ugliness of crime, he'd become a policeman. Or one reason, anyway. Tonight, he simply felt weary and a little bit overwhelmed.

Bradley came out into the living room followed by Buddy. "You see," he told Bradley, "just how bad it can get?"

And she nodded in acknowledgement.

CHAPTER 16

Clement was in his office by six—writing his incident report on Shelly. The photos would punctuate the urgency of the case. Documentation was an important form of bearing witness to an outrage good people had been unable to prevent.

He wasn't exactly the most fluid writer in the world, but he knew, in well-worn tracks, how to write a report. He printed it out, then changed direction and began surfing the web. He wanted to find the episode of *Trial for Murder* from which Christine Holmes had allegedly taken the prototype for the killing of her husband. He did that just out of curiosity, Clement supposed; not that knowing would make any difference, but he wanted to see what the details were. He'd ask the production company to send him a copy. He'd like to study it and see if she'd actually followed the "script."

At seven-thirty, he brought his report on Shelly into Munson's office. Munson was just coming in, a Dunkin' Donuts iced drink in hand, sweat streaming down his face and neck into the collar of a fresh white shirt.

"Another beautiful day in paradise," said the chief.

"Rain and flooding in Houston," offered Clement. He sat down as Munson did and put the report out on his own side of the desk.

"Not going to share?" Munson asked.

"Drink your coffee," said Clement. "I want to talk to you about something else first."

"Yeah?" Munson began wiping his face and neck with a Dunkin' Donuts napkin.

"In 1996, you were a sergeant, but you responded to a call from a distraught father whose son was missing in the Whirlwind area."

Munson had started sipping his drink. "Yeah, I guess so. Am I supposed to recall each incident I responded to years ago? I was a sergeant, but sometimes we were understaffed. Like now." He gave Clement a meaningful look.

"Would you have filed a report on a missing black child?" Clement asked.

"Would I have...?" Munson set his plastic cup down on the blotter in front of him. He stared at Clement. "Well, that's a fairly stupid question." He picked up his cup again to drink.

"You invariably filed reports, I take it," said Clement. "Not one incident might have slipped through because you were simply too busy?"

Munson's cup went down on the blotter, "As if the day weren't already bad enough." Munson looked at his watch. "What are you getting at?"

"If you filed a report—"

"*If?*"

"I believe you filed it, but the report you filed isn't in the records room. I searched those folders from here to Sunday and neither your report nor any that Tolliver claims he might have filed are there."

Not that Clement felt satisfied by the time he left, but he sensed that he had edged up on an important element in the investigation. Or had he? Was the matter of the files just a byway that would take him to a dead end of some type? Had someone perpetrated a civil rights violation? Or was staff simply incompetent? A filing clerk might have tossed reports. But in tossing reports had only thrown out those that he/she didn't care for? Had any other types of incidents been removed?

He would spend a further nice couple of days among the lung-defying dust of decaying papers, and if he found every other type of report in place except those on children who'd disappeared, or no reports filed on black-race complaints, that would be of great interest.

On his way home at the end of his shift, Clement stopped to fill up his tank. In a state that produced a significant amount of natural gas and oil, prices at the pump were stunningly high. He didn't understand at all how those things worked, how the international oil cartels told Oklahoma gas pumps selling Oklahoma gasoline what to charge.

He tended to believe Munson, even though despite Tolliver's repeated assurance, Clement wasn't certain that *Tolliver's* version of the past was authentic. Munson, at least, had filed the report on Lonnie Harding. Probably.

Instead of going straight on to his house, Clement drove to Rod's. The boy might be sleeping since his job started late and ended in the wee hours of the morning, but Clement rang from downstairs. He'd told Rod to call him on his cell last night, no matter how late he got in, and Clement had kept the phone beside him in bed, but Rod hadn't called.

"It's Dad," he said into the intercom and his son buzzed him up.

Rod greeted his father at the door dressed only in a pair of briefs. As predicted, Clement had disturbed his sleep.

"Hey, you're working out," said Clement. "I have to get back to that, too." He came into the apartment feeling uneasy. The place was neat, a good sign, or a sign that Rod compartmentalized—walled off his emotions, just like his father.

"Sorry I didn't call you last night," Rod mumbled. "I got in about two. During the hot weather, I like to do setup the night before."

Clement sat on the couch. Starting what he had to say was the hardest part.

"Is Mom okay?" Rod asked, suddenly awake and alert. "I talked to her last night from work."

"It's Shelly," said Clement. "I found her—by accident." He didn't want Rod to think he'd done anything admirable, since he hadn't. "She's in bad shape."

"Bad shape?" Rod sat down alongside his dad. "What do you mean? Like drinking or something."

"I think she was kidnapped. Anyway, she's had a very bad time of it. She was walking along a back road when I found her, and I took her to the hospital."

Rod stood up in alarm. "I'll get dressed and go see her."

"No. Not yet," countered Clement. He patted the seat beside him, to urge the boy back down. "We need to see what she wants first. She's been through a terrible time." How to explain without telling more than Shelly would want said...

Rod sat down. He looked about the way Clement would have expected him to look—shocked, confused, disturbed. "I don't understand," he told his father.

"I think some...crazy person took her, that she was kidnapped," Clement repeated.

He was sorry that he'd had to tell Rod that much of the truth. Why couldn't a parent protect his own child from the worst parts of life? Maybe the maxim that people's children are only on loan to them was true. Clement felt heartbroken because he hadn't done better and maybe never would be able to. Now, all he could do was leave his boy to suffer what probably constituted the worst emotions of his young life.

The women were sitting in the living room with classical music on the radio when he came in. Buddy didn't get up. Clement might have spent a moment wondering if he'd been transferred to an alternate universe in being greeted by the three when he

126

came home, but he was concerned about how Shelly was coming along and so shifted his attention onto her. Her face was bad, very bad, but she was clean and looked alert.

"Thank you," she told Clement.

He groaned involuntarily. To be thanked for his refusal to recognize what might have happened, what *had* happened! "Shelly, I want you to know if I'd had the intelligence to realize...I would have moved heaven and earth...I never questioned what Rod thought. I'm an absolute idiot."

"Oh no." She shook her head. Tears formed in her eyes. Let her cry. Let her cry. God knew she had something to sob about.

Bradley stared at him in curiosity. Apparently she thought he'd acted oddly or out of character.

The two women were on the sofa, so he sat in his chair. Bradley stood. "I made some lemonade." She left the room and Buddy got up and padded out after her.

"I was just with Rod," Clement told Shelley. "He's in a bad state himself right now. All he wants to do is see you. He was crying." He didn't know if the truth was the best thing for her or not, but here it was. "And I don't know if you want me to call your parents, either."

"I jus' want. I jus' need to be here and to be quiet for a while," she said.

"Of course. I understand." Though how could he really understand? He'd never gone through anything as horrible as she had, had only seen others who had suffered such an extreme. The faces of a few flashed in front of him—mostly women, but not all. Life could get down to the barbaric all too often.

Bradley returned with a tray Clement hadn't known he owned. She delivered glasses of refreshment to Shelly and to Clement and then took one for herself.

Bradley said she didn't mind, so Clement went to church while

Shelly napped. Bradley probably felt trapped in his house, but was being a good sport.

If Clement told his father on the phone that he was going to church, his father would often say, "Do they make you?" as if belonging to a Christian church was like belonging to a cult. "You can take a day off once in a while." But Clement went because he liked to. He looked forward to being there and couldn't imagine why others in their congregation didn't go all the time.

He had the oddest feeling when he returned home, as if he had been blasted back into the past and Judy was waiting for him. Rod might be in his room, putting together some project or other.

In fact, Bradley had prepared a meatloaf for their supper, which made Clement feel kind of embarrassed. "You shouldn't have done that," he said. "I would have cooked."

"You fixed dinner last night," she said. "I want to be fair." As if they were roommates.

He took his plate into the living room and she followed with hers. These days, he only used the dining room table when he had papers to spread out. He turned on the television. Probably rude, but the weather was pretty much on his mind, with flooding to the south in Texas and Louisiana, and wild fires to their west, in Arizona.

But the news was that the Christine Holmes jury had brought in a guilty verdict—big surprise—not—with sentencing to follow. "Life in prison," Clement intoned. "I guarantee it."

"Oh well," said Bradley. "At least she doesn't have to live with him any more." She sort of laughed.

"Yeah, that's to the good," Clement agreed. "And her kid doesn't have to be beat up by his father, either."

"Do you think he did?" Bradley asked.

"No record of it. Yet. Maybe Gregory was just about to start to hit the boy and Christine decided she wasn't going to let it happen. Or maybe she was just sick of being beat up herself."

In an unregulated, so-called uncivilized society—and he didn't know of any left in the world—the law was that if someone hit you, you could hit back. If someone beat you up repeatedly, sneaking up on him and bashing his brains in—or stabbing him 89 or however many times Christine had stuck her loving husband—was a good solution. But now that they lived in these days of cultivation and highly articulated social directives, a victim wasn't allowed to do the natural thing. That was, unless she had a qualified attorney on her side, which Holmes hadn't had.

"Damn shame the way things turn out sometimes," he said.

The two of them looked up as Shelly entered the room. Since the day was overcast (thankfully reducing the intense heat) and the light in here was dim, Clement wasn't sure he could read her mood. He wanted to see some subtle sign of improvement, but he also knew that oftentimes things got worse before they could even begin to get better.

Quickly, he turned off the television. The rest of the news could only be nasty, hard to take for the hearty, and impossible for someone who had been so badly mauled. He jumped up. "Sit here, Shelly. I'll get you some food. Bradley's made a delicious meal."

"I don't want to take you' chair," Shelly said weakly. "I'll be aw right. You don't have to be so kind."

"Kind," Clement snorted. "Kind? It's only natural."

Chapter 17

But Clement wasn't kind, because he had to distress Shelly further that night. The girl ate, and after she ate and after they had talked a little about the weather, Clement began to question her, with Bradley on hand taking notes. Which wasn't to say he hadn't switched on a little recorder he had in his desk drawer, since of course he had. Any small clue could lead to finding the bastard who had done this. And how could Clement not swear in the face of everything that had taken place?

"What do you recall about what happened to you, Shelly? Start at the beginning. Where were you?" he asked.

"I remember some thin's," she said. "I don't remember others. And some thin's I don't want to talk about."

"Just say what you can."

"I finish' schopping at Qwik Trip and got in my car. I thought I had locked it, but he was inthide. He had a knife at my throat. I jus' should have let him kill me."

"No," Clement objected sharply. "No."

Shelly sighed. "I told him he could take the car, but he made me move over to the pathenger side. And he put a cloth over my nose and mouth and I must have passed out."

Clement nodded encouragingly. He had gotten better used to her speech. Her worst trouble was with the "st" sounds, but also an occasional other pronunciation. If she felt up to going to the dentist soon, he would arrange for that.

How long had the beast kept her? He'd kept her for days.

"One of the worsch things was the other girl..."

The other girl? Oh dear Lord. He had let Shelly be for 24 hours in order to spare her, but another life was in danger. Clement was a worse imbecile than he'd imagined.

"See was dead. See was in that little room with me all the while. And see was dead. But I wasn't frightened by that. No. I felt so sorry for her. I just felt so sorry. After a while I pretended that she was alive and then after that, I imagined that we both were dead."

That she had borne that, and that he had thought her a shallow, superficial girl.

"Wouldn't it be wonderful if we could find her?" Shelly said wistfully. "Wouldn't it be wonderful if we could bring her home?"

Outside, later, once Shelly had gone to sleep again, Clement and Bradley sat in the gazebo in order to let Buddy roam just a little. Sweat rolled down Clement's face, but he didn't mind, really, because he liked the dark and the breeze. And the quiet.

Bradley had found Ezra Jackson's family. They'd moved to Boise City, and she'd gone out and interviewed the parents on Clement's second day in San Diego—which seemed about a dozen years ago. She had her notes and described to him the parents' narration of events when their boy had disappeared. For Ezra, like Lonnie Harding and like the Parker brothers, had indeed left home one day, never to return. The parents couldn't remember the name of the policeman who'd taken the report, but they'd given one in, and had phoned more than once after that.

But the Jacksons didn't blame the police, after all. The boy had probably been dead from the first, and how could the police be held responsible for that? Maybe he'd been hit by a car or wound up in a canyon somewhere—somewhere that the boy shouldn't have been and where circumstances had trapped him forevermore. A Christian couple, what more could they have done than what they did? They grieved.

"Listen," Clement said to Bradley, "we found two bodies, but quite by accident. Now we know that two other boys went missing around the same time—boys, mind you—all boys. Where are the other bodies—or bones, I should say? Where are the bones? We searched the park twice trying to find the second skull, so the other boys probably weren't interred there, but serial killers often have favorite burial places."

If they could find the other bodies—sets of bones—and maybe some they didn't expect but that they could identify, this would give them more information and allow them to set their sights on the killer's identity.

That was all a cop could do sometimes, just take it one step at a time. With a cold case like this all Clement could do was chip away and exercise patience.

But Shelley's case was a hot one, and they had to take her out in his car the next day and drive around. He'd called in a report on her car as missing, but so far, nothing.

What could she remember? Surely she recalled the area where she'd escaped. When he'd found her, she probably hadn't gone far since she'd been in such bad shape. Not that she was in much better shape yet.

"This where I found you," Clement said. "Look around. I'll drive up the road. Do you remember any smells, any sounds?" Smells? He supposed she recalled the smell of her dead roommate. But she had taken that well, hadn't she? Better than most women might. She'd remained surprisingly strong throughout her ordeal. He gave her a lot of credit for that. "Did you cut across land, duck under or over any wire?"

"He wa' gone. He lef' every day. So he mus' have gone to

work? Our room didn't have any window's...I had pried a piec'
of metal from the bottom of a foot locker he had in the corner
and worked at unbolting the door by the hinches. Not that
hard. The door wath padloc'ed. Ha." Clement turned and
looked at her. Her face was flushed.

"Good girl," he said. "You outsmarted him. Keep looking
out the window, though, Shelly. Tell me if you recognize
anything. Anything at all. Was there a dog? A fence? Greenery."

"Everything was dried out and dead," she told him. "Jus'
like now."

He drove slowly and let another car pass. "Bradley, write
down the license number of any cars that go by," he called out.
Then he recited the number of that one.

Nothing stood out for Shelly, though they drove the same
stretch of highway for three-quarters of an hour. Then Bradley
took the wheel of his car and dropped Clement off at work
before she accompanied Shelly to the dentist.

At headquarters, Clement first put together a photo array for
Shelly of women reported missing in the last six months, for a
total of four. He would once have considered Holder the safest
spot on earth if you only stayed away from the bars on Saturday nights. He never would have thought that women would be
kidnapped, raped, and murdered in this quiet town. Four
women missing in the last six months?! That was an incredible
number. Had the monster who'd violated Shelly done something similar to all four?

Since Clement had some time, he went into the file room
where the old physical records were still kept and dredged
through the 1996 and '97 records to see if all types of cases
were represented. He found reports of his own of every descrip-
tion.

He even found two missing persons reports, but one concerned an elderly male with Alzheimer's who showed up

eventually and was brought home. The other case was that of a middle-aged woman who was found dead—an ambiguous hit and run on the highway. Why had she been out there and on foot?

Clement tensed in reading that one. The death was mysterious and though worthy of investigation, hadn't been gone into. Still, the report existed. It hadn't been suppressed. He set it aside, to have a look during a quieter period. *Could be a homicide.*

He looked at his watch and went back upstairs to complete a follow-up report on Shelly's case. He was well aware that he hadn't prepared any updates recently on the Parker children. That was, though he had kept good notes and had written documentation in his hotel room and then at home, he hadn't filed anything. He trusted Munson to a pretty good degree, but Clement wasn't ready to present any findings until he had something firm.

Clement's door was open, but he raised his head to a knock—Bradley and Shelly. He suddenly realized he had only one chair and he hustled Shelly into it. Then he struggled with himself, making himself sit and Bradley stand. No preferred seating and no opening of car doors for female officers. He studiously ignored her.

All at once, Shelly smiled at Clement and pointed at her teeth. "Look," she said. "They're just temporary though."

"Wow, nice," he responded. The girl had smiled. He felt terribly relieved and happy himself, though he knew the future for her, and the future of her relationship with Rod were still uncertain. Could she heal and move on? Could Rod? What did Rod feel? He'd thought she'd broken up with him, but she'd been kidnapped, raped, beaten, nearly murdered. That might be too much for a young husband-to-be to deal with.

Clement wouldn't blame his son if he bowed out of the relationship, and he doubted if Shelly would blame Rod, either. In fact, dealing with what she'd gone through might be impossible in the context of a relationship. Clement couldn't predict what would happen, and he didn't even know what he himself thought would be best for either young person, or both of them.

He stopped staring admiringly at her teeth and moved the composite he'd prepared across the desk, facing her. Her smile vanished as she examined the several pictures. She immediately put her finger on the photo of the recently missing schoolteacher. "How pretty she is," Shelly said. "What's her name?"

"Karin Webb, an English teacher at Holder High and local beauty queen at one time."

"Karin," said Shelly. "I wish I had known her before, when she was alive. I'm certain we would have been best friends. I miss never having really met her."

Shelly and Bradley had gone to Shelly's doctor appointment at the hospital. Rape, or repeated rape in this case, implied more than just physical and mental trauma, but included the risk of sexually transmitted diseases—from syphilis to AIDS—and the potential for pregnancy. Clement sighed. He hoped none of the possibilities were realized.

He pulled up the bare bones file on Karin Webb onto the screen. SPO Woodruf was the lead investigating officer.

Webb had disappeared after a cookware party at a friend's home. Woodruf had interviewed fellow teachers who had been at the event, the husband, the woman's parents, her sister, and even her in-laws.

But clues? None. Her car, like Shelly's so far, hadn't been found. That alone had Clement wondering. Where would the "doer" hide two cars? The cars could be broken down and the pieces sold for scrap—or buried. The cars could be put in a lake or placed in a barn or a junkyard, or, given different license plate numbers and paint jobs, placed for sale with forged papers in a used car lot.

Clement contemplated the manpower that would be required

to go through those possibilities. Quite a lot. In order to do the job up right, finding the cars would have to be the department's number one priority, and that wasn't even remotely likely. The unofficial motto here was to do more for less. Beg and borrow, if necessary—though stealing was pretty much considered out.

Clement braced himself and walked over to Woodruf's office in the other wing. Woodruf was a more mainstream guy than Clement was, much more departmental. In another decade, he'd be a lieutenant; of that Clement was sure. Clement himself by then would have been long retired, and he and Buddy Two would be out at his property with a new chain link fence all around to keep out the riffraff from the encroaching developments.

Clement knocked on Woodruf's open door. Doors to officers were open here in the summer as if that would improve the level of air conditioning, which it totally didn't. If they walked around without their jackets and only sweating lightly, the day could be deemed "not too terrible."

"Got a minute?"

"Yeah." Woodruf motioned Clement in. "To what do I owe the honor?"

Clement sat and looked around his fellow SPO's office. This was not a former supply closet but a space with two windows. And Woodruf's diplomas were on the wall, as if he were a doctor or an academic. Good grief.

"I have information on Karin Webb," he told the other SPO.

Woodruf had the decency to seem truly interested, which somewhat mollified Clement's deep sense of annoyance at the man's trappings of success. "She's dead," Clement told the detective. "I have a witness who identified her."

Clement explained briefly, though he had an odd reluctance to tell Woodruf too much—then he went on to lay out his idea for a first pass on locating the cars.

Obviously, he'd been obliged to tell Woodruf where the missing woman was, but Clement really didn't like risking losing control of his own investigation. A little collaboration, however, might work to Clement's advantage in terms of his own agenda. Woodruf likely had more pull with Chief Munson than Clement did and could extract a bit more money for the inquiry.

Chapter 18

Clement, Bradley, and Shelly entered the Church of the Redeemer to the strains of "Amazing Grace" being sung by the choir:

Yes, when this flesh and heart shall fail, and mortal life shall cease; I shall possess, within the veil, a life of joy and peace.

The three, the only whites here today, although Clement had notified both Munson and the mayor's office, sat in the back. Mrs. May, the grandmother of the dead boys finally being granted the simple dignity of burial, sat in the front comforted by what must be friends since family was all gone. The sanctuary was small and the organ not at all grand, which was just the way that Clement liked his church.

Moses and Ezekiel Parker were being laid to rest.

Shelly had said she would come, though why, Clement couldn't quite understand, but maybe simply to be able to sit and freely grieve and not solely for herself.

He would take his jacket off when the other men in the room did so, and Clement soon got the idea that they weren't going to. They were in church!

"These boys will never grow old," said the minister. "These boys will never taste again the fear of death. These boy will never have to confront the devil and will never be tempted to commit a sin. As sad as we are...As much as we have missed them...As much as Sister Eleanor has missed seeing her two little grandchildren grow up and become men...they are blessed. These children are blessed. These innocent children rose straight to their maker on that sad night when they left this world..."

Clement stopped listening. The preaching could be called "making the best of it," or, to his thoughts, "cold consolation." That wasn't his cynicism speaking, because he did feel consoled, but not on the basis that the children had died before their time.

Reborn, reborn, reborn again. When I get to heaven, I'll be reborn again. Reborn, children, reborn again. When I get to heaven, I'll be reborn again.

At the end of the service, they went over to Mrs. May. She grabbed on to Clement's arm and held it, her eyes bright. This was one small thing, but maybe the best he had done in a while.

Or maybe Shelly had come with so she could meet Karin Webb's husband, David, which was where they went next.

"Hot as hell in there," said Clement about the church, once they were in the car with the air conditioning on.

"No. Hell is a whole lot hotter," said Bradley. Clement vaguely recalled saying something silly like that to her a while ago.

He laughed and looked in the rearview mirror. The women had taken their habitual seats in the back. He was the chauffer. He took off his jacket, then drove away.

He'd asked Woodruf to let him bring Shelly to tell David Webb about his wife's death, and Woodruf had agreed. The worst job a cop can do is deliver the news of a loved one's passing and even the conscientious Woodruf didn't appear to mind offloading the task.

Clement had made an appointment with Webb, and they descended on him now like a pack of ardent Bible thumpers determined to bring a hardcore sinner straight to Jesus.

But their intention was nothing like that, of course.

Webb let them in. He was puzzled by their appearance, it

seemed, dazed by his circumstance. Grieving and not knowing if this grief was too soon, since he didn't yet know his wife was gone, gone for good.

"How do I pronounce her name," Shelly asked the young husband. 'Who?' wasn't a question that needed to be asked. David repeated his wife's name—not like 'Karen' but as if she'd been Scandinavian.

The surviving girl started to cry. "I was there," she said. "With Karin. Together, she and I. She was dead. She's dead."

For the first time since Clement had found Shelly on the road, he saw her really and truly cry. She and David Webb both stood and reached out for one another to embrace, and she cried and cried.

In a little while, her sobbing slowed and the two broke apart. They sat, and David offered them all cold drinks, which he brought out a minute later.

"Karin was lucky to be dead," Shelly told the woman's husband. "It's what the preacher told the congregation today, isn't it, Mr. Clement? Death can be a wonderful blessing."

No, death wasn't the blessing, Clement thought. How easily people misunderstood. Death wasn't the blessing. The blessing was…He grappled with how he might explain, if anyone ever wanted to hear. But he hadn't really been called upon to speak, so he didn't. He gave, instead, a weak, sad smile.

The ladies went to wash their faces.

Clement had a dozen questions to ask David, and he listened carefully while taking notes. He wanted that one clue, that one revealing mention that would turn this whole investigation around.

"When was the last time you heard from Karin? She was on her way home from a party?" Clement asked David Webb.

"Yes, she called to tell me she was leaving then. She was in the car."

"I have a list of supposedly everyone who'd been at the party. Did she mention anyone in particular? Any men who came to pick someone up, even? Anything out of the ordinary?" Clement decided he'd like to reinterview everyone Woodruf had talked to. Of course, Woodruf, if he knew, would be annoyed. But did he really have to know?

"Nothing like that," said the husband.

"Did she feel well? Could she have felt sick and stopped somewhere?"

"Well, she was going to stop—at the mall. To bring home a few things…"

"What mall?" Clement pressed. He didn't recall this detail from Woodruf's reports.

"The Muskogee Mall. It's not too far from here."

Shelly had reentered the room. "The Muskogee Mall? That's where I was. At the Qwik Trip."

As if Clement shouldn't have gone to the mall, first thing, and now that obvious fact was brought home to him in graphic terms! But at the same time, although he reviled himself for his own negligence, he felt excited. This small fact was going to lead them somewhere.

Christine Holmes was being kept in the women's unit of the Northern Oklahoma Correctional Facility, an hour's drive from Clement's house out in the sticks. He'd been thinking about visiting her there, and the next day, Sunday, he simply got up, fed Buddy, showered, left a note for the women, and drove off. He was going to miss church, but Jesus had said: "I was in prison, and ye came unto me."

The only compunction he had was in terms of police department politics. But why would anyone check up on him to see if he'd visited Holmes where she was being held? Or why would the Bureau of Corrections notify the Holder P.D.? Neither possibility was a likely one, so his only worry was that he'd run into someone he knew. But this was Sunday, and Holder cops weren't flocking to spend their weekends with guests of the B of

C...Life was short. He'd been astute enough to notice that. And he had to do what he felt he had to do.

The Northern Oklahoma prison was a mixed-use waystation for those being tried in the upper state venues, as well as those serving minimal sentences at low security. After jumping the line and showing his badge, Clement asked what the current population was: 174—117 male and 57 female. Many of the men were housed open-dormitory style once they were sentenced. The women also had a dormitory space for the general population, with the women squeezed in, he was told, because of the phenomenal recent increase in their numbers.

Christine Holmes, already convicted of first degree murder, was a maximum security inmate, so wasn't in with the gen pop. Clement waited for her in an inside conference room rather than at the tables in the rec hall where family and inmates could sit, drink sodas, hold hands, and hug assorted children.

Clement stood up when Christine entered. Her guard stationed himself inside the door to protect Clement from this dangerous killer, who was about five foot three and 112 pounds with sad, dark eyes framed in a pale face. Her face was paler than it had been when Clement had first met her at her home, because today she wasn't smeared with her husband's blood.

"I don't think you'll remember me," he said. "I'm Officer Clement. I came to your house the night your husband was killed." They both sat. He was satisfied with the way he'd phrased that, as he hadn't wanted to say, 'The night you killed your husband.' He also hadn't wanted to remind her that he'd testified at her trial.

"I'm sorry," she said. "I don't recall."

He nodded to say he completely understood. "How are you getting along in here, Mrs. Holmes?"

She actually brightened. "It's quiet and predictable," she said. "It's nice. I have my own room." Her face fell. "I miss my son though. If only my sister would bring him up to see me. I'd like that."

Clement had visited any number of prisoners in his day, but this was the first time one had told him that the circumstances inside were 'nice.' "I've left ten dollars in your account so you can buy something if you want."

She looked pleased. "They sell packages of noodles here," she told him. "I don't eat candy. But the meals are really very good. We have chicken on Sundays. I wonder if you could join us sometime."

Ah, she was still a little crazy. But that was okay. If having delusions made her life any easier, he was all for it.

"How do you like your lawyer, Mr. Alloys?" he asked, coming around to the point of his trip. Maybe he should have come some time ago, but, well, making a good call is always easier long after the moment.

"Oh, he's bad," she said without hesitation. "Gregory would have given him the back of his hand, I can tell you that."

Despite the grim substance of the comment, Clement laughed.

She smiled. "I do miss Gregory sometimes a little, but, really, don't you think he's much better off dead? I mean, we're all better off now. No more yelling. No more violence. I like that, don't you?"

Clement exhaled with a sigh. He supposed he agreed with her, but he couldn't be the one to say. "I know a really smart lawyer, and he'd take your case for free," he told the woman. "He'll pursue the appeals for you. But you have to ask. You have to call him. He's very shy."

Clement gave her Rich's card. "He's an extremely nice man. He has two daughters, and he's very, very kind to them. I'm sure he'd be happy to look after you as well. But you have to call him. You can leave a message on his machine if he's not there. Tell him who you are and ask him to visit."

"We can *all* have supper," said Christine, very seriously. "Chicken burgers for Sunday supper...I hope they're careful of the knives."

The inmates, of course, worked as cooks in the kitchen, so Clement, too, hoped not just that they were careful with the knives, but that the knives were counted after every meal. And they were, of course.

"Call him. Tell him your name," Clement repeated. There, he'd done what he had set out to do. What more could be expected of him?

Judy drove up just after Clement arrived back home with groceries. Maybe she was concerned because he hadn't been at church today. He met her at the door.

"Can I see Shelly now?" she wanted to know.

"I'll go ask her," he said. "Come in though. It's hot out there."

"Oh," said Judy. "Your dog. I'd forgotten." Buddy inspected her briefly, found her less than interesting—she wasn't, after all, a dog—and walked away.

Bradley came out from Shelly's room, where the women had been visiting, he imagined. "I'm sorry," Bradley exclaimed as if she'd interrupted them in a passionate embrace (not peapickin' likely), and turned around.

"Ask Shelly if she wants to see Rod's mother," he called out.

"And that's...?" asked Judy.

"Officer Bradley," Clement said. Her asking irked him. But that was why people got divorced, he supposed—they began to find the other person irritating. Or the other person first found *them* irritating, and acted in such a way as to get on the still willing spouse's nerves. In short, Clement would have remained married to Judy, more or less ignoring who they were together, if only she, herself, hadn't created so much of a stir. But he supposed her having done so, and having left him, was for the best.

He, like Christine Holmes, enjoyed the quiet and the predictability. The lack of yelling.

Bradley came out and stood in front of Judy as if she didn't exactly know what to say. "Please go in," she told Judy finally. "But she hasn't seen a lot of people she knew yet, and she's a little apprehensive. So perhaps you won't stay long."

She'd put it nicely, Clement thought, but had probably gotten on Judy's nerves anyway. This was, after all, Judy's former home.

About twenty minutes later, Judy came out, looking disturbed. Shelly didn't even mention the visit later, at supper.

CHAPTER 19

The arrangement between the three of them was cozy, but could hardly last as it stood. "I think Bradley has to get back to work tomorrow. Maybe even go home," Clement told Shelly when Bradley was out of the room.

"Ohh," said Shelly. "Yes. She must want to go home." She bit her lip.

"Can you stand to be out here on your own during the day?" he asked. "With Buddy, of course." What else could he offer her? She looked a bit...drained. But he couldn't keep Bradley out here, because Shelly really wasn't in any danger at this point, no matter how vulnerable she felt.

"I'll give you a gun," he said, inspired. "Come into the yard and I'll show you how to shoot. You'll be like a frontier woman. What do you think?"

Bradley came back into the living room. "I'm going to teach Shelly to shoot," he announced. "How's that for an idea?"

"Great."

The three went into the yard where he had his so-called practice range. He gave Shelly and Bradley ear plugs and put some in his own ears as well. He thought of the old-cop jokes, most of the last lines of which were "what?" because all of the old cops were at least three-quarters deaf if they spent any time shooting.

He turned on the hose to wet down the area, afraid of the sparks. Inside the house, Buddy barked to be let out. But he wouldn't like the shooting much. Clement wasn't so sure that Shelly would, either, but once she started, she was grimly determined. They shot as long as they had light enough outside. Poor Buddy was under the bed when they came in.

In the summer, people in Holder often went to work early as one futile attempt to maneuver around the heat. That also meant 11 o'clock lunches were not uncommon, and at Clement's invitation, Madge, the personnel clerk, was glad enough to get away by 10:45. He drove them out to Palermo, an Italian restaurant considered extremely exotic by the working class here, a place invariably avoided by all levels of cops...Lest they be seduced by indecent proposals to join the Mafia, Clement guessed.

Madge was thrilled. She had eaten here once as a Christmas-season treat and recalled it fondly. Clement urged her to order the lamb, which, though he himself found the weather awful hot to eat anything so heavy, he also ordered, to encourage her to do so. In a minute, he summoned back the waiter and asked for a hamburger instead.

"Changed my mind," he told her. "Have something to do later today that I can't sleep through."

Apparently, she didn't care. "Osso bucco is always tender," she said. "That's because they cook it so long."

He hoped that didn't mean they would be here forever, as he had to get away by noon.

"So what am I being bribed for?" she asked. "And did you ever do whatever you needed to with Tolliver?" He wondered if she meant the lunch was payment for that prior favor and he could treat her again, some other time, for anything he wanted now. When Christine Holmes moved over to Mabel Bassett after her sentencing, she'd find the politics different, the society among the maximum security inmates much more complex and like real life.

"Say we're talking about 1996 or so," Clement suggested. "Who would have been able to mess with the files—tear up reports, throw them out?"

Madge did look a bit serious for a moment—and shocked. Her Caesar salad arrived with garlic rolls, however, and she didn't answer for a bit. "Very nice," she said. "Very, very nice. So...European."

Clement had been in Germany once for training, but that was all he knew of Europe, and it hadn't been like this. The most foreign thing to him here was the dark wood paneling, which conveyed a sense of coolness on a hot day, if not the actual coolness itself.

"Nineteen-ninety-six," she mused. "Well, officially, me, because I always have access to everything, and I like it that way. Chief Kenny and the head file clerk, Robert...Robert...I'll look it up later. Or I'll remember." Clement recalled Robert Yargee, now that she mentioned him. Very self-contained, a bit of an odd duck, yet very proper.

"But that's officially," Madge went on. "The system has certainly never been set up to be especially secure. If you come right down to it, nearly any officer could have gone into the big file room in the old building and have destroyed files. Is something missing?

"I think so," he said, "but I'm not a thousand percent positive. Just trying to get the lay of the land."

"Oh, really, that was easy," she answered. "I could certainly dish some significant dirt, and I hoped you wanted some. You didn't have to take me to lunch for that little bit of information. Though I do thank you for the excursion."

The heat wilted neither her appetite not her tongue, but Clement was happy to let her talk while he mused.

* * *

Mercifully, by 12:30 Clement was able to make it out to the little private airfield where he'd agreed to meet SPO Woodruf and Dr. Neal for a helicopter search. Woodruf had gotten Munson to sign off on the trip.

Woodruf and Neal were already talking, and Clement hurried them onto the Bell machine, helping Neal with his equipment.

"Perfect," said Neal. "Thanks for the opportunity to test my equipment."

"I hate helicopters," Woodruf said.

Clement had been on a bunch of big military Jawhawks and such in Afghanistan, but not on a small, more or less civilian one like this.

"Okay?" asked the pilot. They didn't have the time to answer before they were up in the air.

Neal took out some photographic equipment and set that up. "We're looking for burial sites," he explained to Woodruf, yelling over the noise of the rotating blade. "The infrared will show any current decomp, but we can also tell if the ground has been disturbed."

"I thought we're looking for cars," Woodruf shouted.

Clement nodded reassuringly. He definitely was interested in finding the women's cars, but would it hurt them to find any dead bodies in the meantime? Or simply skeletons? Neal wanted to test his infrared equipment and find fairly fresh, decomposing corpses, and maybe they could find Karin that way, if the perp had finally taken her out.

Clement, however, was also interested in finding the burial site of bones, boys' bones, from a good long time before. The ordinary aerial photographs might show suspect sites if the ground was exposed—that was, not obscured by trees. Compaction, Neal had said—the ground used as burial sites would show compaction, which actually would leave a void in the soil. Visible cracks in the soil might appear and even outline where the grave had been dug. Different ages of vegetation in the area could also be an indication.

"Why are we going this way?" shouted Woodruf. He was right, of course, since Clement had run into Shelly much further to the east, but the boys were missing on the northwest side of town and might have been buried out that way. He shrugged and pointed from his eye to the ground, indicating they should simply look. He'd brought binoculars and so had Woodruf.

The men focused and did their various types of observations. The area they had to search wasn't that big and the pilot obligingly spun them around over fields and canyons. Clement marked barns and warehouse structures on a map. They flew over a small lake, extremely shallow for this time of year, and calm. If any cars had been dumped there, a roof at least would have shown.

Eventually, they flew back to the airfield. The only ones satisfied were Neal, who was in love with his photographic instruments, and the pilot, who had been paid by the P.D. for three hours of serene flight time over some lovely landscape.

"Everything looks so dry down there. One idiot and a camp-fire is all it takes," said Clement when he no longer had to shout to be heard. He'd seen his house in the midst of all that brown foliage. He simply had to call the county later and scream to make them clear their land. No, better yet, he'd rent a bulldozer this afternoon. He'd had enough of begging so that his home would be spared.

"We're backed up," Michael Keetoowah told Clement when he once again asked about the processing of the rape kit.

"Something is more important than a kidnapping and rape, murder, and attempted murder by a serial rapist?" asked Clement mildly.

"Believe me, I wish I could help you," answered Keetoowah. "And I will. Eventually."

"So when you come right down to it, DNA is irrelevant," Clement said.

Keetoowah gave the SPO a disgusted look. "Funding," he snapped back. "Funding is the important thing. How does a lab operate without funding, tell me that. This isn't TV."

Clement nodded and shrugged. The same old story. Not enough money. Let them murder, rape, and pillage out there. Not enough funds. If they had the DNA results from Shelly's rape kit, he could think about DNA swabs for employees at the mall. But if they couldn't get a rape kit done in the lab, how well would Keetoowah and his helper process 50, 60, 70 swabs? And this in a murder and rape case with the doer at large.

Of course Neal was happy. He would spend the next few days going over his aerial photography with students, comparing the photos he had taken with a set from the early 1980s that he'd gotten from the county tax assessment office. He had free or cheap labor in his classes and funding from grants for his equipment. Well, bless the man. He had done so much already—too bad he didn't perform DNA analysis out there. Without Neal, Clement would never have identified the bones.

Bradley, in uniform no less, lay in wait in Clement's office, reading a newspaper.

"You didn't have to dress up to impress me," he said.

"I'm supposed to go on patrol," she answered. "Too many people out on vacation. We're shorthanded."

"I'll talk to Munson," he told her. "I was thinking you'd be a great decoy at the mall." Once he'd said it, he regretted his words. She was a cop, but she looked so young and vulnerable, he felt frightened for her.

She folded the newspaper and sat up. "Really? That would be fun."

"Not fun," he refuted. "Scary as hell."

"Hell is a whole lot scarier," she said and laughed.

He smiled.

"I can come back to your house tonight and be around just in case Shelly needs me," Bradley added. "I know what I can cook for dinner."

"Ok." Shelly might feel more comfortable that way.

Bradley stood up. "See you later. Don't forget the decoy thing."

"Uh huh."

His cell rang. Rod. Clement answered.

"Hey, Dad."

"Hey yourself. How you doing?"

"Mom said she saw Shelly yesterday."

"Yeah."

"Can I come out and see her, too, do you think?"

"You can call her out there and ask," Clement told him. But he wondered. Shelly might be healing, with the bruises on her face turning from black and purple to a weirdish yellow, and with a temporary bridge in place, but had she begun to repair herself psychologically yet?

Shelly wasn't what Clement had seen her as, originally. But was that because she herself had changed or because his vision of her had? Most likely, both had taken place. And though his opinion of her was no longer the same as it had been at first, he was still, or maybe the word was really "again" doubtful that she would be a proper wife for Rod.

When Clement had first met her, he'd seen her as being too slight a person for his son, someone focused on the outside world, someone without pain. Now she was overly withdrawn and inward, carrying too much baggage for a boy as yet so unbothered by the world. Her suffering would be a heavy burden to any husband. Conversely, she wouldn't survive any attempt to pretend that nothing had gone wrong.

A human being had such potential, carrying around the gift of a divine soul. Yet personalities could be so damaged that many had to endure by feeding off of their own malfunctions. Others soured and became fine feasts for the forces of evil.

Evil. How could evil exist in God's own world?

CHAPTER 20

Clement left work early and drove out to his dad's. Maria, his father's mysterious "girlfriend"—half Cherokee and half Mexican—answered the door. She pretended not to speak English—to avoid talking to people, Clement supposed—but he'd heard her speaking in very unaccented tones to his father. Apparently she was as American as the rest of them when she found it convenient.

Yet, despite that, Clement didn't dislike the woman. He was grateful she could get along with his father somehow and live with him, making his father's welfare less of a responsibility for Clement himself.

"Hey, Dad." His father was playing solitaire at the table when Clement walked into the dining room. "Who's winning?"

"Not me. Who does that leave?" His dad looked up. "You didn't tell me about Shelly," he said.

"No. But then I haven't talked to you."

"That's what the telephone is for."

Clement nodded, but he didn't quite see why he'd needed to tell his father. He sat down at the table alongside the old man. Maria brought in a pitcher of iced tea and a glass for Clement. His father already had his glass.

Clement changed the subject. "Who might have removed something from the files in the old days when all the records were on paper?" he asked.

"Oh I love being interrogated by my own son. Am I a suspect?"

"No, sorry, Dad. You're not. But answer the question, anyway, or I'll turn on the hot lights." His father really could be irritating.

"Well, one of the Gang of Four, I guess." His father gave Clement a self-satisfied smile, that of a man who knew something and would be appreciated for what he revealed.

"Gang of Four? Doesn't sound nice."

His father snickered. "That was me and Malloy, God rest his soul—and I don't mean anything at all by that phrase, Aaron—and Tolliver and his partner, Danvers."

Clement frowned. "I thought his partner was Stan Runninghorse." He'd sort of read Tolliver's file, which Madge had given him, but had apparently skimmed some of the duller stuff. Well, it had all been dull, really.

"For about two seconds," Sam Clement answered. "Tolliver wouldn't have wanted to work with an Indian, for one thing. But things come up and you work with someone for a few days or a few months."

"So did you ever remove reports?" the son asked the father.

"Oh boy, turn those bright lights up a little higher." The elder Clement laughed. "Yeah, well, maybe once, maybe twice. And remember, I worked as a police officer for many years. But those were nothing things—a kid caught speeding or fighting drunk and a parent who would rather not have that remain on the kid's record. So I brought home an extra hundred dollars or two, and what was the harm? I can only assume that the other guys did the same—nothing major, nothing horrible. I was a good cop and they were good guys, too. I wouldn't bother investigating there if you're looking for something."

If his dad had gotten an extra hundred or so for removing a kid's arrest record from the file, how much would a killer have paid to have all trace of his victims pulled? Or was the killer a cop who'd simply removed the file as a favor to himself? "Danvers is still alive then?" Clement concluded.

"Yeah, yeah. I see him sometimes. I mean I run into him sometimes places like WalMart or the bank."

"Good," said Clement.

"Just what do you suspect Tolliver of?" asked his father, suddenly.

"Nothing, I don't think. But I'm kind of bothered by some missing reports."

"Maybe I took them," kidded his father.

"If so, I'd have to lock you up," Clement answered without much humor. He finished the last of his iced tea and said he had to get home. This was Shelly's first day by herself, and he wanted to make sure she was handling it okay.

"I did some target shooting today. I hope you don't mind," said Shelly, meeting him outside the door.

He didn't like the idea for a number of reasons. "It's awful dry out here and I don't want you to burn down my house," he answered without compunction. "Or shoot my dog."

"I was careful," she told him. "But I won't do it again unless you're here."

"I don't want you to shoot yourself, either," he added. "I explained the basic rules of safety, but you have to get used to them."

They went into the house.

Buddy apparently had made his peace with Clement's comings and goings, and the dog's interest in the man as a dog substitute had revived. He came forward and sniffed to check out what Clement had been up since he'd left the house in the morning. A hint of Palermo probably remained from Clement's lunch.

Clement went and washed up. When he returned, he found Shelly in the living room, looking frightened. "Someone's out there," she said in a whisper, barely breathing. Clement walked to the window and pulled away the curtain. "Oh," he said, "it's okay. I know him." Clement opened the door to his lawyer friend, Frank Rich. "Sorry. I was washing up."

"I saw your car, so I figured you were here."

"Well, come on in."

The two men turned at a sound and watched Shelly vanish into her room. "My son's fiancé," Clement told Rich, seeing the wrong conclusion popping into his head.

"Congratulations," Rich responded.

Clement didn't answer that one, but called Buddy away from Rich and showed the guest to the living room sofa. This sofa had gotten more use in the last few weeks than it had in the prior several years since Clement had in a moment of questionable judgment purchased the darn thing. "What're you doing out this way?" Clement finally asked, taking his own chair by the TV, cueing Buddy to settle into his usual place.

"Divorced," said Rich. "Live near West Lake now, in fact. Where Christine Holmes and her husband lived." He smiled.

Clement was interested. "How long have you been divorced?" he questioned.

"About two years."

Clement made an exclamation of surprise. He thought he scoured the papers well enough every day to catch all the local gossip he'd be interested in.

"You have a great house here," observed Rich. He looked up toward the high ceiling. "I love an old farmhouse. How much land you have?"

"Bought at the right time. Got a nice parcel."

"Like money in the bank," Rich commented.

The two men smiled at one another, and Clement leaned over and petted his dog. He knew Rich had come to talk about representing Holmes, and he was glad. But here they were sounding like men of their fathers' day. The conversation was a patterned time waster and a way of coming to what they both wanted to speak about.

"Oh, man," said Rich. "You have a dog, too. I gotta get one, but I live in a condo and the neighbors wouldn't like to hear the barking."

"A condo out by West Lake? That right?"

Just then the door opened and a couple of seconds later Bradley entered, juggling two bags of groceries. Rich got up and took one of the bags out of her hands. She reached back and closed the door.

"Officer Bradley," explained Clement as he jumped up. "Bradley, this is Frank Rich. The attorney."

"Oh, hey, I didn't mean to interrupt anything," said Rich.

"Bradley's helping me out." Clement put Rich to rights.

Bradley and Rich took the bags into the kitchen. That was cozy. If Clement was too old for Bradley, so was Rich.

Rich came back out a minute later and sat down again. "I'm invited to supper," he told Clement. "I said no, but the officer insisted. I'm a law abiding citizen, so I agreed."

"Good," answered Clement. "We have a lot to talk about. I'll show you where you can wash your hands and get you a glass of lemonade."

Shelly came out shyly when called to their meal. Though she had appeared in public numerous times already, the public had been mostly professional, and as anticipated, overwhelmingly understanding. She was a pretty girl, but less so with those bruises across her face—not that she had tried to cover them up, as abused women might. The idea seemed not to have occurred to the girl.

Clement introduced Rich to her. "I'm sorry I didn't answer the door," she said.

"Of course you didn't."

Clement steered them to the dining room. How very odd. His first dinner party.

He couldn't recall Judy and he having guests. Oh, maybe her parents, once, when Rod was little.

Bradley had made them a tuna casserole, which they all proclaimed to be quite delicious. In addition, they had a salad and rolls, with ice cream for dessert. Clement, grateful simply not to have to eat hamburger again, figured it was about as fine a meal as you could expect a semi-adult police officer to concoct. He didn't go as overboard in praising her as Frank Rich did, and Clement wondered if his friend was on the prowl for wife number two.

After, in the living room, with Shelly taking it upon herself to serve the coffee, a first effort from her to resume life's ordinary duties, Rich began the discussion of Christine Holmes. "She called me," said the lawyer to Clement. "I told the woman I'd take her case. But only because you indicated you knew something no one else had. What is it, and why didn't it enter into the trial?"

Clement sighed. "I'm no genius," he said. "That I didn't go to her lawyer wasn't by calculation."

Shelly returned, and because the couch was short and over-stuffed, and now occupied by Bradley and Rich, took the floor. Clement tossed her a decorative pillow he kept on his chair, and Buddy, interested, went over to investigate the whys and wherefores.

"Bradley there told me that she heard the D.A.—Enkan—tell an investigator to get rid of the hospital report, which Bradley had collected for her. Why did you actually get the report, Bradley? Did someone ask for it?" Clement got up and un-locked his rolltop desk to look for the hospital file Bradley had given him.

"You have it a little wrong," said Bradley, "probably be-cause of the way I said it to you."

Clement's heart sank. He found the papers and turned them over to Rich to look at. Prosecutorial malfeasance was one leg Clement hoped to base Holmes' redemption on. He had the entire negotiation with the D.A. wrapped up in his mind. If he'd misunderstood, his plan could easily come unwound. Once again, he'd gone off half-cocked. "Well then tell us," he urged. What a mess.

"Enkan did ask me to get all the files, including any medical records, because she said that the defense was going to get everything, anyway, and knowing from the start was better than not knowing, was definitely how she saw it. So I brought her everything I could get my hands on—Holmes' hospital visits, her prescriptions..." Bradley gave Clement a meaningful look. "...like that."

Rich skimmed the pages while the rest of them waited for him to finish.

Clement continued to admonish himself and to recite inwardly, *I won't jump to conclusions. I won't jump to conclusions. I won't jump to conclusions.* He was old. He was over the hill.

Rich nodded and put the papers beside him, and Bradley went on. "But I was in there later that day when they found out which lawyer was representing her. The D.A...that is, the real D.A., Andrew Sandoval...sneered. Then he told Enkan to tear up the report."

Clement smiled and exhaled in relief. He took a moment to let himself relax. "There you go," he said. "They destroyed exculpatory evidence."

"Not exculpatory," interjected Rich a bit wearily. "After all, she did kill him. And confess to you, as I heard it."

"Yeah, yeah, but mitigating evidence...whatever you call it. They had evidence that could have altered her conviction. You're an attorney. You can twist that to your advantage."

Rich opened his mouth, a fake hurt look on his face.

"Hey," said Bradley sharply. She got up from the sofa and started to pace. "You're saying I have to testify. And I wind up the one who's going to get fired for helping the defense." For the first time since Clement had known the girl, he saw her breathe a little fire.

"No," Clement said simply. "I have that one figured out."

Bradley stopped spinning in her tracks, and Shelly, Rich, and Bradley stared at Clement, all of them seeming to wait for something that would make the case come together the way Clement apparently wanted it to.

Since he had their attention, Clement took a sip of coffee and gave them all an 'I know something you don't know' smile. Then he relented. "Well, look where we are. We're just about to enter the penalty phase. So we don't actually need a retrial. A retrial would inconvenience all of us, wouldn't it? It would look bad, very bad for the prosecution for one thing—and Bradley might have to testify for another. And we wouldn't want that."

Bradley slumped into the old-fashioned desk chair and seemed mollified.

"You..." Clement pointed at Rich. "You negotiate with the D.A.'s office. Tell them what you'd bring out on appeal and at a retrial and give them your terms. If they agree to tell the judge they want her sent to Central State Hospital in Norman, and he sends her, then you won't appeal."

"Oh," said Rich. "I thought you wanted her off."

"Well, she is a little crazy," Clement conceded. "Some psychiatric treatment might not hurt." Christine Holmes *had* killed her husband, and though the man had probably driven her to it and deserved what he'd gotten, the killing likely *was* premeditated. So maybe the woman shouldn't get off scott free. Though Clement didn't know. He really, really didn't know. If the system worked in a more responsible way, he wouldn't have to be trying to decide such things on his own.

CHAPTER 21

They didn't want to spook the perp by monitoring the mall with a marked patrol vehicle since the shopping center was their only "live" clue. So unmarked cars were the order of the day, along with keeping a very low profile. Woodruf, then Clement, then Jackson, then Hirsh alternated driving around out there, but even that was risky if the guy was at the mall very often looking for targets and incidentally counter-monitoring the other cars.

Woodruf, Clement, Jackson, and Hirsh also spent their down-time reviewing surveillance tapes from the mall proper and the parking lot. Though they knew the dates and times when both Karin and Shelly had been taken, the tapes were a jumble and some had been reused. As cheap as tapes were, Clement thought a law against their reuse would be a good idea; the police didn't always know immediately a crime had been committed. This wasn't the first time he'd experienced the frustration of good evidence probably deleted to save less than a dollar.

Clement sat in the video room, making an effort not to nod off from the tedium. He wanted to remain alert because, in addition to trying to spot any abductions—and, yes, others might have occurred—he also hoped to notice any man simply hanging around more than was normal.

This wasn't like watching a movie with a plot: a teenage

couple kidding, a security guard checking cars...wait a minute...a man accosting a woman—but she smiles and they laugh and part like two people who know one another but don't have the time to really chat. More of the same.

Woodruf came in. "No," said Clement, before the other man could even ask. Woodruf set down a Dunkin' Donuts coffee for Clement and popped the top off his own. "Thanks."

Woodruf wasn't as bad as Clement had always imagined, although the younger man was probably a little too "by the book." However, they both had the same goal in this case. Clement recalled Woodruf at the Holmes' murder scene. One of them had been a jerk, but maybe that one had been Clement himself, drawing a conclusion about the killing on scant evidence.

He turned his head for a second and then turned back to the screen. "Anything going on out there?" he asked.

"Nada," said Woodruf.

"A Green River standstill." How many years had gone by on the Green River case before they'd finally caught Gary Leon Ridgway? The little twerp had killed how many? Almost 50 women, or maybe 50, maybe more. These killers didn't always keep accurate count, Clement didn't think, and sometimes they confessed to more than they'd done—sometimes less. Clement's throat constricted. This case was bad enough already, with one murder and one surviving victim.

"What are we going to do?" Clement asked.

"Come back tomorrow and try it again," said Woodruf.

"I know, I know, but it's not going well."

"We can put a decoy out there, but no telling if he'll take the bait," Woodruf suggested.

All the blood left Clement's heart and flooded his extremities. He felt flushed, but his heart wasn't pumping right. He took a couple of swallows of coffee. "I guess we could," he agreed cautiously. "But it's kind of a big risk."

"I realize you're tight with Bradley," said Woodruf. He

turned on the second video player. "She's your partner. But she's attractive enough in street clothes. And she's a cop."

"I know," said Clement.

"Okay. Think about it then," Woodruf told him. "But I've been over all our choices in my mind and I think she's the best. The closest in age to the two vics and similar height and coloring."

"I know," answered Clement. "I have something I want to try tomorrow first though. Then we'll see."

Clement was through working at five. He'd started his day in his office at seven-thirty in the morning, and was due to take a spin around the mall that night after dark. But this gave him time to drive over to Cimarron Village, a nursing home to the east of downtown where Chief Kenny now lived. Clement had called the administrator there and had arranged for a visit. He knew Kenny couldn't be in great shape, since he was 83 and living in a nursing home. As none of the cops Clement had asked had seen Kenny in many years, however, Clement didn't know exactly what to expect.

The investigator was brought into Kenny's room where the chief sat in his wheelchair watching television. "You have a visitor, Mr. Kenny," said the nurses aide loudly. She was Indian and a little overweight. "We sit him up so he doesn't sleep all the time," she told Clement in a quieter voice.

Clement went over and sat down on the old chief's bed. The man seemed to be watching TV. He even had his head tilted up and was looking at the picture, but his face was a perfect blank, though the eyes appeared to try to digest the images. This was a bit worse than Clement expected.

"Chief Kenny," he said.

The man's eyes moved in his head as if something might be going on, but he didn't look at Clement and he didn't respond.

"It's Aaron Clement, Chief. Sam Clement's son."

The chief made a noise. Perhaps Clement's father's name had stirred him. The skin on the old man's face was as smooth as a baby's. He didn't have any wrinkles, just some deep crevasses around the eyes. He didn't look that old. But whoever Chief Kenny once had been wasn't present any more.

Clement, who found old age both hard to comprehend and threatening, studied the man for a while, then took the old chief's hand in his own and held it for a minute. He patted the hand. The old man looked at him. The eyes were blank but working away, trying to come to an understanding though he never seemed able to arrive at one.

"That's okay," said Clement kindly. "That's okay. Everything's okay." He gave Chief Kenny back his hand. He supposed if Kenny himself had destroyed the reports because he'd murdered a number of boys, or if he'd helped someone cover up such a crime, or knew who had helped, none of that even mattered now.

Maybe Clement, too, was demented for wanting to solve the case, to bring justice to someone who might be dead or empty like Chief Kenny now was. Yes, Clement knew all things in life were temporary and that the only eternal was God's ultimate being. Still, he had to do what he felt he must and care about what he cared about.

He cared that the children's deaths should not go unpunished. He cared that women were being stolen from their families and trashed after use like dirty rags. He cared that Christine Holmes might be put away for life for defending herself from an abuser. Maybe Clement was wrong. Maybe he was too impassioned and run by his personal predilections rather than the destiny that awaited him as a Christian. But, nonetheless, that was the way things stood.

In a minute he got up and left the nursing home and drove home. But not to rest.

Sometimes a person forgets to call the parent he phones every single morning. Sometimes he forgets to kiss his wife goodbye when he leaves the house. Sometimes he forgets to take a medication that he's taken for the last two decades. And sometimes, as in Clement's case, he forgets who's living in his house.

When Clement arrived home that evening, he was somehow oddly amazed to find Bradley there, since his mind had been exclusively on Shelly. Moreover, Bradley was cooking dinner— again—and that annoyed him. He wasn't married to the girl, was he? What in the world was she doing in his kitchen?

"I'm not sure we can stay," he said abruptly, and Bradley looked at him in surprise.

"Oh, okay," she said. "Where are we going?"

He couldn't be as mean as he felt and speak his mind, so he calmed down a little. "I want to see if Shelly will take a ride...somewhere. Just Shelly and me. Maybe we can eat first though. What are you making?"

"Spaghetti with meatballs."

"That sounds nice," he told her meekly and went to find Shelly. Stress, he guessed. Had he been angry with Judy often before they'd divorced? He didn't like to think he had been.

Shelly was in the back yard sitting on the steps with Buddy next to her, the dog nestled in the dirt. A little bit of a breeze stirred the leaves on the trees. Clement turned on the hose to water four saplings he'd planted in the spring. Shelly watched. He'd recently checked the regulation and learned he could legally water his own yard from his own well, and that was considered "domestic use." So he wasn't even breaking the law. Clement loved his trees.

Eventually, he turned off the hose, curled it out of the way, and went over and sat down next to the girl. "Listen. I want you to help me out," he said. "Let's have some dinner and then you and me drive out to the mall. Think you could stand that? Think you're strong enough for that?" They wouldn't go into the mall because the perp might see them, recognize her, and be warned away.

165

Shelly swallowed, then she nodded. "I'm strong," she said. "I'm okay. I'm not weak."

"Being weak isn't a bad thing," he told her. "We're all mortal. We're all weak."

"I know," she answered. "But what do you want me to do?"

"We're going to drive around there. And you'll tell me anything that you remember or if you see anyone you think might be him, you'll let me know. Can you do that?"

She nodded solemnly. He even thought going there might be good for her. That she'd feel as if she was doing something to help avenge the crime against her.

She said she was strong and that she was okay, but he didn't think she was anywhere near that. Her face, still swollen, with the bruises still evident but fading, would heal, but he wasn't at all sure about the rest of her.

Nothing in her had yet responded to the idea that she was back in the world. Rod called every day but she hadn't spoken to him to this point, and though she spent the days alone in the house, she didn't do anything useful or active here. Clement wondered at her failure to begin to move on, but imagined that recovery from an ordeal of the magnitude of the one she'd been through would take some time. He hoped she would return to them eventually, but that she might not was a very real possibility.

They went in and ate supper, though none of them spoke much. "Fires in Nevada," Clement said at one point. What he didn't say was that Shelly's rape kit was back and that they'd gotten a good DNA profile of her abductor, which they were now running through the FBI database, CODIS—the Combined DNA Indexing System. He would truly rejoice if they got a hit and could identify the perpetrator, and then maybe even track him down.

Suddenly he felt a bit more cheerful, and he smiled. The women looked at him expectantly. "Well," he said, "things might work out okay." Legwork. Policing was all about putting in the legwork. Then, suddenly, at some point, the legwork paid off, and you got your break.

He was responsible for keeping 67,562 citizens of Holder, Oklahoma safe from crime. God was responsible for their souls, but Aaron Clement had to watch out for their physical well-being.

"Are you going to be okay?" he asked Shelly again, and she nodded. Maybe she would be. He was ready to even be optimistic about that.

CHAPTER 22

Shelly became increasingly agitated as they neared the mall. Not that she was screaming in fear or anything, but she made little nervous movements—picked her lips, chewed her lips, swung her leg, cleared her throat.

He drove into the parking lot. Though Holder was a go-to-bed-early-and-get-up-with-the-cows type of town, the Muskogee Mall didn't roll up its sidewalks until nine, and even after that, people went to the Qwik Trip where Shelly had gone, they went to the drug store, and to Foley's Department Store, while the kids went to the movies—this was summer, after all—or had an ice cream. The idea of a teenage girl being trapped by the same man who had taken Shelly sent Clement's blood running cold.

"Tell me whatever you remember," he suggested in a low voice. She'd spoken about what had happened very little, and though he'd asked her about details on a number of occasions, she often said she couldn't remember or would mention something miniscule, like the broken clock on the table.

"I was a little angry with Rod," Shelly began, "but not really. It was about the wedding arrangements." She laughed. Clement could imagine how not only the argument, but the idea of the marriage would all seem unreal to her now. He realized, finally, with that laugh, that she wasn't going to marry his son.

"Look around as we drive," he whispered. "If you see him or anyone who reminds you of him, let me know."

She did as he said, looked out the window intently.

"Go on and tell me," he urged.

"I stopped in the Qwik Trip because I thought I might as well bring something home to sort of make up. I bought a couple pounds of green grapes. They looked very fresh." She stiffened as if she'd seen something...someone.

"Did you see him?" Clement asked sharply.

"No," said Shelly. He observed her trying to relax. What pressure she must feel under, what anxiety.

"I was so surprised when he sprang up behind me after I got in my car...I wanted to struggle, but the knife was at my throat...I dropped the bag with the grapes out the open door. I wanted to tell him, 'Take my wallet. Take the car.' But look what he took." She fell silent and her eyes fixed on a man going to his car, on a couple holding hands, on a laughing family.

"When I came to, later, I thought I must be having a nightmare. He was on top of me, and a dead woman—a woman dead and decaying—Karin—was staring at us. I thought I was in a nightmare or in hell. Do you think I was in hell, Aaron? Had I done something so terribly wrong that God had to punish me?"

"No," he said, "this earth, it's just..." He wasn't sure what to say because everything he could tell her would sound so trivial, so false, so lame, compared to what she'd just told him. "No," he repeated. "We have something to do here. Each of us has something to do, and we're being prepared for it...I think."

When, then, did the preparation end? he wondered. What about Chief Kenny, for instance, whose mind was completely and utterly vanished, erased? Had Chief Kenny accomplished what he'd been sent here for? Or was God still preparing the man?

Or, did the explanation not even matter? Probably that. They could never know, as humans, and knowing was nothing they needed, in fact. All they had to do was move forward, as best they could. And that, exactly that, was what God had given them.

Clement was satisfied with the way he saw it, and he parked the car and he and Shelly sat and looked as the mall visitors, happy or preoccupied, in a hurry, or simply businesslike, came and went. From time to time, Shelly would become alert, but she never pointed to the man who'd kidnapped her, and when all but the last few cars were gone, they themselves left.

"Thank you," she said on their way home, "thank you," and he wasn't sure what she was thanking him for.

Clement slept in, and stopped for an extra large coffee at a fancy new coffee bar on Chickasaw North, on the square. He got to work at eight-thirty, feeling as if he had a hangover, though many years had gone by since he'd actually had one. He opened the cup and drank off the foam, then sank into his chair. He missed the boys, he missed his bones, though he was glad their grandmother had been able to bury them.

He felt unsettled about everything right now. Last night he'd been hopeful; today he was cast down. His phone rang and he answered as usual, patiently enunciating his last name.

"I'm not waking you, I hope?"

Clement recognized Rich's voice and his sarcasm. "Not yet. Tell me something good and I'll wake up."

"I have nothing good to tell. I had a breakfast meeting with Mrs. Assistant District Attorney Enkan. That didn't work out well."

"No?" Clement drank some more of the hot coffee. He walked the phone to his air conditioner and turned it as high as it would go.

"She's not intimidated, she says."

"No, she's not the intimidated type," Clement agreed. He went and sat down. "But I'm surprised, because she doesn't want to be shown to be in the wrong."

"Yeah, but what I figured out...she doesn't mind the D.A. himself being shown to be wrong, if you know what I mean. She's a bit ambitious. And who knows, maybe she just hates him." Rich laughed.

"Then you had breakfast with the wrong person," Clement said.

"As if the D.A. would have breakfast with the likes of me."

"Call him. He'll speak to you," Clement suggested.

"I know," Rich agreed. "I'll try. But it's sticky. Might have to take the whole thing to appeal. Worst case, if you don't want your girlfriend to testify, I'll try for an appeal on new information—the broken bones weren't brought up at the trial."

"Amazing," said Clement. "She's not my girlfriend," he added belatedly. "She's young. I'm old. You're old, too."

Rich laughed again. "Okay. I don't know what's going on with this or why I let you talk me into it. The sentencing hearing is in 10 days."

They hung up.

Oddly, Clement had thought his strategy would work. He had been so sure of it, he hadn't planned for anything else. Now what? Poor Christine. What about the sleeping pills she had put in Gregory's beverage that night? Why had the doctor prescribed them? Had anyone gotten her mental health history? He hadn't seen any references in her hospital file, but now he wondered what he had missed. Along with the abuse, a history of mental illness would come in handy right about now.

When the phone rang again, Clement thought it must be Rich, calling him back. But it wasn't. Neal wanted to see Clement today, if possible, so Clement decided to drive right out. Neal wouldn't want to see him about nothing, would he? Clement finished his coffee first, turned down the AC to save the P.D. a couple of dollars, and left the building with his face dripping down with sweat and oil.

* * *

The air conditioning at the university wasn't operating too well, either. How could any AC work effectively in this relentless high heat? Clement plodded on toward Dr. Neal's office and knocked on the door, but got no answer. The door was locked. Clement went on, into the lab where Neal was gathered with a few of the summer school students, showing slides.

"Oh, good. Officer Clement will be very interested in this presentation." With a laser pointer, the forensic anthropologist indicated a certain suspect region on photos he had taken from the air—explaining why this spot might contain a gravesite for multiple sets of remains. The man appeared pleased and excited, and Clement, who was chilled and disgusted despite his years of experience with homicide, had to remind himself that the professor was very unlikely to be the perp. Still, such enthusiasm for potential human remains grated on the SPO.

By contrast, the students, jotting down notes like robots, showed oddly little affect. Even the girls.

Clement tried to figure out where the terrain was, but no familiar landmarks clued him in. Suddenly, he realized that the site could as easily be the place where Shelly's attacker buried his victims as the place where the Parker brothers' killer had disposed of his. What a nice little town Holder had turned out to be.

"What do we need to disinter the remains?" Neal asked. Clement thought the man was quizzing his students, then he realized the question was directed at him.

"A court order," Clement said. "I'll get one when I go back into town."

"Great." Neal's fervor hadn't waned. "We can gather our equipment and be out in the field tomorrow morning. As we're unlikely to have rain overnight, conditions are certain to be ideal."

Never mind the 103 degree heat. Clement examined the students' reactions. They seemed, well, more resigned and determined than enthused. He felt sort of the same way, himself.

The students soon left with an admonition to be early for the dig in the morning, and Clement remained to deal with Neal's high energy state. "Hot out there," said Clement, wanting to be sure the professor had some contact with the real world.

"It'll be good for them," countered Neal. "The kids today are incredibly soft." He grinned.

Clement, who didn't really think the heat would be good for *him*, nodded. "Can you give me the location of the gravesite, or suspected gravesite?" He had his pen and notebook out.

Neal gave him the exact latitude and longitude, not what Clement had expected. Then, relenting a bit, Neal named the area—out along a canyon that Clement knew.

"Do you have any idea how old the gravesite is?" Were they going to find fresh remains or old ones? Corpses buried by one of the two killers they knew of, or bodies hidden by some unsuspected maniac? Or even a slew of cattle slaughtered in the 1800s during an anthrax epidemic, an unearthing that could give surviving anthrax spores, a hardy biohazard, a whole new set of victims?

Neal shrugged. "Our weather patterns have been weird and we've had so little rain lately that the land could crack in a very short time, or the graves could have been out there for a while."

"And you're sure they're graves?"

"Never sure until we open it up. But the possibility is strong, and either way, the trip will be good for the kids."

Clement smiled but not with conviction. "I'll call you and verify it when I get the court order. Won't be a problem." He turned to go.

"Oh, wait a minute."

Clement turned back and saw that Neal was spreading some pictures onto the lab table. More aerial photographs, but this time of barns. Gosh, he had to do something nice for Neal. The work he was doing for the department was priceless and the man wasn't getting paid.

"This was the other thing you wanted, right? Someplace cars

could be hidden. I have pictures here of every structure in the area we went over—residential garages aside—capable of holding more than two cars."

Each photo was neatly marked with latitude and longitude and then street address! "I had a couple of students go over these and compare them to the tax assessment photos to give you the locations."

"That's fantastic," Clement told Neal at last with some real emotion. He mumbled a second goodbye and headed, like an automaton, to where he supposed he'd left his car.

If only he, too, had an endless team of students he could send out to do the footwork. Hey, wait a minute, maybe he did. A new class had started at the Holder Police Academy last week. The classes had become progressively bigger because smaller towns nearby had begun to send their own recruits. The new class numbered forty-five.

Clement tried to figure out how many cars they'd need, then he realized these people had brought their own transportation with them. The city could pay them mileage, of course. And they were employees of Holder or their own towns because they were being paid to train.

Munson was a good administrator, which meant he didn't like hassles, including any changes in direction or in schedules. But the chief was also a pretty conscientious cop. He would weigh all the elements. Munson had seen the photos of Shelly and he knew that Karin had been killed. He also knew that Clement might do something drastic to make sure that they found the perp. Clement could go to the papers, for instance—and he would. But let Munson come to Clement's way of seeing things on his own first, Clement decided.

Once again he wondered about the gravesite and which case it would cast some light on. Did all small towns across America have such secrets lurking in their underbrush: burial sites not yet found, evidence of horrors yet to be examined?

The other night he'd watched a show on chimpanzees. They,

like man, were sometimes inspired to kill gratuitously, to kill for sport. Was murder natural primate behavior? Which was the veneer, man's primate nature, or his divine one? Clement believed that the answer depended on the man. He prayed deeply that his own nature was more divine than driven by a heedless instinct. As a cop always so surrounded by evil, he often feared that the evil he saw was in himself as well.

Chapter 23

Before leaving the office for the day, Clement looked online at the weather map. A rain cell was slated to move through the extreme western tip of the Oklahoma panhandle and a little piece of northern Texas. Lucky them. Then he faxed a copy of the court order to Neal and sent an email to Munson, who wasn't around. Hirsh was hitting the mall that night, so Clement wasn't in any hurry to get home.

At five o'clock, the sun still beamed down to fry them all. Hurry sundown.

He drove a few miles south to the old Five Hills section, where a bunch of cops used to live. Sam Clement had nearly moved his own family there, but Clement's mom hadn't wanted to go. For once in her life, she'd won the argument, but mostly because Sam was a little bit too lazy to do the deal and move, or so Clement thought. Tolliver's one-time partner, Danvers, lived here, and he'd agreed to see Clement to discuss "an old case."

The section and the homes had been nice once; now the houses would be considered too small for a family, even a couple.

Danvers came to the door before Clement rang and the older man rushed him into the TV room or maybe it was a den. "Beth is sleeping," he said without apology. "Not one of her better days.

"I'm sorry to hear that."

"Getting old stinks," added Danvers. "But you probably see that in your own dad. And of course your mother...well."

Clement's mother had lived long enough to be divorced by his father, then a year later had died of breast cancer. The progression of events had been cruel, and Clement had missed them, being in Afghanistan at the time. They'd given him leave to come home for her funeral.

"Your dad must be proud of you, though," Danvers went on.

Clement pondered the idea. "My father doesn't show much," he said. Actually, that wasn't true. Sam revealed a lot of disdain and disapproval. "What I'm here about—" he began.

"I speak to Henry quite often still," Danvers said. "I guess you're here on the case of the two boys. "I saw the pictures in the paper and then an article about the funeral. A little late to get on this thing, don't you think? It's all so long ago."

Clement gave a disinterested shrug. "Cold cases are all the rage," he commented. "Remember anything, yourself? You and Henry never filed any missing persons reports for a couple of years—1996 and 1997. You'd think one or two would have come up, wouldn't you? Especially since you were patrolling an area where several children had gone missing." And when Mrs. May, the grandmother of Moses and Ezekiel Parker, recalled that Tolliver had actually taken the report.

Danvers chuckled. "I don't even remember what I had for lunch. But I'll tell you, we did what we had to do to maintain law and order in those days. That was how we saw our jobs— maintaining law and order. Not coddling minorities, not playing nursemaid. But keeping the criminal element out of the community."

Clement nodded without reaction. So catching kidnappers and killers would be considered playing nursemaid and not keeping out the criminal element. An interesting take on the topic of policing. These old guys, his father very much included,

177

really got him. They thought they were something. They didn't just think they were above the law, they thought they themselves were the law. He gritted his teeth and smiled tightly at Danvers.

"I believe Henry," Clement said. "I believe him when he said he filed some reports those years in question. Does that ring true to you? And if you think Henry knows what he was talking about—and I believe he does—then who do you think could have pulled those reports out of the files and gotten rid of them?"

"You're sounding like a bureaucrat now." Danvers shook his head in mock disbelief. "I can't account for you being your father's son."

"I'm not like one of the Gang of Four?" questioned Clement.

Danvers laughed. "He told you all about the old days, did he? Well, then you know. Things were a little wild and woolly back then. We had a lot of responsibilities and we took care of things in our own way. And what was the harm? We did what men had to do in times like that. Now policing is done by a bunch of girls."

Clement let that last remark slide. He'd heard worse from his own father. Arguing policing style was like discussing either religion or politics. The conversation was sure to get you nowhere.

All in all, he wasn't sure he'd expected much more than this, but he'd had to try. He still had Yargee, the records clerk, to interview before he came to a dead end. And he'd moved on beyond dead ends before, so even a dead end wasn't going to stop him. Or so he hoped. Maybe Neal's burial site, if it was one, and was a site that held dead boys' bones, would give them something.

Clement could see a car that wasn't Bradley's in the driveway and for a moment thought maybe Rod had come out to try to force Shelly into seeing him. But as he got closer, he could see the car wasn't his son's.

His place was getting to be a regular Grand Central Station. Ever since he'd taken Buddy in. That was probably the key. Buddy kept having visitors. But, really, what had happened to Clement's peaceful, solitary life, to walking around in his undershorts, the ultimate benefit of living as he did?

Woodruf was sitting on the green couch when Clement walked in. Clement's temper flared up immediately. The other SPO had come out to interview his victim!

Clement literally bit his tongue to keep it in his head. He nodded at Woodruf and kept on going—into the kitchen where he poured himself a tall glass of cold water and drank. He poured some more and got one for Woodruf, bringing both out and handing the glass to the other man along with a napkin.

Clement sat next to his colleague on the couch. "This sofa is annoying me," he said. "Just how uncomfortable is it?"

"It's fine," answered Woodruf, staring at Clement as if he were crazy, but swilling down the water.

Clement stood, then went over to his own chair. How much would a really good sofa cost him? He hadn't realized he'd have so many visitors when he'd bought this one. But then again, in the long run, his house would be quiet again. He'd have to tell Buddy not to invite so many darn guests.

Bradley came out of "her" room, wearing a skirt. Clement, who'd been prepared to cook dinner for them all tonight, was taken aback. Did she have a date with Woodruf? Hey, wait a minute. Wasn't the SPO married?

"Going somewhere?" he asked in what he hoped was a neutral tone.

"We're going out to the mall," Woodruf told him. "Munson called Bradley himself and asked her to be our decoy." That was Woodruf's way of telling Clement not to blame him.

Bradley looked happy about the prospect. "I have a gun," she told Clement quickly, probably seeing his reaction.

And his reaction wasn't pleased. What made her think this was a fun assignment? He himself wouldn't want to be the goat staked down for the tiger. "I have a gun, too," he answered. "And I'm coming with you." Clement looked at Woodruf, not at the girl.

Woodruf nodded. "Okay, but we do have a few other guys who'll be out there. We're going to take every precaution."

"You know he does use chloroform or something like that," Clement warned.

"I've read your reports," Woodruf assured him.

Clement went to let Shelly know they'd be gone for a while and then he changed into a T-shirt.

The three of them each took his—or her—own car. The idea was that Bradley would buy a single item inside the mall—reimbursed by HPD, Woodruf informed her—and then come outside and put it in the trunk of her vehicle. This would allow her several opportunities to be seen and picked up on by the madman.

The men—the four detectives and two other officers who were thrilled to be working the night shift in plain clothes—would lurk in the background and hopefully not be seen. Bradley was wired and had a signal she would use. Hirsh and Woodruf took the old surveillance truck, a genuinely beat-up vehicle and not simply made to look that way.

The others had parked away from the lights, slouched, and wore caps that they pulled over their foreheads. Because of the terrain—an open parking lot with no place to hide—and the fact that they weren't the NY or LA police departments, this was the best that they could do. They were desperate not to blow the operation as well as to protect Bradley from all harm.

After 20 minutes, she came out to her car from the west end of the mall. Clement had never seen her walk that way before and wasn't sure if he liked it or if he was irritated by it. Did a woman need to slink in order to lure in a man? Bradley would have no problems in that department, however she walked. If she wanted to attract a man, that was. Maybe though she didn't want to. Maybe she just wanted to be a decent cop. That was a good and almost sufficient ambition to hold. For an old guy, that was...

He kept his eye on her as she opened her car trunk and placed in a nice-sized package. He hoped she was buying something frivolous that she wanted. On the other hand, Munson would probably make her return what she bought. Yeah, that would undoubtedly be the outcome of the shopping spree.

Thinking the word "spree" set his teeth on edge, since it was most associated in his mind with the phrase, "spree killers." The tension ran through him and he watched her nonchalantly return to the mall.

A little while later, she came out again with another sizable parcel. Didn't the girl have any sense? Sure putting a small purchase into the car might look silly, but she'd be less able to go for her gun while carrying a bigger bundle.

A security guard made his rounds in a little electric patrol vehicle. Bradley fussed with the trunk and her packages until he was gone. Then she finished and started back toward the shops.

A man coming from the other direction approached her.

Clement sat up to get a better look; with care, he opened his door so he could run out to her as quickly as possible. His heart thumped loudly in his chest. He was terrified, overwhelmed by the idea of something awful happening to her.

The man was still with her, in front of her, blocking Clement's view. For what purpose with an innocent explanation would a man stop a woman he didn't know in a parking lot!

Spurred into action by that thought, Clement exploded out of the car. He drew his gun and ran toward the two. The man half turned to see what was coming and Clement had him down on the ground right about then, his Smith and Wesson at the man's head.

The man made incomprehensible noises and Bradley cried out, "It's nothing…" while a whole lot of other action suddenly swirled around this group of three.

"Crap, Clement," said Woodruf. "Now we're exposed." But he made the man slowly empty his pockets on the ground there and then. Keys, change, nothing else in the front pockets. Woodruf pulled a wallet from the man's back pocket and riffled through.

Clement helped the poor guy up. The man was stunned, not even angry, just in a state of total shock. "Sorry," said Clement. He reached out to help brush ground grit from him. The guy jumped back. Bradley laughed. The cops, except for Woodruf, Clement, and Bradley dissolved back to their posts. Clement apologized once again, then heard himself asking the guy what he must have been thinking accosting a woman alone in a parking lot.

"He wanted change for a dollar," Bradley said.

"What did you need that for?" Clement demanded, aggrieved. "What didn't you get it in a store? That's crazy."

They were looking at Clement as if he were insane, but he was irked. This guy didn't have the sense he'd been born with coming up to a young woman alone in a parking lot at night. What an idiot!

Clement turned around and got back in his car. *What an idiot*, he kept thinking to himself, although a while later, the refrain turned to *Maybe I was the idiot*.

They waited a while, then Bradley did a little more shopping, but nothing else happened, and once all the stores closed, though the movie wasn't out just yet, they all went home. Clement tailed Bradley along the road to make sure she wasn't carjacked or anything like that.

After the two parked in his driveway, Bradley waited for him to get out of his car, and Clement did—because he had to, obviously, though he wondered if he was due for a scolding from her. The air was hot, hard to breathe.

"Well, you're something," she told him. Okay, sarcasm was her weapon of choice. But she was so clever, she almost didn't sound sarcastic. "That was fast."

"All right, I misunderstood the situation. But tell me that guy wasn't an idiot."

"I guess he was stupid, but he was harmless," she said. "After all, he didn't know he'd stumbled into a police sting." She grinned. "Thanks, all the same."

"I know I was rash. That's my nature." He frowned. "I apologize."

"I was saying thank you." She gave him a puzzled look and turned toward the house.

"I'm apologizing for ruining the operation and for not letting you handle it on your own," he said to her back. What he'd done was probably worse than opening the patrol car door for her. Now he was going to go to sleep and pretend this whole night hadn't happened.

When they got to the door, he automatically used his key, opened the door, and let her in in front of him. Only after he walked through the door did it occur to him that the ritual of courtesy toward a woman was programmed so deeply in him that he'd just as soon go out on the street completely naked as to not do what he'd just done.

In regard to his trying to protect her at the mall—well, that one was going to get around. Damn good thing he was a loner and didn't have to encounter too much ridicule to his face. But he had to admit it, at least to himself: He'd messed up.

Chapter 24

In the middle of the night Clement heard a noise and reached for his gun, which he always took to bed with him and placed under a pillow nearby. He sat up, but then he saw that it was Buddy, parading around at the window and 'woofing' softly. Clement got out of bed and pulled open the blinds. To the west, he could see a glow, which confused him since he didn't think he usually watched the sun rise from here, and he didn't think so many hours had gone by.

Then he realized that what he was looking at was a fire. He made himself calm down and hurried into a pair of cutoffs and shoes. Then he went and knocked firmly on Bradley's door, opened it, and called in, "Get up, Bradley, and wake up Shelly. We have a fire out there."

He was rattled, but in control enough to get out his cell phone and call emergency dispatch. They'd had some calls from further out, she said, and trucks were already on their way. Clement hoped that the people closer to the fire didn't lose their homes tonight. Just as *he* feared the worst and hoped for the best, so they too were heartsick with worry right now. He pictured anxious husbands and wives, the entirety of whose assets were in that house. He envisioned frightened little children. He himself was unnerved, too.

Turning on the yard lights from the front porch, Clement

went out the screen door, and started the hose. He certainly didn't like this wind, and now that he was in the yard, he could smell the distinctive scent an Oklahoma wildfire gives off. In the distance, he observed the fire tearing through the brush as if being chased by the very devil. One tall pine was completely ablaze like a wick in a candle, and a moment later he heard a 'pop' as the tree literally exploded.

Fortunately, most of the trees on the nearby land had been cleared years ago. Before the developments had cropped up this far out, and before the local airfield had been built across town, someone on the county commission had suggested this site as an airfield. They'd even taken the step of clearing the land.

Clement ought to have set down a firefighting plan for himself earlier in the season. Well, his idea had been to make a bigger fire break, and while he had actually gone so far as to borrow a backhoe and park it close to the county acreage, he hadn't followed through and done the work.

Bradley and Shelly came out of the house now with Buddy, so Clement handed Bradley the hose and told her to just keep watering all around the structure and hosing down the house. How long would the well water last? he wondered.

He looked at Shelly with a curious eye, evaluating her fitness to help out. What was the worst that could happen if he gave her an assignment? She'd fall apart. So? He was on the verge of falling apart, too. "Can you get the shovels and rakes from the tool shed, just in case we have to fight the fire here?" The girl nodded. Good.

Clement hurried out to the tractor on the other side of the yard and jumped on. If only he'd practiced when he'd gotten the machine. He'd never operated it, but the key was in the starter. Stupid of him to leave it there, but his thoughtlessness was working to his advantage with the fire.

He looked out across the vista. What he saw out there reminded him of photos of a lava flow, as the drought's burning anger rushed forward toward his own land, hungrily gulping down this long-awaited meal.

Clement turned on the motor, unsure how much gas the thing had in it. He'd intended to fuel up before he cleared the land next door. He glanced back at his house, standing proud and defiant, but oh so vulnerable to destruction. This could be his last look ever.

Driving around the chain link fence that the county had put up to separate its property from the rest of the world, Clement, inside their domain, started to practice with the blade. Already, he was bathed in sweat, despite the fact that this was the middle of the night and he had on no shirt. The wind was high, but not refreshing. The air that carried the fire forward felt hot enough for him to cook with, a very bad sign.

He'd cleared his own property late last year and followed up regularly, getting rid of any new growth. The view was stark. Well, he had the trees. He should have told Bradley to spray down the saplings. And he had oaks, elms, and pines to the east of the house, but that wasn't where the fire was coming from. He could live without grass, bushes, or flowers, but not without trees. And the trees were fuel.

As he ripped up the mostly dried vegetation and tried to plow it under the dirt and sand, he could hear fire trucks in the distance closer to where the fire was actually burning. If they could stop the fire there, he and the women might go back inside and get some sleep, and he could finish off the firebreak in the morning.

But he knew the firefighters couldn't stop a grass fire just by snapping their fingers. What they had to do was toil—he had seen it, had seen them go to the blackened side of the conflagration and begin to spread foam from behind. Why fight it from the back of the fire? So their trucks wouldn't get caught as the fire moved forward.

But they, too, would try to create a firebreak somewhere ahead of the fire, he hoped. And if his house burned down, he'd sue the county. He'd warned them, even in a letter once.

Probably couldn't sue, however. And the loss of the house would be a crushing blow that money wouldn't make up for. He oughtn't to love his things so much.

The shaking he'd felt from the moment he'd realized what he was finally facing, the nausea and panic, turned to adrenaline as he moved forward. Awkward at first in running the machine, he gained a bit in skill with the blade as the minutes went on. With the wind up as it was right now, he had to be sure the firebreak would be wide enough so no stray spark would blow onto the gazebo or swing set he'd put up years ago for Judy and for Rod.

A wave of depression hit him as he worked. He'd lived such a carefully balanced life since his wife and child had moved out, hadn't taken any emotional risks, yet had invested too much feeling in what he still had. The house, for one thing—his job for another. With a single gust of ill fortune, these could be gone literally within seconds.

Once again, tonight, he'd behaved in an impulsive way, had ruined the stakeout by acting precipitously. His reputation in the department would move down a notch, and he'd begin to be a little less indispensable. He ought to retire while he was ahead.

On the road behind him, he heard a couple of cars approaching. Probably firefighters warning the neighborhood, waking people along the road, even evacuating them. Maybe the fire was simply out of control, and they were going to stop trying to save this sector.

All he could do as he worked was pray—for the safety of them all. He didn't pray that his house would be saved. That was surely too material in nature for him to legitimately make an appeal to God. All he had to do was plow down this whole field. If it took him all night. But he was scared.

The glow crawled forward rapidly as Clement worked and watched. The grass here was higher than he'd even thought, or hadn't he paid enough attention in the last few weeks? He dug. He'd dig with his hands if he had to. But he had so much more to go, he felt a terrible despair. If only the fire crew would hurry up. He was unlikely to hold the line all by himself.

He knew that the risk for him was getting caught in not just the fire but the smoke. He could easily lose his life tonight and he wasn't ready to die, and certainly not this horrible way. The fire continued without slowing, licking out to take what mattered most to the human enemy.

Hearing voices behind him, Clement turned and glanced back across the footage that he'd worked. In amazement, he saw half a dozen men he knew from church hurrying into the field with shovels and such. Out toward his house, then, he saw where they had parked their cars and he saw a few women standing, their eyes out on the backhoe and the horizon.

He wouldn't be able to admit it later on, but tears welled in his eyes and fell onto his face, already soaked with the sweat of his labor. There. He did so have people who cared about him. Many days, he didn't feel so. But with push coming to shove, they'd rushed to help. He felt enormous gratitude.

Though then a minute later, the machine coughed a bit and sputtered and was done for the day. Out of gas and with the fire gaining on them! Clement got down from his seat and realized how the vibration of the thing had shaken him, and how jammed up his back felt now. He took the shovel from the oldest of the men who had come into the field to help. Juran should be inside the house with the air conditioning full blast.

"Thanks," Clement said.

Then, for a long while, the men didn't speak at all, but worked steadily against the chinook winds and the fire, taking down the summer growth.

After a time, the flames approached where they were in the field, and the men retreated back through the cleared land, toward Clement's house. He was pleased to see how far they'd come. The firebreak might hold. Oh, Lord, that the firebreak would hold! He stood on the edge of his property and abated his breath, evaluating what they'd accomplished.

The air currents might shake their fists, but he didn't think the strength of the motion would be enough to carry sparks to the house. Moreover, the forestry trucks carrying water and foam had driven up on the blackened earth behind the blaze and were making to douse what was left of the danger. He shouldn't love his house so much, or his child, or his job. He shouldn't even love his church the way he did, but only the Lord God.

When the men went inside the house, Clement saw that the women were setting out some nice cold drinks. Even water would feel wonderful to his parched throat. And then he saw that his father was here, sitting on the sofa as if he dropped by every day.

"You got up in the middle of the night?" Clement asked his dad.

"I sleep by a police scanner," his father explained.

"Maria must love that." Clement passed a glass of iced liquid to his father, and when his dad refused it, drank the fluid in one long gulp.

Buddy came over to Clement, no doubt interested in what the upshot of the nighttime work was. The dog, after waking Clement at just the right moment, had certainly called together a lot of folks to help save their home, and Clement was grateful. Now Clement wished everyone would go home. The men were tracking dirt, sand, and dried grass onto his floor, even the area rugs he shook out almost daily—or avoided walking on—to keep them clean.

He guessed he was supposed to make a speech to thank them all. But he didn't want to. So, tired as he felt, he shook every person's hand, as those who had come to help him left, a couple at a time.

A minute later, he looked behind him and saw Rod. When had the kid snuck in and how had he known? How had anyone known? Of course in this part of the country and during fire season, not just Clement's dad slept next to police scanners.

189

Rod had gone over to Shelly to talk. Clement kept his eyes on the two. Shelly's face had healed and, as pretty as ever, she seemed to have gone through nothing much, certainly not the nightmare of the underworld, of Hell itself. Clement wasn't sure which of the two kids he felt the more protective of at this exact juncture.

One of the women had begun to sweep. When she looked up to notice Clement watching her, she smiled. He came over and thanked her. "These men! They had to track in whatnot, and you sure keep a nice house. We can all thank God He saved it for you."

Almost too tired to talk, Clement agreed, and thanked her again.

Clement's dad summoned him over and patted the couch, but Clement sat on the floor, instead. Too tired to stand, he nonetheless didn't want to soil the green velvet covering.

"I thought of something after you left the other day."

"The other day?" Clement couldn't recall even having been at his dad's.

"We were talking about Tolliver and I mentioned Danvers."

"Oh, yeah. Danvers," Clement agreed. As his dad said, every time Clement went to visit, he went about a case and not really to see his father at all. Clement would have to do a little better from now on. Grateful that his house was safe and that people had flocked here to help, he resolved to make up to those around him for any misdemeanors over the years.

"I remembered that Tolliver had another partner for a couple of years—Grant Simpson. Frank and me didn't like him so well and we kind of shied off of Tolliver around that time. Something about the guy didn't smell right. I'm sure you know what I mean."

"Yeah." Clement could have made a joke and say *he* didn't smell so good right now, either, but he hardly had the strength to bother.

"Kenny let him go after a while, so I guess he didn't seem

none too good to Kenny, either. He wasn't a guy's guy, I guess it was."

Clement didn't have a clue as to what his father meant by that.

"He was an oddball."

Clement nodded. Clement was an oddball, too, and he knew full well that if his father hadn't been in the department at the time he'd started, Clement himself might have been let go. So, the guy's being an oddball could mean anything from their sense that he was homosexual to the feeling that the guy was an independent thinker. Or their perception that he was a serial killer of young black boys.

"Stick around, Dad, if you like, and watch TV or nap in my chair over there," Clement said. "I have to get some sleep before I go in to work though." He stood up, feeling as if he'd just run a marathon.

Rod and Shelly had disappeared. Whether that meant a serious talk about their breakup, or a reunion, Clement really wasn't able to even guess.

He found Bradley in the kitchen, finishing the cleanup. Clement didn't mind that all the cold beverages were gone, and he drank one more glass straight from the tap. His well had survived and was still able to offer up some fresh, delicious water.

Before finally collapsing, Clement made sure to top off Buddy's water bowl as well. Buddy, the hero. The dog had earned his place in this house for sure.

CHAPTER 25

Clement slept late. He saw that Munson had called his cell, but ignored it and didn't even retrieve the message. He wasn't in a rush to be scolded about last night and didn't think that the dressing down was a crucial law enforcement action. Munson and his criticism could definitely wait. Instead, Clement headed out to the excavation site first thing in the morning, as he'd promised the forensic anthropologist.

With a few cars parked on the shoulder of the road, Clement knew this must be the place. He didn't like parking here exactly and tried to pick the spot where his car would be the least likely vehicle to be sideswiped.

Down the slope, he spotted Neal with a gaggle of students. Neal held a long, slender metal probe that he pushed into the ground, lecturing all the while. Clement went down to them, taking care not to slip. He saw that they had begun a dig at another nearby spot and that bone structures had been exposed and not far from the surface.

Though Clement knew very little about all this, he thought he recognized a human pelvis alongside a femur. And since he'd lived with the boys' bones for a number of months, he decided this was the skeleton of either a juvenile or a female.

Neal greeted Clement and came over to the cop. "What a find," he said, a little more subdued than the day before. "It's grisly, if you actually think of it. I've never really found any-thing in situ like this. Of course it's a great experience to detect a site from the aerial photography and then uncover the graves. Great technology."

The man appeared to be a little done in by the heat or by emotion and Clement knew he didn't look too chipper himself. "More boys?" he asked.

"I think the pelvis is, but we can't be sure for forensic pur-poses until we get the DNA, though sometimes we can tell from the clothing. But you know—forensic standards." Neal turned back to look at where the students had started work again. "It's a wonder the bones weren't disturbed by foraging scavengers and then found by someone. Maybe because we're right off the highway here, and a road with traffic might be tricky for an animal to cross from up in the hills."

Neal frowned as if the explanation didn't make sense to him. "Or...well, we'll see. Lime on top of the bones? Don't think that would discourage a hungry fox."

Contrary to what Neal implied about the traffic, Clement didn't think this was a much-traveled road, especially at night, and he could see why this might make a good burial spot, in general.

But he wondered if a psychological reason for picking the gravesite accompanied the physical practicality of the place. A serial killer, he'd read and heard time and time again, even if not a ritual killer, often used symbolism in choosing a burial spot. Clement studied the terrain. They were at a low point of the valley. Did that mean something? Or was this place just a convenience for a killer who lived out this way? "How many are buried here do you think?" he asked at last.

"Several," said Neal. "Maybe as many as five."

Only two, other than the Parker brothers, had been identi-fied as probable victims. That meant at least three more children Clement didn't know about had been killed.

"We're going to set up some tarps over the gravesites, even

though we don't expect any rain." Neal smiled—no doubt at the irony of protecting the graves against potential precipitation. If only it *would* rain in this part of the state. Clement took out a tissue and wiped his face and neck.

"You need to send a policeman out here to protect the dig at night," Neal added. "But we'll take care of the photographs and chain of custody for the evidence and all that, if you'll let us. This is a great teaching opportunity." A hint of his delight at the circumstance returned.

Clement smiled. "Coincidentally, our piggy bank is always on empty, so we're very grateful for the help. If there's anything I can do for you..." Clement hoped Neal wouldn't be able to think of anything, especially at this time when Clement was dizzy with the number of tasks he had to accomplish.

"Hire all my students when they graduate," suggested Neal, but Clement was glad to see that the man was just kidding. As things stood, Munson would grouse when he received the request for another warm policing body.

As Clement entered the P.D. and headed for his office, three different people were happy to stop him and let him know that Munson had been trying to find him for the last three hours. The SPO had to admit the apparent fervency of Munson's search irritated him. Was chewing Clement out really that important?

He stepped into his office first and took off his jacket. Surely Munson wouldn't fire him just yet. That would be rather ridiculous and Clement didn't really see it as Munson's style.

The chief's door was open and Clement walked right in. Woodruf sat there as if he himself were a stick of furniture, and the two men had what seemed to Clement to be sour expressions on their faces. He decided to derail their little hanging jurisprudence. "The site Neal pinpointed out by the highway is positive for human remains. Oh, yeah, and Neal wants a cop to watch the site overnight—keep out the grave robbers." That was guaranteed to grab Munson's attention.

And it did. Munson let out an almost grinding sort of sigh, startling Clement. "Something going on I don't know about?" Clement asked, despite his intention to stick to the subject of the dead boys.

A second agonized noise emerged from Munson.

"We have a woman reported missing from last night," Woodruf answered into a subsequent silence. "Probably from the Five Tribes Mall."

Clement's sigh was a great deal more subdued than Munson's, but inside his head he pictured Shelly as he had met her on the road that day. Her face had been so swollen and bruised he hadn't even known who she was. *It's Shelly, Mr. Clement.*

All the questions he wanted to ask were trapped in his throat. What was the latest victim's name? Who had reported her missing? How old was she? Around what time had the woman been abducted?

This was another scenario he was able to picture all too clearly. Say at eight-fifteen last night the perp had been watching Bradley with intent. At eight-thirty Clement had popped out at the jerk guy, blowing their cover. The perp had peddled off to the Five Tribes Mall and had grabbed this other girl, who like Shelly, had awakened in Hell. Clement was the direct cause, then, of the woman's misery.

"The question that keeps sticking in my head is about the cars," said Clement. "Can we finally go ahead and mobilize the academy students and try to find the cars? The barns...I gave you the pictures...The ones nearest where I found Shelly are marked in red."

"All right," said Munson. They all knew the exigency of the case required whatever they could throw at it.

Another thought hovered, too: What about the perp's own car? Holder's system of public transportation was limited, not really great for the carless criminal especially at night. And yet, this rapist/killer took the women's cars with his vics. Did this mean he left his own car in the mall lots? Did this mean they had to review the tapes again and look at cars—compare the cars sitting at both the malls? Talk about your needle in a haystack. But if they had to, they had to, over time. By then, this woman would be dead.

"The DNA," pressed Clement. "Since the CODIS database hasn't given us a hit yet, we have to take DNA samples from all the male mall employees. And we have to cross-check who could have been at both malls. Vendors at least. Delivery guys. We have to run criminal records on all the workers."

Munson gave a bitter laugh. "Yeah, we can do it. With enormous difficulty. And you do know how long processing the samples will take, don't you?"

"Let's do it," said Woodruf. "It's a stone we have to turn over eventually. Sooner will be better than later."

Munson shook his head as if he was going to refuse, but he didn't. "All right. I'll get the sergeants to organize a group. First thing tomorrow—first thing after the holiday—they'll be out there doing swabs." Clement knew Munson wouldn't want to be accused later of being lax in the investigation, even if he didn't think this would turn out to be an effective approach. "As far as criminal records' checks, a lot of the stores may have done them to avoid civil liability. Someone else needs to coordinate that."

Finally, Clement had to ask, "Does anyone know what time this last vic was picked up?" He noticed that he'd simply stopped breathing while putting forth his question.

"The husband expected her home by seven o'clock," Woodruf told him. "So she must have been taken between the time she left work—a little after five—and, say six-forty-five. Before it got dark, I guess. The guy has nerve."

Then Clement hadn't ruined the operation and their chance to take the doer down last night. Bradley had been irrelevant as bait by the time she'd stepped out into the lot around a quarter to eight. Their guy already had his victim bundled up into her car and was driving off into the countryside excitedly intent on ruining, then taking, the poor girl's life.

Clement's not being the direct cause of the woman's downfall was a balm to the SPO's own sense of self, but that didn't help this woman at all, not at all. Though Clement hadn't hurt her, he still had to make sure that she was saved.

"Let's get last night's mall tapes," he said, "and Bradley and Hirsh can review those. Me, Woodruf, and Jackson will try to get lists of vendors and deliveries, and cross-check between the malls." Did that jibe with the transportation problem? Wouldn't someone have noticed a delivery truck left in the lot? "Or mostly just vendors for now," he said. "Sales guys."

"Five Tribes does digital monitoring," added Woodruf. We've already downloaded yesterday's surveillance to our own computers."

Woodruf and Clement drove out to Five Tribes to pursue the dual tasks of canvassing for anyone who might have seen yesterday's incident and to get the stores' vendor lists if the managers would or could cooperate. Although getting the lists had been Clement's own idea, and it wasn't a bad one, the sheer magnitude of the task struck him as absurd. Going door to door everywhere in northwest Oklahoma to see if a madman was holding a woman inside was just about as good an idea.

At the stores, Clement was able to get the vendor lists because he was simply a persuasive guy. He presented himself as assuming that everyone in Holder would be willing to cooperate with the police. *Hey, this is Holder, Oklahoma. Never mind the corporate policy made up by guys in New York or Los Angeles.*

Being a cop had made him something of a salesman over all these years. He sold a product he believed in and he would pose in any way required to obtain the information he needed for a case. Any cop who couldn't act the role of cowboy, best friend, hick farmer, or priest was doomed to a career stuck in a radio patrol vehicle.

At Patty's Dresses, he met Valene, young at 70, if she was a day. She was Southern, a Texas transplant, who preached him the Lord until his smile muscles were weak. Hadn't Jesus told his followers to enter into their closet when they prayed? And didn't that imply a certain closed-mouthedness in regard to a person's religious life? Not to Valene.

After she finally got around to printing out a list of vendors, she then explained, "But we do a lot of pickups from the Muskogee Mall ourselves, of course, and sometimes have our dresses for both stories delivered there. I used to have my own dress shop, you see, but I got out of the business 20 years ago." And she started to tell him the story of her financial and marital life.

"But let me ask you, Valene," he stuck in anyplace, because she didn't seem to need to take a breath in between sentences. "Who would do the pickup and delivery from one store to the other?" This was a prospect he hadn't accounted for.

"Oh, one of the girls, or our stock boy."

"Who's the stock boy?

"Well, let me see, I think his name is Manard. That's his first name."

"And might he have made a pick up or delivery between the malls, say yesterday?" Clement wasn't sure what he was getting at here, but something about the possibility certainly piqued his interest.

"Well, no, maybe not yesterday. I think he was out. Anyway, of course all the stores that have a branch in the other mall do it. It's not just us." What had seemed so promising a minute before was now collapsing. He'd have to start knocking on all the northwest Oklahoma doors, after all.

Good heavens, had she just batted her eyelashes at him? He worked his smile muscles yet one more time.

"Well, tell me, Valene, how would a stock clerk travel between this mall and the other one? His own car? Some other way?"

"Patty has a delivery car," said Valene, "with a cute Patty's logo." Clement nodded in response, but couldn't make any sense of the answer in terms of the case.

He had to think of a better way to track down this pervert— and soon. Because every minute they were out here asking nonsense questions, and getting answers that didn't ring a single bell, was a minute longer some poor girl was suffering and on the road to a premature death.

CHAPTER 26

The two men met in the food court and settled at a table with their cold drinks. Today was a weekday, though the next day would be the Fourth of July holiday, and the mall was much quieter than usual.

Clement shook his head. "Nothing brilliant comes to mind," he told Woodruf.

"You go home," replied Woodruf, as if it were an order. "I'm going to pick up the husband and bring him down to the station for an interview. We've assumed the wife was abducted by the rapist, but we don't know that. Could be a spousal murder, after all."

"Yeah, would be oddly comforting, God forbid," agreed Clement. He'd made so many stupid suppositions of late, he couldn't dispute the fact that this could be another one.

They talked a little more, pretty much about nothing, and Clement told Woodruf about the fire of the night before. "If I'd done what I'd set out to do and plowed down the field next door, I would have just gone back to sleep with the fire in the distance, or watched it from my front porch." He searched for an analogy to the present case, but couldn't imagine how they might have prevented the kidnapping—if such it was. "Maybe if we'd gone to the papers to warn women," he suggested.

Woodruf shook his head in rebuttal. "Then he would have

taken a female mall employee. Or gone elsewhere for his predation. The only way to stop him is to catch him."

"Then let's catch him," suggested Clement. He smiled. Then he stood, cold drink in hand, more or less sketched out a goodbye to Woodruf, and dragged himself off. Out in the parking lot, he studied the terrain, trying for a fresh idea on how the girl might have been taken. But nothing, nothing, nothing came to mind.

He was wiped out, down to his shoes, yet he wasn't going home. He wanted to visit with Grant Simpson, Tolliver's other partner, the guy his dad had thought quite hinky. Clement wasn't sure what to expect, but with a "to do" list a mile long, he might as well cram in the interview. Doing a little more than he should or he could was his trademark, and he wasn't finished being a cop until he was ground to below the nub or until Munson said "get out."

Madge had given him Simpson's phone number and his address out in the Wheaton section, a part of town, like that of Danvers, with older homes. Simpson received a very small pension from the P.D. each month since he hadn't worked for the department long, but long enough to qualify for a minimal payout.

No one had answered the phone and no machine had clicked on, so Clement thought of turning around and just going home and crawling into bed. He kept driving, however, and intermittently dialing the number. When he found the house, he parked, got out, and rang the doorbell. No answer. He went back to the car and sat there, waiting. He must have fallen asleep, because the next thing he knew someone was tapping on the window. He rolled it down and shut off his air conditioning.

"I see you have a Holder Police Department decal on the windshield. Can I help you?"

The guy was older than Clement, of course, but not old, and

seemed in pretty good shape.

"Grant Simpson?" Clement asked.

The man didn't answer—just invited Clement to come inside the house, where an overweight dog of indeterminate breed staggered to his feet to see if Clement was likely to produce any treats. Clement was sure the dog must detect eau de Buddy on him. In fact, to the dog, Clement must reek of the former stray.

Simpson showed the SPO to a seat in the kitchen, put ice in two glasses, poured himself a scotch, and seemed puzzled when Clement set a hand over his own glass. Clement got up and ran some tap water into the tumbler and swirled it until he thought the temperature was fit for drinking. Meanwhile, Simpson's drink had disappeared and he poured himself another one.

"We finally found where the bodies are buried," said Clement. "Out by Old Stable Road on S-13, around the bend they call Fisherman's Hook."

"That's right," said Simpson. "Jesus Christ, it took you 20 years. What the hell's the matter with you guys?"

"We're only cops. We're not psychics," Clement told him. He drank some more water, trying to appear relaxed, as if this were an ordinary conversation. He suddenly felt wide awake and as excited as if he'd won the hundred-million-dollar Oklahoma lottery. "Maybe you can fill me in on the events." He tried to slow his breathing and not show his eagerness to hear the ex-cop's story.

"I waited 20 years for you idiots to come." Simpson downed the second drink without hesitation.

Clement wasn't going to walk out or leave this guy alone and let him blow his brains out. That was what he had to be most careful of right now if Simpson, the killer of more than half-a-dozen children, had finally been caught.

"I need for you to come down to headquarters with me," Clement said with as firm a tone as he could muster. He wanted to seem as if he'd intended this next step all along.

I've solved the case, he shouted inside himself. *I've solved the case.* And the solution was truly inadvertent, so not really a credit to Clement at all. And when you came right down to it, his dad had been the one who'd actually solved it.

"I suppose you do," observed Simpson. He poured himself another shot. "Wait a minute, until I finish this."

Clement wasn't going to let the man change his clothes or go to the bathroom, that was for sure, and he frisked Simpson inside the house, before taking the suspect out to the car, but the SPO didn't handcuff him.

So at ten after six, Clement and Simpson strolled into headquarters. A couple of guys said hi to Simpson as if he belonged here, because of course he had once, and they sort of remembered the face as being that of a peer. Simpson didn't seem the slightest bit drunk, either, after three what must have been doubles. Practice, practice, practice.

Clement brought the suspect up to the second floor interview rooms and gave his own gun over to Strum, the black sergeant in charge of the night watch. Strum monitored the rooms from his desk and taped the interviews from there.

Inside the interview rooms, the chairs were bolted to the floor, as was the table. A lot of police departments would never do that, because cops often liked to use the chair and table arrangement as a part of their interrogation strategy. But after an incident two years before in which a suspect had overpowered an officer using a chair and had then taken the cop's gun and used it to kill him, this set of precautions was the standard here.

"Can you buzz us into two?" Clement asked Strum. He liked interview room two because he had gotten a couple of confessions in there.

"SPO Woodruf's in two with the husband...of the woman." Strum let the sentence trail off, not sloppily because Strum was never anything but crisp, but, as Clement immediately understood, with a view to giving out the information discreetly. And, indeed, that was appropriate behavior since Clement had a murder suspect with him, not a guy to say hi to, or gossip in front of.

Clement brought Simpson into room one. "I can get you a soda," he offered the former cop.

"If you can't get me a scotch, then I'd like a glass of water." Simpson at least had a sense of humor.

Clement walked out, ostensibly just to get the water, but also because he wanted to peek into Woodruf's interview. He felt torn between the two cases and sought to have his curiosity satisfied in regard to both.

He went into the observation room for two and sat down. The husband, in a white shirt with the first two buttons undone, looked as if he'd been crying. One glance at the red-rimmed eyes and Clement felt immediate sympathy.

To counter that all-too-human reaction, he tried to recall killers who'd been all broken up over their victims, and he could remember several, clearly. A couple of those were remorseful and confessed at once. A few, who he was certain were guilty and even had the physical evidence on, admitted to their grief but not their misdeeds and sometimes left Clement wondering if he should believe them or his own lying eyes. How many killers? Well, this wasn't L.A., but he'd met a few bad people over the years.

Clement turned on the sound.

"What did she say on the phone?" SPO Woodruf asked.

"I told you three times already. She said she was stopping to get takeout at Five Tribes. That it was too hot to cook."

"Which restaurant?"

"She didn't say."

"Did you have a favorite?"

"No. We hardly ever brought in food. We didn't like to spend the money."

"Money problems?"

"No more than anyone. What does that have to do with it?

"Nothing, really. I just ask these things. You never know."

"You never know what?"

"You never know what answers will matter. For instance, money problems might lead you to say something about someone who'd been bothering you for money...or anything like that."

"No. Nothing like that."

The husband began to cry again. "I know something's wrong," he said. "I know something happened to her. We had plans."

"What plans?"

Clement shut off the sound. The husband hadn't done it. Unless he, Clement, was being a sap. That reminded him of Holmes. Time was slipping away and her sentencing was coming up pretty soon. He had to finish what he'd started in regard to helping her, and he did have some calls in on that. Okay, maybe he was a softy about her situation, but he still felt the way that he felt.

He went out to the vending machines in the corridor and got change so he could buy a few bottles of water. Every police station he'd ever been in had vending machines.

The husband was always guilty; the wife was always right. Clement believed that generally, and most of the domestic murders he had seen were cases of the man killing the woman. Maybe the Holmes' situation was different than some, but in incidents where women killed their partners, almost always abuse of the woman lay at the heart of the unfortunate act. Once in a while, of course, money was the motive. The Holmes family had only been affluent in a middle class sense, however, which meant they were more in debt than holding assets free and clear. Christine Holmes hadn't killed her husband for the money.

Strum buzzed Clement back into interview one where he handed Simpson two bottles of water then opened one of the other bottles for himself. The room, though air conditioned, was rather warm. He was likely to fall asleep, but then, too, after three double scotches, so was Simpson. Clement pictured the two of them, each peacefully sleeping in his chair. Strum, technically Clement's superior, would be entitled to kick Clement's butt.

"Tell me about the boys buried by Fisherman's Hook," Clement invited. He was going to get a confession here. He was saving his job in the same week he had saved his house—with God's help. After this, maybe he could save the kidnap victim.

"What a disgusting mess," Simpson said. "I told that freak that I wasn't going to cover for him, and I didn't, but you aren't going to find what happened anywhere in the record, are you? I waited. I waited for you guys to come and ask me. I'd really like to know why it took you people so long."

"Hold on, hold on, let's go back a minute. Go back to the first murder, in fact. Start with that." Clement didn't have the vaguest idea what Simpson was referring to. His rambling diatribe had no particular handle for Clement to grasp. Clement shifted in his chair, but of course the chair didn't move.

"I don't know about the first murder." Simpson's glare accused Clement of stupidity.

"Yeah, I know," Clement agreed. "I mean the first you were aware of." He was trying to find his way in the dark here, trying to seem knowledgeable so Simpson wouldn't hesitate to tell all.

"He acted so weird that night, I had to follow him. I said good night, got into my car outside the old precinct house on Broken Arrow, you know? And then I waited."

Clement waited with him, now, silently. "Was it night?"

"Not when he went into the precinct, but when he came out. Then it was late evening—winter, so the sun was down. He drove the squad car out of the precinct lot, which in itself was strange. After all, we were only allowed to use those cars if we were on police business. The shift was over, so what kind of business did he have?"

"And the business was?"

"He came up by Fisherman's Hook and stopped. I'd been driving without my headlights and far behind him. I turned off the engine way down the road, off on the shoulder, but I was really afraid someone was going to come up from behind and clip me."

"I know what you mean," Clement acknowledged. He'd had exactly that feeling out there today.

"He carried a bundle out of the car and he seemed to know just where he was going." Simpson closed his eyes as if watching an old movie inside his head. "I didn't know what the hell he was doing and when he was down there, I drove away. I didn't want him to catch me spying."

"So how did you discover what he'd brought down the incline there?"

"I wish I had a drink," said Simpson. "I wish to hell I had a drink."

Clement nodded. He was so close to finding out the rest of the story, so eager that he could tear his hair out by the roots. He wanted to shake the man across the table from him and force him to speak. But Clement sat still.

"I went back the next day and saw the fresh dug ground and a couple of days later came back with a shovel. When I saw what he'd buried—a boy! A child! I reburied the body, thinking maybe there had been an accident and he was just scared. So I went and confronted him."

Simpson's eyes bulged out of their sockets and Clement gave him another water, a third, his own unopened one. He didn't want to leave the room and he hoped Simpson wasn't going to have a heart attack. That would be quite an ending to the story, wouldn't it?

"And he said?"

"Oh, he was sorry. He didn't mean to do any of it. He wasn't going to do it any more. So I realized then that he'd done more than one. More than one! And I said I wasn't going to cover for him, and that I was going to Chief Kenny with the story. Well, he begged me not to." Simpson opened the third water and drank it down as if it would get him high.

"Then you didn't go to Kenny?" Clement asked.

"I went to Kenny. I told him what I'd seen and Kenny said he'd take care of it. But nothing happened. I couldn't work with Tolliver any more and I was disgusted by the entire department. You don't happen to be related to Sam Clement, do you?"

"Sam Clement?" Clement shook his head in a negative response. "He was working here when I got here and I knew him though—a distant cousin. Then Munson took over and Sam left." No, he didn't know his father, didn't know him at all. "Was Sam Clement one of those involved in the murders?" Murders? Racial murders? Clement's father?

"I don't know anything about all that," Simpson said. "The only one I saw was Tolliver, and that's all I know about."

"Another question, Mr. Simpson. What exactly did you tell Tolliver you knew?"

"I told him I'd seen the body in the trunk, that was all. Because I was afraid if I told him I knew where he'd buried it, that he'd move it."

Clement had been wondering exactly that. Why hadn't Tolliver moved the bodies? That Tolliver didn't realize how much Simpson knew could be one possible answer. The other possible answer was that Simpson had buried the bodies there, himself.

But Simpson had said "it" after having been to the burial site. He'd only said "it." He only had one body in mind, as that was all he'd seen at the time. Which meant that the others came later on, after Simpson's threat to go to Kenny and after Tolliver allegedly had told Simpson he was going to quit.

First Tolliver had killed the Parker brothers and he'd laid them to rest in Holder Park. The next boy he'd buried up at Fisherman's Hook and Simpson had seen him. Then later, Tolliver had used the spot for more.

"Weren't you scared of Tolliver? Afraid that he'd come after you?" Clement wondered.

"Pretty much," said Simpson. "One reason why I left the department. One reason why I started to drink." He shook the empty plastic bottles one by one in the way he must shake the empty liquor bottles at home. "I waited for you 20 years ago. Why didn't you come then."

"Yeah," Clement told him. "I wish I had."

Chapter 27

Clement walked out of the interview room shaken. His sense of honor and justice had been pulled from its socket. He pointed Simpson toward the men's room, still very much aware that Simpson could be lying in order to hide his own crimes. But who could prove the truth, one way or the other? Reports were missing. Kenny's brain, if he'd ever had one, was erased. Tolliver was some sort of a monster—or he wasn't.

But the bottom line was that boys were dead, and this week or next or the week after—depending on when they found the abominable who was capturing women, or gave up for the moment—Clement would have to return to California and reinterview Tolliver, no matter how morally, emotionally, and physically exhausted the SPO was. He'd brace himself and prepare for the mission tomorrow or thereafter. Right now he didn't have the wherewithal.

But a moment later, he remembered—he was getting near to the resolution. The arm of human law was going to reach out and take in a wrongdoer. Good people were about to say, "This won't be allowed."

Woodruf came out of his own interview, hollow eyed, ushering the distraught husband before him. "I thought you'd gone home," he said to Clement.

"They let us go home?" Clement asked.

* * *

After he'd driven Simpson back to the Wheaton section, he turned on the radio and slowly and carefully took himself home.

Bradley was out swinging on the swing set when Clement parked in his gravel drive. The smell of wildfire still hung in the air. Clement thought he had the 20-yard walk left in his legs, just about. He went over and sat on the swing next to hers. The fit was tighter for him than it was for her.

She stopped pumping her legs and little by little let the swing bring itself down to earth. She set her feet on the ground. "You look bad," she said.

He couldn't even make a joke out of that. "A lot going on. Since last night. Today."

"You guys have all the fun."

Clement gathered all the energy he could muster and smiled. "Lots of fun," he said. "You come the day after tomorrow and do DNA swabs with us. You'll have a good time."

She smiled, too and pushed off to swing again.

Though he didn't want to, Clement stood up. The house seemed awfully far away. Who knew when he'd put the swings out here how far away from the house they were. Who knew how heavy the porch screen door was, or the front door to the house. He crept in.

Shelly was in the living room, watching the picture on TV with the sound muted. She sat in his chair and he signaled her to stay. He wanted to lie down on that stupid green couch, which he did. "No sound?" he asked.

"I don't like to hear things," she said. "Everything I hear scares me. Everything."

"You need to see someone." He'd said that to her a couple of dozen times.

"Maybe I'll get some medication," she finally conceded.

He was pleased and just about drifting off. The couch wasn't quite long enough for him to nap on, but he didn't care.

"What are you going to do about Bradley?" Shelly asked, waking him slightly.

"She can come to the mall on the Fifth. We're swabbing for DNA," he answered. His muscles began to relax just a little.

"I mean about the fact that she's in love with you."

Clement didn't quite understand the statement, or was it a question? He must be dreaming...someone in love with him? Not very likely.

Wednesday morning, the Holder P.D. hit the mall, and not to shop except for male DNA. Seven of them took up residence in the mall management office, and employees willing to donate a bit of saliva lined up. Clement knew that likely wouldn't include the killer, and asked managers to report who didn't volunteer. Of course, the rapist/murderer could be a manager, too.

"Needle in a haystack," Woodruf muttered. He wasn't complaining—just stating a fact.

With a woman currently missing and presumed still alive, action was preferable to inaction, of course.

Shelly had come along to watch. She'd wanted to and Clement thought the idea a good one. She could see more males now than when they'd merely driven around the lot.

He knew very well they were unlikely to catch the perpetrator this way, but the crime was horrible, and the potential payoff, gold.

After a while, he saw that Shelly was increasingly restive. Maybe she didn't like being cooped up in a small room again—understandable. Maybe she didn't like being surrounded by so many men. That would no doubt be a given. He accompanied her out into the hall.

"Do you feel as if you can walk around a little with me?" he asked. He could always have Bradley take her home.

"I'm okay," she said, but she broke down trembling. He hadn't seen such a thing since he'd been a radio patrol officer and a bomb had gone off, and that was a long time ago.

Footsteps right behind them made Clement turn around. Only Woodruf coming to check on them. "Okay?" he asked Shelly directly.

She nodded as if she could no longer speak, and Clement led her ahead gently, while Woodruf fell back. A security guard for the mall walked toward them, maybe to help with the DNA, maybe to make his own sample available, or maybe thinking management was still in the office today. Clement, ever trying to be kind, smiled to let the guy know that he had nothing, really, against mere guards.

Then he noticed that Shelly had taken something heavy out of her purse. A gun. Clement's gun. Suddenly, with two hands she pulled it up, pointing at the security guard. And who the guard must be at once became obvious.

The guard—the rapist—though an obvious psychopath—wasn't stupid. He saw the gun, too, and knew what Shelly intended to do. He ducked and ran in a zigzag pattern, while Clement struggled to force down Shelly's hand. Then, as the security officer ran, Woodruf swung into motion, also at a young man's sprint.

Clement had the gun. His match with Shelly hadn't been too arduous. "My gun," he complained. He checked it to make sure it was...well, clean, at least. But he hadn't taught her how to clean a gun. Damn.

"I...I...I..." She began to cry and grabbed on to his arm.

"You're certain, right?" he asked. "He's our guy? You're sure?"

"I...saw...him...last...time," she gasped out between sobs. "I decided...to kill him. Kill him."

If only she'd told Clement then. If only they'd arrested the bastard at that time. Gretchen Paulson wouldn't be missing. But Clement would never tell Shelly that. Never of his own accord.

* * *

He expected Woodruf had arrested the perp by now, and anticipated a "got him" call on his radio any second, but when he heard the crackle, that wasn't the message. The perp had taken off in his car and Woodruf had found his own car and taken off after the doer, having to search, though with the help of a patrol car in the vicinity.

"We need a helicopter," Clement muttered. Officers and technology, an efficient lab—how could they maintain the thin blue line protecting public safety without these things?

He called Munson on his cell in case the chief wasn't in touch with dispatch, but Munson was already on his way—in the armored van.

One interesting if uninspiring fact about Munson was that he tended to have a penchant for military toys. He'd gotten a bunch of M-16s from the U.S. Department of Defense's Defense Logistics Agency for five dollars each to equip the nonexistent Holder SWAT team. The DoD armored van was certainly slated to be used, once a Holder P.D. driver had been trained. Now Munson was himself driving the van to the scene. Not to where the rapist killer was on the highway, but to the place from which the man had fled.

You can't hit a home run every time.

Bradley came out. Clement wanted to give her Shelly to look out for, then drive off into his car to find the perp, but he was the responsible officer with underlings right here. "Tell the guys to discontinue the swabbing," Clement said, "then you come back here."

Shelly had stopped crying and looked weary, so he brought her over to a stone bench next to a sturdy plastic palm. He was old, but not so old that he wanted to sit here while another man was out on the chase.

Bradley emerged again, and through the glass wall Clement could see Munson drive into the parking lot in the armored van. Clement was up and out the door of the mall and didn't look back. Munson stopped the vehicle—just about the same type as vans that carried cash to and from banks—and stepped out. "Now then," he began.

"I'll drive the van," Clement said.

"I'll drive," shouted Bradley from behind. "I know how."

"Chief..." Clement made his tone sound strict but fair. "Look after Shelly. She's our witness." He started to get in the driver's seat, but Bradley aggressively pushed him aside and he decided if she knew how to operate the thing, he ought to let her. He trotted around to the passenger door and jumped in a half-second before Bradley tore off onto the road in front of the mall.

They drove and listened to the radio conversation between Woodruf and the patrol car driver, and Bradley began to take the van out to the highway where the other cars were apparently headed.

"How'd you learn how to drive this thing?" Clement finally asked her.

"I saw it done in an L.A. car chase," she said.

"Huh?"

"I saw an L.A. car chase on TV," she repeated.

"You're crazy," he told her. "God help us all. Please don't kill us."

"I know exactly how to do this thing."

Just about idiotically, he believed her.

Woodruf described the blue 1999 Chevy that the subject was driving and read the license plate off to them so there would be no mistake. Luckily, the car chase was at a fairly low speed, probably because the Chevy seemed to be overheated, and the van was able to make progress to where the three ahead were.

Patrol cars on either end of this stretch of road had evidently been able to stop most of the traffic flow because the highway was fairly if not completely empty.

"There they are," pointed out Clement. He sat up and angled forward to get a better view.

"Sit back," Bradley ordered. She called over the radio that the two cops giving chase were to pull over and let the armored van through.

"I think you ought to—"

"Shut up," she said.

Yeah. She was in the driver's seat. Clement shut up. He listened to Woodruf on his PA system warning the driver to pull over, and the patrol car advising other traffic on the road to get out of the way.

Bradley moved up quickly behind the subject's car. Clement, who wanted to have a good look at the perp, could hardly wait until they had the guy in cuffs. Truth to tell, Clement wanted to annihilate the guy, but he most certainly wouldn't. This was one trial he was going to enjoy.

Bradley tapped the Chevy on the right rear with their armored car. Then she fell back. Clement thought it was a no go, she hadn't bumped him hard enough, but then the Chevy skidded into a turn, to face the van.

"Exactly," Bradley cried in triumph as she stopped their vehicle. And Clement and Bradley both pulled their guns, opened their doors, and crouched behind them. The man sat in his car—maybe making up his mind. His options were limited. He couldn't turn his car around—they'd just knock his car again—and he couldn't rush them because they were the 800-pound gorilla and he was the chimp. Or ultimately the chump. Clement saw the rapist had some kind of a pistol though and tensed. Suicide by police was all too common.

"Throw down the gun," Clement yelled. "Put your hands up and come out."

The man opened his door and Clement thought the monster might be about to do as he was told—but men like this one had to be in charge, no matter what the cost to others or themselves. This time, in thumbing his nose at the rest of the world, this particular idiot was the one who paid the highest price.

The subject put a gun to his head and pulled the trigger.

After the blast, came a moment of dead silence and general shock.

Woodruf, who had parked behind, came forward then. When he reached the corpse, he kicked away the gun. Good training, certainly, but with the guy's brains splattered all over the highway, the subject was highly unlikely to pick the gun back up.

CHAPTER 28

Although they'd found the rapist/murderer and he'd so conveniently killed himself, the complex aftermath remained. Clement had on latex gloves and was in the deceased's pockets within seconds—never mind the gore. Following the trail of all the perpetrator's crimes wouldn't be simple obviously, but for now the objective was to find the still-missing woman. And to pray that she remained alive. Clement thought of her despair and the fact that she might be locked in a small room with a still-unburied Karin. The circumstances would be enough to drive anyone mad.

The driver's license read "John Stevens" and the address was on Pioneer Road. "We're going," Clement told Woodruf. He beckoned Bradley to the van. "I'm driving now," he said.

Once he'd started the engine he then thought to add, "You did good." He gave her a thumbs up and sped off. "We go in without a warrant under 'exigent circumstances.' Any judge would agree this is an emergency."

"The circumstances seem pretty exigent to me." She wiped the sweat out of her eyebrows. "I really am a good driver, aren't I?"

"Yeah."

"So why aren't I driving?"

He puzzled that one out as he exceeded the speed limit. "Male chauvinism," he answered eventually.

"Aha. Oh well. Only to be expected, I guess."

"Yeah."

"He saved the state some serious money by killing himself," Bradley said.

"You do the crime, you should be willing to do the time. But noooo. He didn't want to pay for it."

She shook her head. "He paid with his life."

"He didn't believe he was paying when he pulled the trigger on himself, because he didn't know the value of life," answered Clement. "He only knew that he wasn't going to let himself be taken in the same way he took his vics." He concentrated on his driving, then spoke again. "Death was an act of one-upmanship for him, not payment for his crimes. He got off on the cheap." Oh, yeah, Clement believed something or someone probably damaged Stevens early on, but that didn't matter. Wrong was wrong.

Then he thought of Christine Holmes. But that was different. She'd killed a man who wasn't innocent. Well, not innocent according to Clement—although the court and the law so far hadn't seen the case the same as Clement had.

He hunched forward over the wheel of the van and accelerated. The image of a young woman trapped in a small stifling room with a corpse spurred him on. She was dehydrating in the heat and very, very fearful.

They parked outside of 11 Pioneer Road and rang the bell. The guy who had lived here was dead, of course, and no one else seemed about to answer. Clement drew his gun, nonetheless. How did they know Stevens hadn't had an accomplice? They didn't know, and Clement would hate for the two of them to be killed out of mere stupidity.

Bradley drew her gun, echoing his action. "Just stay here," he said. "I'll go in the back and open the front door for you.

He went around the house to an unkempt yard that hadn't

been mowed so far this summer. Why would someone leave a yard this way in the fire season, anyway? To keep people out?

He tried to peer into the back entry, but the windows were too grimy and the interior too dark to see anything. He knocked firmly, waited, then got out his utility knife and cut the screen. After that, he tapped out a pane in the door near the knob with the butt of his gun. In a second, he was in. *Let this be a lesson to you homeowners who think you're safe because your door is locked,* he thought. Inside, the house was a garbage pit and smelled, but not of death. The odor was of dirty dishes in the sink and maybe even vermin.

Carefully, Clement made his way through a sea of newspapers and trash to the front, where he let in Bradley so they could execute a standard search. Nothing but rubbish, old furniture, soiled sheets, and an electric clock reminding Clement that a woman was waiting to be saved. The basement held a rusting furnace, pipes, and more broken old furniture. A scuffling sound set his heart to pumping. Maybe...But no. A mouse scurrying across the floor on urgent business didn't even glance his way.

Clement wanted to find Gretchen alive. He wanted her to live and to heal. He tucked his gun back into its holster and climbed the stairs.

"Hey, house, he's not coming home," Clement told the peeling walls. He walked into the kitchen again, Bradley on his heels, and opened the refrigerator. A bottle of soy sauce and a jar half-filled with mustard sat inside on a rusting shelf. Even the empty refrigerator smelled bad. Clement saw no sign that Stevens had eaten here lately or had cooked anything for his latest captive.

"Where is she?" asked Bradley.

Let her be alive, let her be alive. "Here's what we have to do," he said. "We have to search every square inch of this rathole and see if we can find a dug-out space separate from the basement below or a room built into the walls. That's first.

Then we've got to talk to the neighbors and see how much he's been around here lately. Finally, we have to see if any papers or mail might reveal where else he might have hidden her."

He looked around them with revulsion and called headquarters to get a couple of warm bodies in to help. Then he called Woodruf, who was still processing the scene and would come when he was free.

"No one could have lived here. This is disgusting," said Bradley as they began to work their way through the living room.

"Some people live this way. Just wait until you're on the job a while longer—you'll see. Mostly they have a mental illness and collect—newspapers, items from dumpsters, dogs and cats."

"Women."

"Yeah, women, too, in this case." Again, Clement had on latex gloves as protection from the filth, and pressed, probed, and knocked at the walls, progressing through the room with the precision and familiarity of a surgeon examining a candidate for his kind of treatment.

The idea of a hidden room was, sadly, not at all far-fetched. A special place in which to torture and/or rape wasn't limited to grotesque fiction.

In the end, however, after about an hour of this exercise, they gave up on her being held anywhere here. Clement felt frustrated, worried, desperate to find her. *If only, if only, if only.*

Right after that, two patrol officers finally showed up and Clement had them put on their latex gloves and set them to gathering all handwritten or printed documents—but no newspapers unless those had pen or pencil markings or were folded so as to indicate special interest in a topic.

Clement and Bradley separated and went out to ring doorbells. *Let her still be alive, Lord, if you will.*

"Can I help you?"

Clement had gotten some of his best tips from the elderly, and this woman was maybe a thousand years old.

"Ma'am. I'm Senior Police Officer Clement." He showed her his badge and she actually came closer so she could look. Annoying, sure, but he liked that kind of attention to detail in a witness.

"Do you know your neighbor, John Stevens, ma'am?"

She shifted on her feet. He could tell she wasn't going to be able to stand very long. "No one to know. John Stevens is dead."

Clement was struck dumb. How could she have found that out already? How much had gone out to the media this soon? Yeah, police scanners and reporters. "Can we sit at your kitchen table and talk, ma'am."

"I've seen your badge, but that doesn't mean I'm going to let you in."

"Of course not, ma'am. Very sensible. What can you tell me about John Stevens?"

"He and his wife, Hilda, died three years ago. Since then a cousin or something has been living in the house. Haven't seen him lately. He needs to clear the yard. I think he has rats there and we certainly don't want them in our house. Can you give him a violation?"

"Ma'am? The youngish security guard is a cousin?" Clement was startled, to say the least. He looked at his watch. How time could fly when you were looking for an innocent woman in mortal danger.

"I suppose so. Or a nephew." She shifted her stance again, which told him she wasn't going to tolerate many more questions.

"When's the last time you saw him, ma'am?"

"He drove a pretty nice red Honda up to the house one day a few weeks ago. Must have just bought it. A friend of his came by and the two of them drove off."

"The friend, ma'am? Had you seen him before?" An accomplice? An actual friend, as if this swine could possibly have a real human connection? An acquaintance?

"No, I don't recall…"

She shook her head and he could tell she was going to shut the door. He moved back so she wouldn't catch one of his body parts in the process. "Thank you, ma'am."

Okay, okay, okay, what did it mean? John Stevens—the one who'd just killed himself—wasn't John Stevens, or was a different John Stevens, or…What the hell? The car? Karin's, probably. Had he sold it to a stolen-car dealer? That was a possible lead.

How long would all of this take to investigate? Too long. Gretchen was dehydrating. Her heart was beating hard. Did she have any pre-existing medical conditions? He felt as if he himself were waiting in the terrifying dark, waiting for the police to come.

He looked around to see if he could find Bradley, then called her on his cell. "Got anything? Okay, well, meet me at the house."

On the way there, Clement checked the mail box in front, which was empty. Everyone in America got mail, surely. Even the dead.

Back at the subject's house, or the house the man had been squatting in, the officers were wading through the trash that covered the floor and smoothing out any crumpled papers that might count.

Clement picked up what they had and flipped through it. Anything dated was from prior to the end of April. Nothing pertained to the rental of another property.

Bradley came in. "We're going now," Clement said. "We have to hurry. Carry on, gentlemen. SPO Woodruf or I will get back to you." Someone had to process the house, and, moreover, he'd left the back entrance exposed so anyone might walk in. Liability, sure, although which of the dead John Stevenses would sue?

"I'm driving," Bradley insisted. She snatched the keys.

"We're going to the branch post office on Coyote," he told her then. No use arguing with a woman, was there?

She drove fast enough so that he was satisfied and she didn't bother to use the siren, either. Good. Although people were used to nutcases driving all over the road, sirens confused them and often caused accidents.

He got out at the post office while she parked. They were just about in time since, stupidly, the place closed at four. How were working people supposed to conduct their business during such hours?

Clement hurried to the head of the line, pushed in front of someone at the window, showed his badge, and demanded to see the postmaster immediately. The clerk was frightened, the customer respectful, and those still in line who probably hadn't seen his badge—or maybe they had—muttered against his going out of turn.

In a minute the door to the back of the post office opened and a balding man with a fringe of overly long hair brushed oddly forward came out. Clement showed his badge yet again, and explained his business concisely. He expected delays and a lot of bureaucratic mumbo jumbo, but to his surprise, the postmaster immediately led Clement into the heart of the back office and to a desk with a computer.

He looked up the address with Clement hanging over him. "Yeah, I see. It's being forwarded permanently." Without fuss he wrote down the new address for Clement.

That was the fastest Clement had ever been in and out of a post office without exception. He'd have to use his badge more often.

Bradley was just coming inside to meet him and he put his hands on her shoulders and turned her around. "God willing we'll find Gretchen now, and we'll find her alive." But in his heart of hearts, he wondered. Though he prayed, he knew full well that not everything a human being might ardently want would be exactly what he got.

Chapter 29

The trick was finding an address in a rural area neither of them knew. Dispatch had a map and tried to guide them, but on the ground, streets without street signs could deceive. Of course Clement recognized this wasn't far from the area where he'd picked up Shelly, so he believed they must be on the right trail.

Finally, they stopped at a farmhouse and asked direction. "I think that's the old Cooper place," said the woman, peering at them in puzzlement and mistrust. "No one has lived out there since old man Cooper died probably 10 years ago. I doubt anyone's out there now."

Bradley assured her that was where they wanted to go and the woman detailed the way, citing landmarks probably known only to the local residents. Clement took notes. So what their dead perpetrator had done was to somehow locate abandoned property and move in. That struck Clement as being even more nervy and devious than kidnapping, rape, and murder, which were felonies so extreme that only the criminally insane could even contemplate them. Still, fewer psychopaths or sociopaths would have the cold steel bravado to take over a residence they didn't own.

Once they'd found the desolate place and got out of the van, Clement unholstered his gun once again. Even if he hadn't heard the story of the car and a second male, he would have, not knowing who might be living here alongside the suddenly no-name doer.

The house ahead needed a paint job to check its obvious deterioration, and the porch, which had fallen to the level of the crawlspace, would have to be pulled off and replaced, along with the roof. Golden brown weeds grown more than a foot would bring what was left of the home down should a single spark ignite them.

Bradley, also taking her gun in hand, followed Clement's lead. For a second time today, they entered a residence and cleared the rooms one by one. Clement checked each closet for the kidnap victim. *Oh, Lord, no, where is the girl? Help us find her.*

Just like the other house, this one, too, had been used as a giant garbage can. But here, the kitchen seemed to have been employed for some kind of meals. Shelly had told Clement she'd been fed cold hot dogs and cereal and that's what he found in the refrigerator—two packages of the meat and a large box of oatmeal. Was that what the monster had eaten, too, the reason why he thought such odd fare sufficient nourishment for his captives? Or was it just enough to let them live without a thought for long-term nutrition, since their chances of ultimate survival were zilch.

Then back of the house, only a few yards from the door, they made a find.

They smelled it first, an unmistakable and dreadful smell, and came up upon a rat gnawing on its evening feast—a corpse. Clement stomped his foot and forced the rodent to retreat. *Which girl?* he wondered. Gretchen, already? But the body, when they turned the cadaver face up, was obviously long dead, so rank that even the killer had proclaimed it foul and turned it out of the house. "Karin," Clement said.

They left her where she lay, and he called dispatch for a crime scene unit and a coroner's truck although he knew the Holder crime scene unit, such as it was, must be still processing the first scene on the other side of town. The coroner tech—probably little Alice Drummond on this shift—would find herself waiting a while for the CSU to finish before she could retrieve Karin's body. That was, unless she, too, would be late since she also had the other corpse to handle first. They were big-city busy in Holder on this day.

"Where on this earth is Gretchen?" Clement agonized.

They continued to walk the perimeter. Then Bradley tripped and nearly fell, but caught herself. "Something here," she called out.

Another body? He hurried to her. They got down on their knees and felt gingerly with latex covered hands. "Yeah, something," he agreed—a grill of some type. He began to pull the weeds out of the dirt around whatever Bradley had literally stumbled on. The ground cover came up in a clump as if torn out previously and then simply shifted back over the spot.

"It's one of those precast tornado shelters," Clement exclaimed in sudden realization. He pulled at the entryway to the underground unit. Locked! Of course.

"Here, I found a ventilation pipe," Bradley told him. She cleared around it so he could get a look.

"Gretchen?" he shouted into the pipe. "It's Officer Bradley and Officer Clement. Don't worry, honey. We're going to get you out. Can you hear me, honey? Are you down there?"

The "yes" that came up was very tentative and weak, but Clement was so relieved to hear it that he felt overcome with a rush of joy. He met Bradley's glance and saw the same strong emotion in her own face.

"Talk to her," he told Bradley. "I'm going to see if there's anything in the van that will help us open this thing." The van was intended to double as an emergency services vehicle and might well have extraction cutters—the so-called "jaws of life" routinely used to extricate people trapped in cars.

He thought he was heading toward the van but something drew him past Karin's corpse and back into the house. Maybe what led him was his stubbornness and a half-formed thought that even if the fake John Stevens had the key to the shelter in his pocket when he killed himself, he might have had a second copy here. Surely he wouldn't take the chance of losing his key and being unable to reach his plaything.

Okay, Clement was crazy, stupid, and the key wasn't where he'd hoped it was. He walked through the house to take the front exit. And hanging on a hook inside the door, he found a brass key beginning to dull from oxidation and scratched with use. Why not? he thought. Worth a try. He trotted back across the path he'd created through the house and went out the rear, where he was hit again by the rank odor of death. Corpse was a smell that stayed in your nostrils for days afterward, but he was glad the family would at least be able to bury her.

When Clement returned to where Bradley sat sending a flow of reassuring words into the pipe, he tried the key in the lock and nearly shouted for joy when it fit. But he didn't want to scare the victim.

"I'm opening the door," he told her, "and I'll get you out."

He pulled back the steel lid and he and Bradley stared down at the girl whose eyes were too round for her thin and frightened face. She made no move to come up the steps, so he went down, taking off his shirt as he descended, so she might clothe her naked body.

"The man who took you is dead," he told the girl.

Relief and satisfaction welled up in him, a feeling that he had overcome not death, but evil. Nothing can give a man more pleasure than the sense of banishing the wickedness of the world, at least on a momentary basis.

When they got her into Holder Medical Center, the nurse who had been on duty when he brought Shelly in took out another rape kit. He was going to tell her not to bother, but something about that didn't sit right and he just nodded. Having the rape kit done was like taking out his gun when he entered an empty house. The one time he allowed himself to skip a procedure would be the time he'd be caught short. Might as well prove the dead man to be the perp and give them all closure.

He and Bradley drove the armored van back to headquarters.

"Where's my car?" he exclaimed, not seeing it in its usual spot. Someone had stolen a cop's car in the P.D. lot? Then he remembered his car was parked out at the mall.

They went inside. He had to admit that he was tired. He'd had a day off; he knew he'd had. But that seemed like a long, long time before. Yeah, yesterday had been forever ago.

He led Bradley to the administrative wing, and she hesitated. "I can wait for you in your office," she said. He beckoned her on to Munson's door, open now because the workday of the ordinary world was over, and the chief's secretary was gone, though the chief still had the burden of horrendous crime and the bodies of the dead to deal with.

Clement led Bradley into the inner office of the chief and when Munson looked up, Clement took his seat. Bradley stood awkwardly until Munson pointed her to the second visitor's chair.

The SPO wiped the sweat off his face and relaxed in the air conditioning as he caught Munson up on any details the chief might not have had relayed to him.

Then Clement realized. He looked around. "Where's Shelly?" he wondered. Hadn't he asked the chief to take care of the girl?

"I took her to her friend's," Munson assured him.

Clement felt perplexed by that. "To my son's?"

"Yes, David's."

"David? Who's that?"

He and Munson looked at one another in confusion.

"Oh," said Bradley, "Karin's husband."

Ah, certainly Shelly would think of him from the first. The realization would have come to Clement and to Woodruf in a few hours time, but she, of course, would think of David from the moment she'd decided to shoot Karin's killer.

Clement would pick her up once he got his car and tell David that they'd found his wife's body. And he and Woodruf would have to talk soon. About Shelly, about forgetting her little misstep with the gun. Because what would be the sense in charging the girl with any crime? No jury in the world would convict her even of a misdemeanor.

"The paperwork will have to wait until tomorrow," Clement told Munson. "I'm fried. Come on, Bradley. You can drive me to the mall."

Buddy, having been alone all day, was no doubt miffed when his adopted family finally came through the door. He barked to let them all know just what he thought of such a desertion. He explained, Clement supposed, where their real obligations lay. Clement hustled to set out the dog's dinner. He was a lousy human pal, apparently.

Just as he was emptying the can into Buddy's dish, Clement's cell phone rang. Oh, Rich. "Hi," said Clement. "I haven't forgotten. I'm working on it."

"Forget about it then," Rich told him. "We'll do it on appeal, on the grounds that her lawyer was incompetent and that she was abused and that wasn't brought in. Well get her a hearing on that basis and a lesser sentence."

"No, no," Clement disagreed. "I'm working on it. I'll have something soon." In the meantime, he had a long-cold case to finally clear up. He was, after all, Holder's cold case detective. Yeah, that was it. He'd just about forgotten that one. He'd been working on something entirely different than a present day murder and multiple rapes.

CHAPTER 30

Clement had actually put on his suit to talk to Enkan, the head of homicide prosecutions for the D.A.'s office. No one in law enforcement was wearing a suit this summer, so Clement did it as a kind of joke on himself—and only tangentially on her. He wanted to appear humbled by the magnificence of her office and to seem apologetic for any past recalcitrance, especially in preparation for the Holmes' case. She didn't need to know that he was now hard at work in opposition to her office on Christine Holmes' behalf, and that soon he hoped to cause the D.A. some acute discomfort in the sentencing phase.

Not even sitting, he presented Enkan with a signed statement by Simpson of his observation of Tolliver's actions and of finding the corpse of a child—that he had reported this to Chief Kenny and that nothing had subsequently been done by the chief. Clement had the transcript of the tape, but didn't offer it to her in accord with his belief that the more you tell people, the more confused they become. All he wanted from her was an extradition request. As Tolliver—hopefully—had committed no homicides on California soil, the state should happily send the old man back to Oklahoma.

"And where is Chief Kenny in all this?" Enkan wanted to know. "What does he say?"

"He's in a nursing home with advanced dementia, ma'am."

Had he ever called her "ma'am" before this moment?

"Well, then, easy to make an accusation against him," she concluded.

He didn't reply. She'd be a fool not to ask for Tolliver's extradition.

"There might be no merit in this at all," she added.

"We have the bones of seven boys," Clement answered. Then, because she was getting on his last nerve, he added a warning. "I'd hate for Holder to be sued for civil rights violations in the case. My fear is that the feds will get wind of it, you know. Things could get very public and very ugly."

Without another word, Enkan's signature went on the extradition request.

As soon as all this was settled then and the killer brought to stand before a jury of his peers, Clement would retrieve the envelope he'd mailed so many weeks ago to his FBI contact, Special Agent Carrie Roberts.

Maybe he'd retire to San Diego, himself, Clement mused as he walked in the pleasant breeze of that city's downtown. But he knew he really never would. His life was in Holder, though that life was rather routine, small-town, and dull. But maybe that was all he needed for himself: his church, his house, his son, his dog, his job for a few more years.

Okay, here was the building that held the California Department of Justice, San Diego County office. He'd already spoken on the phone to the attorney, Elizabeth Cohen, who handled interstate requests. He waited in the bustling cool of the wood-toned waiting room until Cohen came out. Hmmm, she seemed a bit in manner like Enkan—brusque and with a probing eye, though rather pretty and probably no older than Bradley was. The cranky attitude must be the standard to the position of litigator employed in a government post.

In her office, Cohen went over the papers and took out an

official stamp, marking both copies he'd handed her and then signing them. She kept one. "You give this to the county sheriff and someone there will help you execute it," she said. She kept pulling a strand of frizzy brown hair out of her face and appeared rather bored by what must be a repetitive business here—someone from another state come to haul away a serial killer.

He didn't have the power to arrest a man in California, so his next stop was the county sheriff's office. They, like attorney Cohen, seemed to find the taking in of a serial killer rather humdrum.

"Dangerous?" asked the patrol officer assigned to help Clement.

"I had breakfast with him a couple of weeks ago. He didn't seem overly dangerous then, but you never know what a cornered animal will do." Clement got in the front seat of the vehicle. He recalled a time when riding in a car like this had seemed to be his entire life.

"What he do?" asked Officer Hudlin.

"Killed seven little boys."

Hudlin was black, but Clement didn't feel like going into which color the little boys were. Discussion of race, everyone's consciousness of color, tired Clement out. Jesus had never mentioned race. And yet, looking at the map and thinking of how men traveled and traded across various routes, a person could see that those from Africa of darker skin had swept up across the Holy Land on missions of commerce. Jesus was not oblivious that the world was made of people of different hues. Yet he'd never said a word on that subject, even by parable.

They arrived at Tolliver's. "Let me go in myself and speak to him first," Clement suggested.

"I'll go in with you and make the arrest," countered Hudlin. He was telling Clement what he would do. And in his place, Clement would surely make the same move. The word was "responsibility." The officer responsible did the job. Laxness could kill, and death, if it wasn't that officer's own, could mean termination of employment. Most of the time Clement liked the system pretty well, so he went along with it now.

The two stood at Tolliver's door and Clement rang the bell. Tolliver's wife answered and Clement smiled, a bit embarrassed. Her husband was a serial killer, yet Clement was the one embarrassed. "Is Henry in?"

"Practicing a little putting in the den. I'll get him. You men come in."

"We'll just go right there and say hello," Clement told her. His worst fear was Tolliver, alerted, would do something rash.

Doris looked at them in surprise, but she stood back. Clement led the way into the den.

"Henry Tolliver, you're under arrest and an extradition hearing will be held to send you to Oklahoma to stand trial for murder," said Hudlin. He provided cuffs and Clement almost wanted to stop him from cuffing the old man, but didn't. A cuffed prisoner can resist temptation to do something evil much more easily than an uncuffed prisoner.

"What are you doing?" Doris shrilled as they passed her on the threshold to the room. "You must be crazy. He's a policeman, not a criminal." She followed the three men to the door. "Henry, tell them…What's going on?"

Henry glanced back before they left his house, but he never answered his wife, not even a word.

Before they put him in the back of Hudlin's car, the San Diego officer very properly read the ex-cop his rights. Tolliver could waive his extradition rights or not, but a judge *was* going to send him back to Oklahoma.

As the car pulled away, Clement watched Doris standing outside the door, crying. Then he turned to see if he could tell what Henry was thinking. Tolliver's wispy old man hair was mussed and he seemed to be trying to gather himself. Clement wanted to say something cutting, like "You thought you got away with it, you bastard, but you didn't." However, he refrained. And Tolliver had enjoyed a lot of good years that those children hadn't, so maybe he was the one who'd had the last laugh, after all.

Clement sat with Tolliver in the sheriff's interview room. "Going home, Henry. Back to Oklahoma." Clement liked to claim that his interview technique was to act like an idiot, and sometimes, indeed, his approach was idiotic. He said nothing useful, asked nothing, but waited to hear what the subject had to say.

"I hope you let Doris know where I am." Henry's eyes blinked rapidly, as if all of his energy was going into that one display of nerves.

"Yes, of course. I called her. She's mystified, really at a loss. You're going to be flown to Oklahoma City and then taken directly to McAlester." Tolliver knew McAlester, of course—the Oklahoma State Penitentiary. Built early the last century—the 1900s—McAlester wasn't air conditioned. And they called *Leavenworth* the Hothouse.

Clement wondered how Tolliver would hold up physically. Probably not well, but then they'd take him to the hospital unit. Clement felt some compassion, but he also felt great satisfaction at bringing Tolliver to human justice.

What would be the key to making Tolliver talk? Getting an extradition had been possible on Simpson's say-so alone, but getting a conviction? Cold case convictions usually depended on strong DNA evidence, the testimony of more than one accuser, and/or confessions. Clement hoped for a confession.

"I've been wondering about Chief Kenny," he began. Kenny's failure to take action was a thread that bothered Clement. Had Kenny been involved in the murders? Or had he "simply" looked the other way.

"Kenny wasn't much of an administrator, as you already know." Tolliver smiled. "He didn't pay attention to much."

Kenny's Alzheimer's was so advanced now that maybe he

had been already suffering from it while he was still the chief. Maybe after Simpson came to him with the electrifying news that Kenny had a killer cop on the rolls, he merely forgot. The thought was somewhat frightening, but surely possible.

"They don't like pedophiles in prison," Clement said suddenly.

"Pedophiles? Of course not." Tolliver looked clueless as to what Clement meant. Not a pedophile then? If true, that would be a surprise.

Clement waited a minute, but Tolliver seemed unaffected and perhaps his mind was wandering.

"I wouldn't have taken you for a racist, Henry," Clement tried next.

Tolliver's gaze snapped back to the present and he look at Clement with a bit of heat. "A racist? I'm not."

"The boys were all black."

"No. They weren't." And then Tolliver smiled but a smile that held knowledge; superiority; and a deep, deep malice.

"Seven boys," Clement shot back.

"More than seven." Again, that smile from the pit of some frightening, demonic realm. But an admission, almost an admission, anyway—certainly a statement that would play rather well in court.

"Ah, you had me fooled, Henry. I thought you were a racial killer."

"You're a poor psychologist and not much of an investigator, either, Aaron. I remember when you were just a boy yourself. Even your father didn't like you then."

With interest, Clement watched Tolliver's face flush and anger arise. Anger was a good emotion for the interviewer—in the subject. People were much less careful when they were angry. "If not race, Henry, then why kill black children?"

"Not children, Aaron. I killed boys. Not girls. Only boys." He'd said it and the San Diego's sheriff's office was kindly recording the conversation. "Because boys are nasty, brutish bullies. It's that simple, Aaron. Undoubtedly like you were as a child. Nasty and brutish, pushing the weaker children around. I think that describes you."

That completely didn't describe Clement, who had been a well-behaved, thoughtful, mamma's boy without being effeminate. And he'd been glad to be that way as well, because he had never wanted to be anything like his father, Sam. He hadn't even wanted to be a cop.

Clement nodded. "A bully," he said. "I would have pushed you around, Henry, you worm. But why black children? More brutish, you thought?"

"Easier to kill. No one cares. Even their parents wouldn't miss them."

Clement, thinking of the relentless heartbreak Tolliver had caused, was nearly speechless. "You thought the parents wouldn't grieve?"

"Grieve? No. Why would they grieve?" Tolliver stared at him. "These were boys. Brutish boys. Like the boys who...never mind."

Clement waited, gave Tolliver the time to go on, but he didn't. "Did anyone help you, Henry? Kill with you? Cover up for you? Pull the reports?"

"Every step of the way was a piece of cake, Aaron. I didn't need any help."

Clement had done it. By the grace of God, he'd completed the investigation and could look forward to an eventual conviction. "I'll come and visit you in McAlester, Henry. We'll talk some more there, I hope. And if you want to come home to Holder for a while, you can show us the gravesites that we missed. I'm sure Doris would like to have you home in Holder."

Clement was tired, emotionally wrung out, and as he stood, he realized what a long trip he had ahead of him. Not just to return home, though that would take hours, but with this case and the unanswered questions.

* * *

237

Rich came out for another dinner, which Bradley had insisted on preparing. Chicken! This was a first and Clement guessed she was showing off. She must have taken quite a fancy to Rich, despite the attorney's many deficits in Clement's eyes. First of all, Rich was a lawyer, and second of all, he just didn't seem suitable, and third of all, well, what was wrong with the girl, anyway, running after an older man?

Clement, Rich, and Shelly praised the chicken mightily until the tributes grew tiresome and the talk died down. Clement was thinking about the pile of papers on his desk and when he could get over to McAlester to reinterview Henry. Maybe Clement should just let Henry sit a while, growing bored. He'd then appreciate the opportunity to talk his head off. On the other hand, though he was in segregation for his protection, maybe an angry prisoner would have killed him by that time, and all opportunity to learn where the other bones were buried would have been lost.

"I have kind of an announcement," Shelly said.

They all looked her way.

"I'm going to move back to Ohio, where my parents are," she told them. "My mother has been begging me. I think I'll try to go to graduate school. I'd probably like to help rape victims as a psychologist."

Now they all moved to congratulate *her.* And from Clement's point of view, her move back home really was probably for the best. She'd have a lot more time to heal with her family's support. Though he did wonder if she'd told Rod yet. Whether she'd thought a lot about his son at all. Though Clement knew this was the better outcome for his boy, he knew Rod would be sad for a long while.

As they moved into the living room a few minutes later, Shelly pulled Clement aside, toward the hallway. "I didn't know how to tell you," she said. "I owe you so much. Much more than I'll ever be able to say or to pay back."

"Pay it back to your counseling clients," he said.

"I didn't know if you were aware that I broke it off with Rod some time ago," she added. "I guess I thought he should be the one to tell you. Too many things have changed for me."

"Of course, Shelly." No, Rod hadn't told him. No one told him anything. Maybe that's why he'd become an investigator, in order to find out something once in a while. "I completely understand."

"You didn't owe me anything, and yet you did so much for me." Shelly's face flushed.

"You deserve all the best," Clement said. "I should have noticed that before, when I first met you. I want you to be happy."

"David—Karin's husband—and I have agreed to correspond." The red deepened.

"Life goes on," Clement assured her. He patted her awkwardly on the shoulder.

They went to join Rich and Bradley in the living room, Clement sharp-eyed to see what had passed between the two. Oh Lord, more chicken talk. Clement had eaten a lot of chicken in his time, and this chicken had been a fine one—but really! If Rich was looking for a new wife who could cook, Bradley probably wasn't the one he should pick.

"So what am I supposed to do about Holmes, Your Honor?" Rich asked Clement as the SPO sat.

"Funny you should ask that because I rounded up a few things today—my first day back to work after arranging to bring a serial killer to MacAlester." Yeah, he was sort of bragging on himself, but Clement held up his hand to stop them before they started slinging a load of compliments his way. All this politeness had become rather irritating.

"When I first heard about it, I became interested in the testimony of the forensic psychiatrist in the Christine Holmes' case. He told the jury that Holmes had followed the steps set out in an episode of *Trial for Murder* on the Criminal Justice channel." Clement didn't feel like delivering the personal detail that *Trial for Murder* was a show he often watched. "I looked up the show on the internet and tried to find the episode cited—which I couldn't. So I called the production company several times after and finally wound up talking today to one of the producers who had worked on that episode."

Clement smiled with satisfaction. "That is, they'd started to work on an episode like that and had consulted with Norman Parks, the psychiatrist who'd testified at the trial. Then, the producer told me, they scrapped the episode because some oddball things about the case left them open to a lawsuit."

Rich sat up straight. "No kidding," he exclaimed.

"Yeah, no kidding. You see, the episode was never shown. And the testimony about the episode was a key piece of evidence for premeditation." Clement was pretty pleased with himself. He could have been completely mistaken in regard to what he'd set out to do here, but he'd been right.

He went on. "We have that, along with the information about the D.A.'s office burying the hospital report and the obvious fact that Holmes's attorney was incompetent. I think just the threat of bringing Parks' misinformation to the judge prior to sentencing and maybe having the judge declare a mistrial should convince the D.A. himself to request leniency for Christine."

"A mistrial." Rich laughed. "That would certainly be one for the books. A mistrial after a judgment but before sentencing. Yeah, maybe."

"And I'm working on getting her psychiatric history," Clement added. "Though I have been a little pressed for time this past week."

When Rich had gone and the dishes were done by the host and hostesses, Clement got out Buddy's leash.

"I'll come with you," Bradley told Clement. "I'll ride shotgun. In case of any mountain lions."

Once they were outside and Buddy had begun searching out excellent smells, Clement returned to thoughts of all the work that had piled up on his desk in the last few days.

"Since Shelly is leaving, the time has come for me to go back home," said Bradley.

That seemed to Clement to have come out of the blue. While Rich might have asked her out, surely no offer of marriage had been tendered thus far.

"You don't like my house? My company? My dog?" Clement asked.

"People are talking, as is," she said.

"You're worried about your reputation? I see."

"Well, no, not really that…"

He snorted. "I guess you're right though." He snuck a look at her.

She looked at Clement. "I could stay on a while. It is convenient if we're going to work together going forward."

"If? Well that depends on if you want to. And on Munson." He suddenly felt as if he'd stepped into a dangerous, engulfing swamp. "Oh, come on, Bradley, hang around. We'll see how it goes. I'm not looking to get married…"

"Neither am I," she responded, alarmed.

"We can just see," he said. "Of course I'm old."

"Not so's, I've noticed."

They walked on in silence for a while until he put an arm rather companionably around her shoulder, listened to his heartbeat, then turned and kissed her.

Either that was an impulsive act, or an action that was long overdue.

G. MIKI HAYDEN recently published two martial arts literary novels and before that several action-adventure novels, but her first novel in print, *Pacific Empire* (an alternate history), won a rave in the *NYTimes* and was on that paper's Summer Reading List. Other novels of hers have been in print including *By Reason of Insanity*, a mystery, and fantasy novels for middle grade and young adult. Miki has had many stories published, including in *Alfred Hitchcock* and *Ellery Queen* magazines and in several Mystery Writers of America anthologies (winning an Edgar for one). Miki has two writing instructionals in print—*Writing the Mystery* in its third edition and *The Naked Writer*, a style guide in its third edition. She has taught at Writer's Digest University online for more than twenty years.

On the following pages are a few
more great titles from the
Down & Out Books publishing family.

For a complete list of books and to
sign up for our newsletter,
go to DownAndOutBooks.com.

The Killing Rain
Left Coast Crime Anthology 2024
Jim Thomsen, Editor

Down & Out Books
April 2024
978-1-64396-362-4

The Killing Rain is collection of short crime fiction, ranging from the cozy to the hardboiled, with each story depicting the Seattle area as a real or imagine place.

It's in conjunction with "Seattle Shakedown" — the slogan for the 2024 Left Coast Crime conference, slated for April 10-14 in nearby Bellevue.

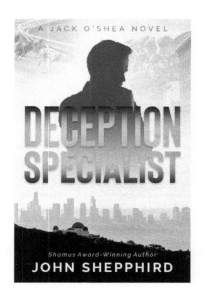

Deception Specialist
A Jack O'Shea Novel
John Shepphird

Down & Out Books
April 2024
978-1-64396-363-1

Reformed-swindler-turned-private-eye Jack O'Shea was first introduced in a series of short stories published in *Alfred Hitchcock Mystery Magazine*. The debut won the Shamus Award. The second in the series was a finalist for the Anthony Award.

Seeking redemption from his criminal past, Jack investigates a murder at a shadowy Northern California mountain college—a "visa mill" with ties to Silicon Valley. As he uncovers the truth, Jack's life of crime catches up with him. Nothing is as it appears.

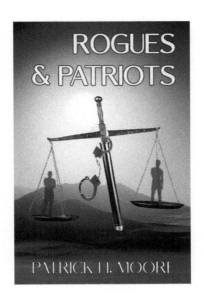

Rogues & Patriots
A Nick Crane
Patrick H. Moore

Down & Out Books
April 2024
978-1-64396-364-8

Patrick H. Moore's new novel *Rogues & Patriots* is Book Two of Moore's taut and topical three-volume series in which veteran LA PI Nick Crane finds himself locked in a life or death struggle with Miles Amsterdam and "the Principals," a terrifying group of aristocratic, right wing "super patriots."

With its well-drawn characters, non-stop action, and sharp, first person narration, *Rogues & Patriots* will leave the reader breathless and begging for more. Once again, Nick Crane stands tall as a world-weary PI everyman who takes on all comers in his battle to make America safe again for everyone.

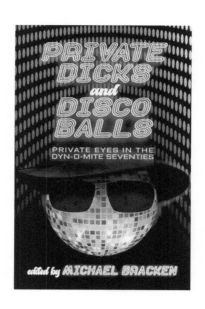

Private Dicks and Disco Balls
Private Eyes in the Dyn-O-Mite Seventies
Michael Bracken, Editor

Down & Out Books
May 2024
978-1-64396-365-5

The Sixties were a time of great cultural upheaval, and that upheaval continued into the 1970s. In the midst of all this, private eyes worked with clients across the generations, from those still clinging to the social mores of Nixon's "silent majority" to those who embraced the rapid societal changes that began in the 1960s.

From old-school private eyes to the Baby Boomers coming of age and entering the trade, these private eyes will take readers on a funky frolic through the Dyn-O-Mite Seventies.